"You will do exactly as I say, Nicole."

Those long, tanned fingers tightened to the precise point just short of pain. That silvery gaze darkened as Ian pulled her closer. "The issue is not up for debate."

Nicole met his intense glare with lead in her own. "Then you'd better be prepared to stick to me like glue. To watch every move I make," she warned. "The first time you turn your back, I'm out of here. I've had the same training as you, and we both know I'm very good at my job."

Loaded silence followed that summation. A muscle flexed rhythmically in his chiseled jaw. Heat mushroomed between their almost-touching bodies. Nicole's heart pounded so hard, she felt sure Ian could hear it threatening to burst from her chest.

"Look at me," he demanded softly, the sound of his voice wreaking havoc with her senses.

Nicole's breath caught when her gaze connected with his once more. Desire, hot and fierce, burned in his eyes. She blinked. That one thing was all they had ever truly shared—overwhelming attraction, soul-shattering desire. The kind that diminished all else.

D0957870

Dear Reader,

I certainly hope you have enjoyed the stories from the COLBY AGENCY series so far. This month I have the pleasure of bringing you Ian's story. Ian and Nicole are two of my favorite characters. The suspense as well as the sexual tension heats up very quickly between these former lovers. Their story begins in the Chicago office of Victoria Colby. I invite you to follow their breathtakingly dangerous journey from Chicago to our nation's capital, and on to the beautiful state of Virginia.

Ian Michaels is the kind of tall, dark and handsome hero that steamy fantasies are made of. Nobody is better at getting under Ian's skin than the very woman who betrayed him three years ago, Nicole Reed. Nicole is tough, sexy and beautiful, a lethal combination under any circumstances, but the fact that Ian still loves her makes the situation even more explosive. Putting the past aside, Nicole desperately needs help. And Ian is the only one she can trust. His heart won't let him turn her away. So hold on to your seat as you turn those pages!

Protective Custody is the third of my COLBY AGENCY stories. I hope to bring you many more engaging characters from Victoria Colby's private investigations firm. The Colby Agency is the best in the business, and so are the men and women who make up its ranks. As Ian and Nicole's story unfolds, you will learn about one of the agency's legends, Trevor Sloan. Broken by his haunting past, Sloan has risen from the emotional depths of losing his wife and son to a ruthless assassin called Angel. The loss has hardened him, effectively wrapping steel bars around his heart. Watch for Sloan's story in January 2002. I promise you not only pulse-pounding suspense, but also heart-stopping emotion.

Please let me know how you're enjoying the Colby stories. You may write to me at P.O. Box 64, Huntland, Tennessee, 37345.

Enjoy!

Debra

PROTECTIVE CUSTODY
DEBRA WEBB

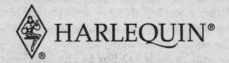

HARLEQUIN®

TORONTO • NEW YORK • LONDON
AMSTERDAM • PARIS • SYDNEY • HAMBURG
STOCKHOLM • ATHENS • TOKYO • MILAN • MADRID
PRAGUE • WARSAW • BUDAPEST • AUCKLAND

ISBN 0-373-22610-1

PROTECTIVE CUSTODY

Copyright © 2001 by Debra Webb

All rights reserved. Except for use in any review, the reproduction or
utilization of this work in whole or in part in any form by any electronic,
mechanical or other means, now known or hereafter invented, including
xerography, photocopying and recording, or in any information storage
or retrieval system, is forbidden without the written permission of the
publisher, Harlequin Enterprises Limited, 225 Duncan Mill Road,
Don Mills, Ontario, Canada M3B 3K9.

All characters in this book have no existence outside the imagination of
the author and have no relation whatsoever to anyone bearing the same
name or names. They are not even distantly inspired by any individual
known or unknown to the author, and all incidents are pure invention.

This edition published by arrangement with Harlequin Books S.A.

® and TM are trademarks of the publisher. Trademarks indicated with
® are registered in the United States Patent and Trademark Office, the
Canadian Trade Marks Office and in other countries.

Visit us at www.eHarlequin.com

Printed in U.S.A.

ABOUT THE AUTHOR

Debra Webb was born in Scottsboro, Alabama, to parents who taught her that anything is possible if you want it bad enough. She began writing at age nine. Eventually she met and married the man of her dreams and tried some other occupations, including selling vacuum cleaners, working in a factory, a day care center, a hospital and a department store. When her husband joined the military, they moved to Berlin, Germany, and Debra became a secretary in the commanding general's office. By 1985 they were back in the States, and finally moved to Tennessee, to a small town where everyone knows everyone else. With the support of her husband and two beautiful daughters, Debra took up writing again, looking to mystery and movies for inspiration. In 1998, her dream of writing for Harlequin Books came true. You can write to Debra with your comments at P.O. Box 64, Huntland, Tennessee, 37345.

Books by Debra Webb

HARLEQUIN INTRIGUE
583—SAFE BY HIS SIDE*
597—THE BODYGUARD'S BABY*
610—PROTECTIVE CUSTODY*

*Colby Agency

HARLEQUIN AMERICAN ROMANCE
864—LONGWALKER'S CHILD

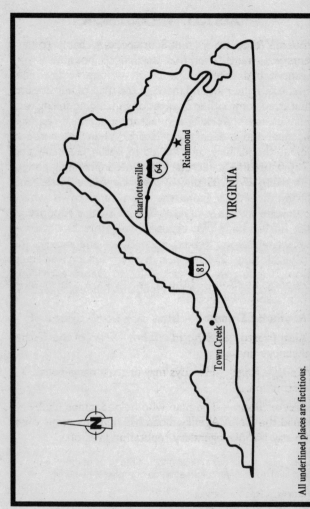

All underlined places are fictitious.

CAST OF CHARACTERS

Nicole Reed—Someone knows her secret and that someone wants her dead. There is only one man she can trust: Ian Michaels.

Ian Michaels—Nicole betrayed him once, but he cannot turn his back on Nicole when her life is in danger.

Victoria Colby—The head of the Colby Agency.

Ric Martinez—The Colby Agency's newest investigator. He has a lot to learn, but Ian is a good teacher.

Director Landon—Did he die protecting Nicole's secret?

Agent Daniels—Was he murdered by the assassin stalking Nicole?

Leonna Landon—Is the grieving widow safe from her husband's assassin?

Raymond Solomon—Is his case worth dying for?

Alex Preston & Ethan Delaney—Two of the Colby Agency's finest.

George Reed—His toys may prove a dangerous distraction.

Trevor Sloan—The man who helped James Colby build the Colby Agency. Sloan has demons of his own to slay, but his legendary reputation lives on.

This book is dedicated to a very special lady,
Mary Bauer.
Thank you, Mary, for being a cherished friend
and an inspiration to us all.

Prologue

"Absolute trust is essential." Nicole Reed's solemn gaze settled heavily onto Victoria's. "Both our lives will depend on my being able to trust your investigator completely. I know Ian Michaels. I can trust him."

Victoria Colby considered that last statement for a time before she spoke. Not a single doubt existed in her mind that Ian would be the wisest choice. He was not only the Colby Agency's most experienced investigator, he was a man of his word. With Nick Foster's retirement, Ian had transitioned into the position of second-in-command. Victoria employed only the finest in their fields at the Colby Agency, and Ian had proven no exception during his three years of service.

"Miss Reed, I understand your need for a civilian investigator. Obviously, you can't trust anyone in your own organization."

"I can't trust anyone even remotely connected to the bureau or the Witness Security Program." Nicole sighed. "I wish that weren't the case, but it is. There have been two attempts on my life already. My director is dead, as well as another agent I've worked closely with in the past. Until I get to the bottom of what's going on, I need someone I can trust to watch my back. Your agency has an impeccable reputation, Mrs. Colby, and I *trust* Ian Michaels.''

Victoria relaxed into the soft leather of her chair and studied the client seated across the wide expanse of her oak desk. The woman's features were striking. She looked as if she had just stepped off the pages of *Vogue*. A navy silk jacket and trousers lent an air of professionalism as well as elegance to her image. Blond hair fell around her shoulders. Wide, assessing blue eyes highlighted a face that could only be called beautiful. So, Victoria noted, this woman was the reason Ian Michaels had walked away from a promising career as a U.S. Marshal.

Victoria arched a speculative brow. ''Your history with Ian may be a problem, Miss Reed.''

Nicole frowned. ''I don't understand.''

Victoria almost smiled at the look of innocence Nicole Reed could adopt. ''Before I employ anyone at this agency, I research their background thoroughly. I evaluate their strong points as well as their weak points, and I familiarize myself with their past mistakes. You worked with Ian Michaels on a high-profile case just over three years ago. The Solomon case, I believe.''

Nicole's expression grew guarded. ''That's right.''

''I'm aware of your personal involvement with Ian, and the subsequent outcome of that involvement,'' Victoria added, leaving no question as to the point she intended.

''Raymond Solomon died, Mrs. Colby. We did our best to protect him, but he died anyway. End of story.''

Between the suddenly blank look in the other woman's eyes and the emotionless tone of her voice, Victoria had her doubts as to whether the story had ended. But that wasn't the issue here. Nicole Reed needed help, and the Colby Agency had made its reputation by providing the kind of help she required. Victoria straightened, then pressed the intercom button. "Mildred, ask Ian if he's free. I'd like him to join this meeting."

Nicole blinked, then looked away. Asking for Ian's help couldn't be easy, Victoria imagined. After all, it was Nicole who had helped end his former career. And if Victoria had Ian pegged right, which she likely did, Miss Nicole Reed had probably broken his fiercely guarded heart as well.

"You need help," Victoria told her finally. "And I believe this agency can help you, Miss Reed." Nicole relaxed visibly. "However, I don't feel Ian is the proper choice considering your shared history." Their gazes locked, Victoria's firm, Nicole's hesitant. "But I will allow him to make the final decision."

Nicole lifted one shoulder in a semblance of a shrug. "Fair enough."

The moment Ian entered the room Nicole knew she had seriously overestimated the healing value of time. His stance stiffened and those silver eyes frosted with indifference when his gaze collided with hers. His expression was exactly the same as it had been the last time Nicole had seen him, filled with unmasked contempt. No matter, he was the one person she could trust. She might be a fool for even asking for his help, but it was worth a shot. Besides, that's the way their relationship had been from the beginning, overpowering attraction, yet bordering on enmity.

"Ian, I'm sure you remember Miss Reed," Victoria announced, breaking the awkward silence.

His icy gaze never left Nicole's. She didn't miss the slight hesitation before he spoke. "Yes. Of course."

Nicole steeled herself against the shiver generated by the low, raspy sound of his voice. Deep, sexy as hell, and laced with a hint of European flavor. Ian Michaels had the kind of voice erotic dreams were made of. Tangled sheets and long, hot nights immediately leapt to mind. From the moment they had first met, the man's tone and speech pattern had tripped some sort of desire trigger deep inside Nicole. He only had to look into her eyes, speak, and she melted. Despite what had happened between them and the passage of three years, his effect on her remained unchanged. But she couldn't let him get to her this time. This time she had to maintain strict control.

Nicole swallowed, then stood. She extended her hand and produced a smile. "It's good to see you again, Ian."

Ian's gaze traced her body with painstaking slowness, making Nicole too warm despite her determination not to react. Then he stared, long and hard, at her hand before taking it in his own. Long, tanned fingers wrapped around hers and she fought the added reaction his touch evoked. She could not allow this. Too much depended on the next few minutes and this one man to permit emotion to override reason.

Ian acknowledged her greeting with nothing more than a ghost of a nod, then released her hand and turned to Victoria. "You wanted to see me."

"Yes. Please, have a seat." Victoria indicated the remaining chair in front of her desk.

Seemingly from some faraway place, Nicole listened as Victoria recounted their earlier discussion, the words barely registering. Nicole could not take her eyes off the man now seated next to her. Still tall and amazingly handsome. Still a commanding presence that stole her breath. He wore his hair longer now, she noted with reluctant admiration, its dark length curling at his nape. Nicole almost smiled as her greedy gaze swept over his body. Though the suit was more elegant now, probably Armani, the color was the same. Black. Ian always wore black.

And he would certainly be as good at his job today as he had been three years ago. No fugitive ever eluded him for long. No witness ever failed to make it to court or to safety when Ian was assigned the case.

Ian Michaels never failed. That's why he had been assigned to the Solomon case three years ago.

And that's the reason Nicole had received her assignment as well. To see that Ian failed in his.

Now, with the memory of betrayal still screaming between them, she had come to ask Ian for help. There was no one else she could trust. Nicole held her breath as she waited for him to respond to the request that he handle her case personally.

"I'm sure you'll be pleased with the investigator Victoria assigns to your case," he said coolly, his icy gaze once more connecting with Nicole's. "But it won't be me."

"YOU'RE COMFORTABLE with your decision then?"

"Yes." Ian didn't turn around. He knew Victoria was disappointed in him, but right now he didn't care. All he wanted to do was watch Nicole storm across the parking lot four stories below. She had left Victoria's office as if his refusal to help her didn't matter, but he knew better. He had seen the uncertainty, then the defeat flicker in her blue eyes. Whatever her current situation, she considered Ian's refusal to help her a significant loss. Ian almost smiled. However, it didn't come close to evening the score.

"You're not concerned with her refusal to work with Alex?" Victoria again interrupted his moment of savoring victory with another dig at his already chafed conscience.

"Why should I be?" Ian clenched his jaw at the denial that crowded his throat. He no longer gave one damn about Nicole Reed. No matter that his traitorous body had reacted as if three years had not passed…as if Nicole had not already cost him dearly. Had she really despised him enough to purposely get in the way of his work? Had her own ambition meant more to her than a man's life? Ian would likely never know the answers to those questions. Did it even matter? No. He couldn't change the past. It was over, done with. Solomon was dead.

"Nicole can take care of herself," he said in answer to Victoria's question. His voice sounded harsh to his own ears. Reacting on emotion was not something Ian allowed, but he hadn't been able to help himself today.

The squeak of leather alerted Ian when Victoria stood. She had more to say on the issue, of that he felt certain. Three near-silent steps later and she was at his side watching Nicole's determined march toward whatever vehicle she had arrived in.

"I know very little about what happened between the two of you, but I do know a woman in trouble when I see one."

Ian kept his gaze glued to that mane of long blond hair fluttering in the September breeze behind Nicole. How could the mere sight of her still make him ache with need? Even knowing what he knew. Why in hell would Nicole come to him for help? She had to know he would refuse. She had to be desperate.

Victoria had made the decision his, and he had decided. Nicole's subsequent refusal to work with another investigator was not his problem, Ian reminded himself as that annoyingly restless sensation twisted inside him. The feeling was all too familiar, but he intended to ignore his instincts this time. Nicole was on her own.

"Perhaps she'll change her mind," Victoria suggested.

"She won't," he murmured. A thought spoken. Nicole

had entirely too much pride. The fact that she had come to him at all spoke volumes about her proximity to the edge. But she definitely would not come crawling back for what she would consider second best, and begging had never been her style. Remorse trickled through him before he could stop it. He knew her too well.

"Well, then, I hope you're right." Victoria folded her arms over her chest. "I hope she *can* take care of herself."

"I stopped caring one way or another a long time ago," he affirmed aloud. Who was he trying to convince? he wondered with self-disgust. Victoria or himself?

As if to refute his words an earthshaking explosion rattled the glass in front of his face. Debris from what used to be an automobile flew in a dozen directions. Black smoke mushroomed skyward as flames licked the remaining, mutilated frame. Ian's heart lurched. He frantically scanned the parking lot. Panicked pedestrians rushed toward the building for cover. He clutched the edge of the windowsill as his heart stilled in his chest.

Nicole! Where was Nicole?

Chapter One

The ground trembled beneath Nicole's feet. An invisible wall slammed into her face, shoving her backwards until the pavement stopped her. Her head hurt. Badly.

Nicole struggled to open her eyes...to fight the vortex of thick, heavy darkness sucking her toward oblivion. She had to wake up. To run from the danger! But her body refused to cooperate. She couldn't move...couldn't scream.

Nicole heard herself groan, the sound giving her hope that she wasn't dead after all. Pain exploded inside her head. She clung to the pain. You had to be alive to feel pain. She felt herself move, a simple side-to-side motion of her head, which initiated another burst of fiery pain at the back of her skull. She groaned again. Louder this time.

"You're safe, Nicole."

She stilled. That voice...

Ian. Her lids fluttered open and her eyes labored with the effort to focus in the near-darkness. The face that had invaded her dreams for more than three years finally came into focus.

"Ian?"

"It's okay," he said soothingly.

Nicole closed her eyes and savored the erotic sound of

his voice. Memories flooded her mind. The explosion. Hitting the ground. And then Ian was there...taking care of her. A weary sigh eased past her lips, her body aching even with that tiny exertion. He had insisted on having her examined at the ER, then he had taken her back to his place. She remembered falling into an exhausted sleep in his arms.

"My head hurts." She opened her eyes, and her gaze connected with his. Those emotionless gray eyes gave nothing away.

"I know." With gentle fingers, he brushed a wisp of hair from her face. "I'm sorry."

Ian's refusal to accept her case suddenly hit with the same impact as that invisible wall. "Why are you doing this?" Nicole sat straight up with the surge of adrenaline that accompanied that thought. Pain twisted inside her head. She rubbed at the tender spot on the back of her scalp.

"You were badly shaken. The doctor said you shouldn't be alone," he offered quietly.

Bracing her hands behind her to maintain her upright position, Nicole leveled her gaze on his. "The explosion?"

"Your rental car apparently." He searched her eyes. "I've taken care of things with the police. Why don't you tell me what's going on?"

This time had been too close. Nicole clenched her teeth and forced herself to breathe deeply and slowly. She needed to be calm—to think. She surveyed the darkened room. Ian's bedroom. His scent, so familiar, suddenly enveloped her. That clean, subtle musky scent that was his alone. That stirred her blood even under current circumstances.

His bed. She was in his bed—with him hovering over

her. Why had she let him bring her here? He wasn't going to help her. He had made that point quite clear. Anger shot through her veins, sending her heart back into double time.

"I have to get out of here." Nicole scrambled from beneath the covers. She wasn't safe here. She wasn't safe anywhere. She had to run as fast as she could.

"We need to talk."

Instinctively Nicole rolled to the other side of the bed, out of his reach. She jumped to her feet and immediately regretted both moves. The insistent throb inside her skull erupted with a vengeance, threatening her unsteady legs. Not quite a concussion, the doctor had said she would be fine. She had been very lucky to only be close enough for the force of the blast to knock her to the ground. Nicole squeezed her eyes shut and focused on blocking out the pain. There was too much to be done. No time to waste. She had to reschedule her flight. She had a witness to relocate and protect. And she couldn't trust the regular channels to handle it. Someone wanted her and her witness dead. How had the bastard tracked her to Chicago? She had been so careful. No mistakes! No one knew her location.

No, that wasn't true, Nicole realized grimly, because *he* had found her. And he would find her again. She needed her things. Did she dare go back to the hotel and get the few items she had brought with her? She would need a change of clothes.

Clothes.

Nicole stared down at herself. The shimmering glow of moonlight from a nearby window confirmed her sudden realization. Her clothes were gone. She wore nothing but her skimpy, lacy bra and matching blue panties.

"Where the hell are my clothes?" Nicole looked up to

find Ian towering over her, his tall, dark frame almost lost in the shadows. Something, some emotion flitted across his features too quickly for Nicole to analyze, and then that mask of iron control fell back into place.

"I thought you would be more comfortable like this." His gaze moved slowly over her. "I sent your clothes to be cleaned," he added in that maddeningly calm way of his.

That tone. That controlling, no-arguments-tolerated tone. He had no intention of working with her, yet he had taken charge of the game strategy. She was no different than one of his fugitives. He would handle the situation until he could wash his hands of her. That was his way. Ian Michaels always did the right thing. He never deviated from the straight and narrow—never failed.

Except once.

And then he had turned his back on her as if nothing had happened between them. As if what they had shared hadn't mattered in the final scheme of things. He hadn't given her the benefit of the doubt. Hadn't waited around for her to explain. Ian had simply walked away. From her. From everything.

Because she had betrayed him. The fact that she had only been doing her job was of no consequence—even if she had been able to tell him the truth. Nothing she could have said or done would have altered his opinion of her. If the man were capable of emotion he might display some sort of reaction. Anger, pain, remorse, something. Nicole almost laughed out loud. But this was Ian Michaels. She glowered at him. He didn't allow himself to feel. Hadn't she learned that three years ago? Hadn't she learned anything at all?

"Where are my clothes?" she repeated with all the force she could marshal. She should have known better than to come to him. Why would he care if she lived or died? And how could she blame him?

"I've already answered that question."

"This was a mistake. I shouldn't have wasted my time." Nicole attempted to brush past him only to be halted by his half step to the right.

"You need to tell me what's going on, Nicole," he argued quietly.

"Get out of my way, Michaels." Nicole darted to his left. Ian moved more quickly, effectively blocking her once more.

His unreadable gaze locked on hers. A hint of a smile curled his irritatingly full lips. "You have no clothes, no transportation, no money. How do you propose to leave?"

He had her clothes and her bag. Another rush of anger flooded Nicole. She stood before him exposed, emotionally as well as physically. She glared into his handsome face, his perfectly controlled emotions angering her all the more. She manufactured a caustic smile of her own. "Don't sweat it, Michaels. I'm sure I can get a ride." Nicole ran the fingers of both hands through her hair, allowing the long strands to drift down over her shoulders. "In fact," she added tartly, ignoring the protest of her sore muscles, "if push comes to shove, I feel certain I can earn myself some fast cash." Not that she would ever resort to what she was suggesting, but he didn't have to know that, and if it hit the mark... "You don't need to worry about me at all. I can take care of myself."

Nicole knew she would not soon forget the collection of emotions that danced across his handsome face. But it was anger that ultimately took center stage and held his features captive. The uncharacteristic outward display fascinated her for about two seconds then trepidation kicked in. Before she could take a step back, he grabbed her by both arms.

"You will do exactly as I say, Nicole." Those long, tanned fingers tightened to the precise point just short of pain. That silvery gaze darkened as he pulled her closer to him. "The issue is not up for debate."

Nicole met his intense glare with lead in her own. "Then you'd better be prepared to stick to me like glue. To watch every move I make," she warned. "The first time you turn your back I'm out of here. I've had the same training as you, Michaels, and we both know I'm very good at my job."

Loaded silence followed that summation. A muscle flexed rhythmically in his chiseled jaw. Heat mushroomed between their almost-touching bodies. Nicole's heart pounded so hard she felt sure Ian could hear it threatening to burst from her chest. To her utter frustration, her gaze drifted to his lips. She licked her own, her mind immediately conjuring up his taste.

"Look at me," he demanded softly, the sound of his voice wreaking havoc with her senses.

Nicole's breath caught when her gaze connected with his once more. Desire, hot and fierce, burned in his eyes. She blinked. That one thing was all they had ever truly shared—overwhelming attraction, soul-shattering desire. The kind that diminished all else. "What do you want from me?" she demanded. Nicole searched his eyes for an answer beyond the heat and memory that connected them body and soul.

"When that car exploded and I couldn't see you, I thought..." He released her arms only to gently cup her face in his hands. His thumb glided across her cheek, sending shivers down her spine. The breath of his reluctant sigh whispered across her lips. "I thought I'd lost you."

Nicole steeled herself against what she wanted to feel. Just words. That's all they were. She couldn't trust Ian with her heart any more than she could trust her life to the bastard who was trying to kill her. She understood Ian's probable motivation—revenge. Would he take this opportunity to do to her what she had done to him three years ago? If he only knew...

Ruthlessly squashing the tiny spark of hope his words elicited, Nicole encircled his wrists with trembling fingers and attempted to remove his hands from her face.

Ian swallowed...hard, the play of muscle beneath tanned skin doing strange things to her stomach. "I can't lose you again," he murmured.

"You never had me," she assured him with forced contempt.

He laughed softly and raised one dark brow in mock speculation. "I can recall having you at least four times, Nicole." That eclectic accent he had gained from growing up in half a dozen European countries thickened as his voice lowered to a more seductive level. His fingers slid around her neck and urged her closer still, his thumbs working a sensuous kind of magic. "I remember every detail of every moment we spent together. Each time we made love proved more intense than the last. Don't try to tell me you've forgotten."

He pressed a silky kiss to her cheek, Nicole shivered as much from his words as from his kiss. "Stop," she whispered hoarsely.

He stopped but didn't pull away. His lips remained only a hairbreadth from her skin. "You want me to stop?"

"Yes," she lied. Nicole didn't have to look to know

he smiled, she felt it. Electricity crackled between their heated bodies.

"And if I refuse?"

Nicole closed her eyes and released a shuddering breath. She shouldn't have come to him. Did she really expect to be able to spend five minutes with the man and not want him? Only a few hours ago she had eluded death for the third time in less than two weeks. And right now all she could think about was how it would feel to make love with Ian again. To have him touch her in that slow, thorough manner of his. To have him whisper sweet things to her in that lightly accented voice. To make him believe that she hadn't meant to hurt him three years ago—that she had only been doing her job.

What if she had died today?

Nicole blinked. She would never have had the opportunity to make things right with Ian. She lifted her gaze to his, watched the renewed desire turn those silvery depths to a deeper, gunmetal gray. *One last night.* They could have one last night together and then she would disappear from his life forever. She would face whatever the future held for her...alone. If death awaited, Nicole decided she would just have her taste of heaven now.

She moistened her lips and smiled up at him. "Well," she said languorously as she began to slowly unbutton his shirt. "I suppose that leaves me with no choice." Nicole slid her hands inside and over his muscled chest, the feel of that sculpted terrain making her weak with want. How she had missed him. No man would ever be able to make her feel the way Ian had. Would this thing between them still be as it once was—even after what she had done to him? Nicole cleared her mind. She didn't want to think...she wanted to feel. To touch...to forget.

He remained absolutely still as she plunged her fingers

into his long, dark hair and pulled his head down to hers. She nipped his lower lip with her teeth, then traced that sexy cleft in his chin with her tongue. He moved then. His hands slid over her shoulders and down her back, caressing, arousing her naked flesh. And then his mouth captured hers.

His kiss was slow, thorough, tantalizing, with a kind of erotic finesse only Ian possessed. Her heart thudding with anticipation, Nicole watched the intent expression on his face as he deepened the kiss. Then her eyes closed with the ecstasy she could no longer deny. Desire burst inside her like shattering glass, sending tiny shards of heat throughout her. Her head no longer hurt, her muscles no longer complained of their bruising. All conscious thought vanished. Ian's masterful hands squeezed her bottom, then pulled her against his thick arousal. Nicole shuddered with the need now gripping every fiber of her being.

She wanted his bare skin against hers—now. Nicole jerked his shirt open, scattering the remaining buttons across the lush carpet. She reveled in the feel of his strong back as she slid the material down, then pressed her body to his. Smooth and hot. His skin singed hers as their bodies melded. Ian groaned his approval deep in his throat, the sound urging Nicole's own frenzied desire. She tugged his shirt from his slacks, then slowly peeled it off his body.

He lifted her against him and she instinctively wrapped her legs around his lean waist. His mouth continued to torture hers, his tongue delving inside, tasting, tempting, then retreating. That slow in-and-out pace foreshadowing what she knew would come. Her legs tightened around him, pressing the moist heat between her thighs more firmly into his hardened length. This was what she had fantasized about a thousand times in the last three years.

Ian carried her to the bed and lowered her gently onto the tangled sheets. His body aligned over hers, he looked down at her, those amazing gray eyes analyzing her too closely. Nicole struggled to read the emotions cluttering his face. Sadness, maybe, or pain…almost. Had he missed her half as much as she had missed him? Did he want her as she wanted him?

"You do have a choice," he said softly.

Nicole tried one last time to decipher that distant look in his eyes, but to no avail. "I know," she whispered, then smiled. "I choose this." She unbuttoned his fly, then lowered the zipper. His eyes closed on a tortured groan as she eased his slacks and briefs over his hips, then caressed him intimately. Her own need suddenly careened out of control. Instinctively her body arched against his, the resulting friction making her cry out with want. One solid yank was all it took for Ian to relieve her of the tiny, strappy panties.

And then he was inside her, filling her, turning her world upside down. Their movements turned frantic, out of control. His powerful thrusts propelled Nicole closer and closer to the climax that had begun the moment he touched her. Ian kissed her again, hard and fast. He murmured desperate words in a language she didn't understand. She gripped his broad shoulders, trying to hold on longer…to make it last. But she couldn't, one more thrust and she tumbled over the edge. Heat and light and pleasure cascaded over her, swirled inside her. Ian followed close behind, driving into her one last time.

His taut body relaxed, his forehead rested against hers, their ragged breathing the only sound in the room. "You should rest now." He brushed a soft kiss across her lips. "I'll keep you safe."

Nicole nodded, suddenly feeling totally exhausted all

over again. "I trust you, Ian," she murmured, her gaze holding his. "I trust you with my life."

"Sleep, Nicole," he insisted gently. "I'll be right here when you wake up."

IAN PARTED the blinds and checked the parking area outside his town house once more. Still no sign of Martinez. He paused to listen for Nicole. The sound of water spraying in the shower continued. Good. He wanted her occupied until after Martinez arrived.

He had spent the entire night watching Nicole sleep, memorizing each delicate feature of her sweet face. She was as beautiful as ever. Her body slender and feminine, yet toned and amazingly strong. Ian swallowed back the emotions he knew he should not feel. Merely touching Nicole aroused him to the point of insanity. The sudden image of water sluicing over all that satiny skin made his groin tighten. He closed his eyes against the memory of her scent, her taste. Nicole did things to him…made him feel things he could not begin to describe. Ian sighed and shook his head slowly from side to side. This could not be.

He was a fool.

His foolishness had cost a life once before, he refused to risk a repeat of that mistake. Ian plowed his fingers through his hair and crossed the room once more, silently cursing his compunction every step of the way. He had paced this room for the past ten minutes.

Guilt gnawed at him for feigning sleep when Nicole had awakened this morning. She had kissed him tenderly on the cheek, then slipped quietly into the bathroom to shower. And what had he done? He had immediately called Martinez and hastily dressed. Nicole would not be happy when he informed her of his plan. But her displeasure was of no consequence in the matter. Ian understood what had to be done. He knew no more now regarding her case than he had known yesterday when she had left Victoria's office. But he did know with complete certainty that he could not stay objective where Nicole was concerned. And her survival depended on the kind of objectivity and focus he lost all sight of in her presence.

The moment he had set eyes on her in Victoria's office, Ian had experienced a sense of rage unparalleled by anything he had ever known before. She was the last person on the planet he would have helped do anything. Or so he'd thought. When that car had exploded, and he hadn't been sure if she were dead or alive, the truth had hit him like a bullet between the eyes. He still had deep feelings for Nicole. The past changed nothing. He couldn't bear the thought of losing her forever.

But, after last night, Ian realized that he could not determine the threat to her safety with her so close. It was true three years ago and it was still true today: when he was with Nicole, he could not maintain the necessary focus required to perform his mission. Taking that kind of risk was out of the question. She would simply have to go into hiding with Martinez while Ian did what had to be done.

The issue was closed in his opinion. Nicole would do exactly as he instructed. He set his jaw determinedly.

Or else.

The anticipated knock came just as Ian turned to retrace his path across the room. He repositioned the Glock tucked into his waistband at the small of his back, then made his way to the door. He breathed a sigh of relief when he checked the peephole and found Martinez on the other side. Finally. Ian opened the door only wide enough for Martinez to enter, and quickly closed it behind him.

"Thanks for coming on short notice."

"No problem, man." Martinez, the Colby Agency's newest investigator, scanned the room. "Nice place."

Ian nodded. He wasn't accustomed to having visitors in his home, but there was no getting around it this time. The spray of water in the other room stopped. Ian glanced in the direction of the bedroom door, Nicole would appear at any moment. He was out of time. Without preamble, he related the details of her case as he knew them to Martinez.

"Good morning."

At the sound of Nicole's voice Ian turned slowly to face her. He did not relish the next few minutes. "Good morning," he returned with a tight smile. An unfamiliar sensation squeezed his chest at how vulnerable she looked in an old pair of his sweats, her long blond hair still damp from her shower.

Her gaze darted from Ian to the other man, then narrowed with suspicion. "I didn't know you had company," she said stiffly.

Ian glanced at the man standing beside him. "This is Ric Martinez." Ian leveled his gaze on Nicole and steeled himself for her fury. "He will be keeping you company at one of our safe houses until the investigation is over."

Pain, then anger stole across her features. She gave a jerky nod. "I see."

Ian took the four steps that separated them. "It would be a conflict of interest for us to work together," he explained quietly.

Nicole lifted her defiant chin and glared at him. "Whose interest, yours or mine?"

Irritation flared. "It would be in both our best interests for you to cooperate with Martinez." He matched her insolent expression. "And that's what you're going to do."

She shoved a handful of hair behind her ear, the fight-or-flight urge already evident in her posture. "Last time I checked this was still a free country."

Ian snagged her arm when she would have pushed past him. "If the story you told Victoria is true, then walking away from our help would be a serious mistake. Someone has tried to kill you three times already, Nicole. You're not leaving alone."

She glowered first at his offending hand, then at him. "Just try and stop me, Michaels."

His grip tightened. "Don't be a fool, Nicole."

"Miss Reed, I think maybe you should listen to him," Martinez suggested soberly.

Her disdainful glare flicked to Martinez. "This isn't your fight."

He held up his hands stop-sign fashion and backed off. "Whatever you say, lady."

Ian pulled her closer to him, an unspoken demand for her full attention. "You know the rules of survival as well as I do," he ground out.

"Why don't you tell me about the rules, Michaels." She struggled against his hold, but he tightened his grip, angering her all the more. "What was last night all about, huh? Survival or retribution?"

One beat turned to five, the tension growing thicker with each. "You had a choice, you decided," he reminded coldly. "I have a choice this morning, and I have decided."

"Go to hell."

"I've been there, Nicole. Don't you remember?" Watching Solomon die and knowing he was responsible had been pure hell for Ian.

She blinked, but not before he got a glimpse of the regret in those wide blue eyes. Nicole sighed defeatedly.

"Fine," she relented, then lifted a repentant gaze to his. "I suppose you know what you're doing, Ian. And I—" She shrugged halfheartedly. "I'm just totally confused."

Ian relaxed his brutal grip on her arm and exhaled his own burst of relief. "Good. Martinez will stick close to you and I'll work the investigation."

"And what will I be doing?"

"You'll lie low until we know exactly what's going on. That's standard operating procedure. You know the drill."

Nicole nodded. "Sounds as if you have everything covered."

Ian held her gaze, urging her to understand. "I will do whatever it takes to neutralize the threat to you, Nicole."

"Well." She smiled, her lips trembling with the effort. "I guess we should get going then." She glanced in Martinez's direction. "No point dragging this out."

"You'll be safe as long as you do exactly as I tell you," Ian assured her.

She paused and turned back to him. That crystal-blue gaze softened, grew misty. "No kiss good-bye?"

Ian's chest constricted with regret and something else he refused to acknowledge. Before he could stop himself, his hands went immediately to the face permanently etched in his memory. The feel of her skin ripped him apart inside. How could he let her out of his sight? But, how could he permit this thing between them to get in the way of what had to be done?

As if in slow motion, he lowered his head, his mouth yearning to mate with hers. His eyes closed at the first brush of their lips. Nicole's arms slid beneath his suit jacket, around his waist, caressing him as she had last night…as she had in his dreams so many times.

She had the weapon in her hand two endless seconds before his body accepted the command to react. Nicole backed away from him, her expert aim shifting quickly to Martinez. "Get your hands up where I can see them," she demanded sharply.

"Think, Nicole," Ian suggested calmly, while mentally cursing himself for the idiot he was. He never made mistakes like this. *Only with Nicole.* "You came to me for help. How can we help you if you won't let us?"

"Just yesterday you refused to help me. Now I've decided I don't need your brand of help, thank you very much." She moved cautiously toward the door, skillfully alternating her focus between him and Martinez. "Your keys," she said to Martinez when she reached the door.

He shrugged as if he didn't understand, his olive skin a good deal paler than when he arrived.

"Your car keys. Give me your car keys," she ground out impatiently.

"Okay, lady, just stay cool. My brother is going to kill me. That Explorer's brand new." Martinez reached for his pocket with his right hand.

"Wait! Hold your hands up high and turn all the way around," Nicole instructed curtly.

Martinez glanced uneasily at Ian. Ian nodded for him to do as she said. Martinez turned around slowly, his hands held high. The form-fitting muscle shirt, which he wore tucked into his jeans left no doubt that the man was unarmed. Ian swore silently. He should have warned Martinez to be fully prepared. Not that it would have done any good since Ian obviously had been ill-prepared himself.

"Now give me those keys—with your left hand," Nicole ordered.

Martinez complied without hesitation.

Nicole reached behind her and opened the door. "Nobody moves until I'm out of here. *Nobody.*" She allowed

Ian one final look before she stepped across the threshold and slammed the door behind her.

Ian hissed a four-letter word. How in the hell had he fallen for that old trick?

"Hey man, are we going after her or what?" Martinez asked uncertainly.

"Go out the back. See if you can get around behind her to cut her off," Ian told him roughly as he stormed across the room. Dammit, the woman was going to get herself killed. She knew better. Nicole knew the code of survival and protection. So far she had done nothing but act like a frightened civilian, breaking every rule.

Ian cursed again when he stepped into the early-morning sun. Fortunately it was Saturday and his neighbors would likely still be in bed at this hour. He quickly scanned the seemingly deserted street. But his neighbors weren't the concern at the moment. He shook his head in disgust. Nicole was a damned open target standing there fumbling with Martinez's keys. His gut clenched.

"At this rate you won't make it very far, Nicole." Ian took the steps two at a time.

Nicole's head jerked up. Instantly, she focused a bead on him with her left hand, while continuing to try and manipulate the keys with her right. "Stop right there, Michaels."

"I suppose you're going to shoot me if I don't."

Her head came up again. Ian smiled when her resolve visibly faltered. "I didn't think so," he concluded aloud, his supreme annoyance making his voice sound more lethal than he had intended.

He walked right up to her, the muzzle of the Glock pressed into his chest. "Give me the weapon."

"No way. I don't need any help," she said tightly, her

eyes suspiciously bright. "I decided last night that I wasn't going to involve anyone else in *my* problems."

"Was that before or after we made love?" Ian held her gaze. His entire being reacted to the uncharacteristic fear he saw in her eyes.

"It'll be better this way." She drew in a shaky breath, but firmed her grip on the Glock. "Now get the hell away from me, Michaels. People are dropping like flies around me. First my director, then Daniels."

"No."

"Now who's being the fool?" Lowering her weapon, Nicole jerked the vehicle door open and slid behind the wheel. "Goodbye, Ian."

Without warning, glass shattered, the sound echoing in the otherwise quiet street. Fragments from the truck window sprayed in Ian's direction. Simultaneously, something propelled him back a step, the impact and burn clicking an instant recognition in his brain and sending him diving for cover. Thankfully Nicole was in the vehicle. He hoped like hell she stayed put. Ian hit the ground. A stab of pain knifed through his left shoulder and radiated down his arm.

The squeal of tires and the roar of an engine pierced the still morning air. Then the report of Ian's Glock, three shots in rapid succession, echoed. Nicole was returning fire. Ian swore savagely and pushed to his feet. Nicole whipped around and quickly surveyed him.

"Where are you hit?" Worry traced lines across her face, her gaze darted back to his left shoulder. "Damn," she breathed. Gingerly she pushed his jacket away to view the damage.

"It's nothing."

She gave him a look. "Yeah, right."

Ian gritted his teeth when she unbuttoned his shirt partway and pulled it from the wound. He winced inwardly. "I am now fully convinced that you're trying to get yourself killed, Nicole. Why didn't you stay in the truck?"

"Shut up, Michaels." She grimaced. "You need a doctor."

"I got a partial on the license plate," Martinez reported breathlessly as he skidded to a stop next to Nicole.

"We have to get Ian to a hospital." She tugged him toward the passenger-side door of Martinez's borrowed truck as she spoke.

Ian manacled her right wrist and halted her forward movement. "I'll take this." Before she could protest he relieved her of the Glock, then tucked it into his waistband beneath his jacket. "And don't even think about leaving my sight."

"Fine," she snapped, her eyes shooting daggers at him. "As long as you get in the damned vehicle."

Martinez quickly brushed the glass from the driver's seat and dropped behind the wheel. "My brother is definitely going to kill me," he muttered.

"Drive, Martinez," Nicole ordered as she slid in next to him, "or he won't get the chance."

Chapter Two

Blood…

Oh God.

Nauseated and feeling more than a little faint, Nicole stared down at her bloodstained hands. This was by no means her first time to exchange gunfire with a hostile, nor was it her first up-close encounter with spilled blood.

But this was Ian's blood.

The hospital's medicinal smell didn't help. Nicole swiped her palms against the baggy gray sweatshirt she wore. She squeezed her hands into tight fists and dropped them to her sides. Moistening her dry lips and careful not to make eye contact, she slowly lifted her gaze to the man seated on the examining table. He sat on the very edge, poised, intent, as if anticipating the need to make a tactical move at any given moment. His torn and bloody shirt lay on the exam table behind him, the damaged suit jacket next to it. Nicole closed her eyes against the panic that still threatened to suffocate her each time she relived those few seconds between the sound of the gunshot and the moment she confirmed with her own eyes that Ian wasn't mortally wounded.

The sound of Ian's smoky voice as he answered some question the doctor asked dragged Nicole back to the here and now. Young and obviously nervous, the doctor pulled another suture through the nasty wound on Ian's shoulder. He kept muttering something about the injury looking like a gunshot wound to him. Poor guy, Nicole thought to herself, he had to be an intern. Otherwise Martinez would never have had him even half believing that idiotic story about Ian's falling into a window.

Ignoring the doctor's concerns, Ian did nothing to lessen the thick tension. His dark, brooding presence would unnerve a war-zone veteran. He had refused the offer of pain medication, and, in that arrogant, dangerous tone of his, had ordered the doctor to do what he had to do as quickly as possible. The wound wasn't so bad, Nicole told herself again. Just a nasty slash through skin and muscle. Had the angle been slightly different Ian might be in surgery now—or worse.

Shuddering with a chill that went bone-deep, Nicole wrapped her arms around her middle. Ian could have been killed. And it was her fault. She should never have gotten him mixed up in this. How could she drag him into her problems with no regard for his safety? Had she been so absorbed in saving her own skin that she hadn't thought through the consequences of her actions? Nicole let go a heavy breath. She closed her eyes and willed the mixture of fear and frustration to retreat. Ian was going to be fine, she told herself again. He was safe.

And she was leaving.

She could do this alone. She was a highly trained federal agent. All she had to do was make sure she wasn't followed when she made live contact with her witness. She didn't need Ian. Denial rushed through her at that thought. She needed him all right, but not in the way she should.

Suddenly, more from some innate need than true courage, she met Ian's gaze for the first time since their arrival at the ER. He hadn't taken his eyes off her since they'd entered the examining room. It wasn't necessary for her to look to confirm her suspicions, she could feel his gaze on her. Steady and relentless, those piercing gray eyes held hers even now, then reached past her defenses and touched her.

Nicole trembled with reaction. The only indication that Ian felt anything at all was the flexing of that muscle in his rigid jaw. He was probably just annoyed that her stupidity had got him shot. Whatever he was feeling, one thing was certain, Ian Michaels was planning his next move. Nicole knew his methods as well as she knew her own. No matter that he was surely in serious pain, Ian would develop a plan, and then a backup plan for that. Analyzing her current emotional state would be part of his strategy. He read her too easily. Nicole looked away. Why give him any more ammunition?

A cell phone chirped, startling Nicole. She took a slow, deep breath and ran a shaky hand through her hair. She was seriously rattled. Of course, dancing with death would do that, she reminded herself. Next to her, Martinez murmured responses to his caller.

"It's for you," he announced, offering Ian the compact phone. "It's Victoria."

Ian accepted the phone, then placed it on the examining table next to him. Nicole knew he was still watching her, so she kept her gaze purposely averted from his. He reached beneath his jacket lying on the table beside him and retrieved his weapon. He handed the Glock, butt first, to Martinez.

"Don't take your eyes off her," he warned. "If she makes a move for the door, use it."

The doctor made an odd, choking sound of disbelief.

"Did I see a badge? Are you gentlemen police officers? If this is a gunshot wound—"

Indignation exploded inside Nicole. "Screw you, Michaels," she hissed, cutting off the doctor. Those tender emotions she had felt only moments ago evaporated instantly.

Ian held her gaze for one long beat. "I believe you've already taken care of that."

"You bas—"

"Miss Reed," Martinez interrupted firmly. "I'd like you to have a seat. Please," he added quickly as he tucked the weapon into his waistband.

"I…I really need you to be still," the doctor said hesitantly, his gaze darting to the weapon at Martinez's waist, then back to Ian. "I can't do this properly unless—"

Ian waved him off. "In a moment." His formidable focus remained fixed on Nicole, watching, waiting for her reaction to Martinez's request.

One second lapsed to five before Nicole gave in and plopped onto the molded-plastic, institutional-orange chair. Knowing Ian, he would have sat there and bled to death before relenting. Still stinging from his remark, she mentally recited every vile word in her vocabulary and Ian's connection to each. Martinez stationed himself between her and the door. Did Ian really believe he could prevent her from leaving whenever she got good and ready to go? Nicole smiled to herself. She would just see about that.

Obviously satisfied that he had won, he picked up the cell phone and turned his attention to Victoria. "Yes." He paused, listening. "No, I'm fine. There's no need for you to rush back. I have everything under control." Another brief pause. "Yes, I'll do that." He flipped the mouthpiece closed and tossed the phone back to Martinez.

"I do have other patients, Mr. Michaels," the doctor said pointedly, obviously finally finding his courage. Or perhaps just anxious to rid himself of present company.

"Of course." Ian leveled one final warning glare on Nicole.

She produced an exaggerated smile, then, while he watched so intently, she silently mouthed a most descriptive adjective—one that fit Ian perfectly in her opinion. The promise of a smile tilted one side of his usually grim mouth, making her pulse react. Nicole released a weary sigh and for the first time today had the presence of mind to thank God that they were both safe.

But how long would either of them stay that way?

The door suddenly swung open and Ian's attention jerked toward the intruder.

"We've got another bleeder, Doctor," an efficient-looking nurse called from the doorway. Her gaze immediately flew to Martinez, and then the weapon at his waist before he could turn away. "A seventeen-year-old with a knife wound to the right forearm," she added slowly, her eyes widening with fear.

The doctor spared her a brief glance. "Prep him, I'll be right there. Almost finished here," he said distractedly. The nurse managed a smile in Ian's direction before she disappeared into the hall. The wide door closed soundlessly behind her.

Ian gave Martinez a discreet nod, then angled his head toward the door in silent instruction. No doubt, Ian reasoned, that nurse was at the desk calling the police at this very moment. When the police arrived, there would be confusion, distraction. Too much opportunity for Nicole to give them the slip. Not to mention he didn't want her position with the bureau brought to the attention of the locals.

"Let's take a walk, Miss Reed," Martinez suggested.

Nicole looked him up and down as if he'd just suggested something lewd. "I don't think so, Martinez."

"Do as he says, Nicole," Ian ordered quietly. She shot him a drop-dead look, then heaved an impatient sigh before pushing to her feet. Reluctantly she followed Martinez out the door.

"Hold still just a little longer, Mr. Michaels." The doctor paused, surveying Ian with a look of concern. "Now that we're alone, are you sure you don't want something for the pain? That local can't be doing much for you."

"I'm fine."

The doctor shrugged and returned to the business at hand. Ian needed his head clear. He would have to deal with the police, which wouldn't be that difficult. Victoria had a great many influential connections. Known for following the rules and cooperating, Colby Agency investigators rarely got any flack from the local authorities. Maybe this time Ian was stretching the rules, but that couldn't be helped. He set his jaw hard against a particularly fierce stab of pain.

Nicole was anything but simple. Dealing with her required Ian's full command of all his senses. His strategy was as straightforward as you could get. First he planned to get the truth out of her—one way or another. She knew a lot more about the threat to her life than she was telling, of that Ian felt certain. Secondly, he intended to stash her away someplace safe while he handled the situation.

Then, he would walk away and never look back. Ian refused to acknowledge the protest that twisted inside him. He couldn't deny what he felt for Nicole. The emotions were fierce, overpowering. But he couldn't trust her. She had betrayed him before, what was to prevent her from doing it again? Ian almost smiled at the memory of her reaction to his comment earlier. He closed his eyes and allowed Nicole's image to envelop him. All attitude and sass on the outside, but soft and vulnerable on the inside, Nicole was the one woman who could make him lose control. She held a power over him that defied all else. Ian blinked away the vision. But he wasn't a masochist at heart, nor was he without pride. He had allowed that mistake once.

Nicole cared only about her career. She was attracted to Ian he knew, but that was all. Her complete allegiance lay with the cloak-and-dagger stuff that epitomized shadow operations. Ian bit back a laugh at the thought of Nicole as someone's wife. But the rush of jealousy that surged through him was no laughing matter. Ian frowned and quickly reined in his wayward thoughts. No more, he determined. From this point forward his every connection with Nicole would be strictly business.

A quick rap on the door drew Ian's gaze in that direction. Two uniformed Chicago police officers entered the room. Both looked entirely too young to own a weapon, much less use it.

"Ian Michaels?"

"Yes," Ian replied.

The doctor looked up; a frown knitted his brow. "Sorry, guys, you're going to have to wait until I'm finished here," he warned as he placed a bandage over the newly sutured wound. "My patient's health comes first."

"No problem, sir," the taller of the two replied. "We've got all the time in the world." The look he shot Ian was arrogantly challenging.

Ian answered that bold gaze with bored amusement. This was going to be a piece of cake.

The door suddenly flew inward again. The two officers whirled toward it in a flash of dark blue. Martinez stumbled in holding his nose with both hands, blood gushing between his fingers and down his shirt front. Ian bounded off the exam table amid the doctor's protests.

"Where's Nicole?"

"She's gone." Martinez used one hand to swipe the blood from his mouth. "Hell, man, I think she broke my nose."

Ian's heart shifted into warp speed. "How much head start does she have?" he demanded curtly.

Martinez shook his head defeatedly. "Five minutes maybe."

Suddenly everyone was talking at once. The doctor shouting for a nurse. The policemen demanding to know what was going on. And Martinez trying to explain how a female he outweighed by nearly a hundred pounds and towered over by at least a half-dozen inches had managed to beat the hell out of him, leave him stunned on the floor and get away.

The voices and faces around Ian faded into insignificance as his mind raced forward. *Where would she go?* She was breaking every rule of survival in the book. In Ian's experience, when an agent broke code there was compelling motivation. Something worth the risk.

What was Nicole hiding?

"I'VE GOT IT," Martinez announced in a distinctly nasal voice as he rushed into Ian's office. The white tape stretched tautly across the bridge of his nose looked stark against his dark skin. "The car the shooter used was stolen. And Nicole had a room at the Sheraton downtown. She checked out just over an hour ago."

Ian glanced at his watch, one-fifteen. "Did she call for a cab?"

"The doorman said she got into a Ford Explorer parked

on the opposite side of the street.'' Martinez swore. "My brother is going to *enjoy* killing me."

"It'll show up at the airport,'' Ian said distractedly. He needed to know where Nicole was headed and from which airport. And he needed to know now.

"I'm sorry I lost her, man,'' Martinez offered again.

Ian met the other man's concerned gaze. Though inexperienced, Martinez was a good investigator. In time he would be a force to be reckoned with, and there was no time like the present to gain valuable experience. Ian knew he could trust Martinez completely. Besides, Nicole was a formidable opponent. Ian didn't know anyone, not even himself, he mused, that she couldn't best if she put her mind to it. Martinez might as well learn the hard way.

"It's okay, Martinez. Nicole is not your typical vulnerable female client.'' At least not on the surface, Ian amended silently.

Martinez huffed. "You got that right."

"Mr. Michaels, I have that information you requested."

Ian motioned for Mildred, Victoria's secretary, to come in. He accepted the documents she offered.

"Miss Reed has a reservation on every flight on all airlines headed to D.C. and New York that are scheduled to leave O'Hare and Midway between three o'clock and eight o'clock today."

Ian scanned the list of flights. Eight different flights arriving at five different airports. He shook his head. Nicole had no intention of making this easy.

"And here's the report on Miss Reed's car. I asked Murray at city's lab to put a rush on the preliminary and fax me a copy ASAP.'' Mildred smiled with satisfaction. "He came through, as usual."

Ian returned her smile. Mildred had been with the agency since the beginning, when Victoria's husband had been in charge. The vivacious middle-aged woman knew the Chicago PD like the back of her hand, and had something on anyone who was anybody employed there.

"Thank you, Mildred." A frown creased Ian's brow as he scanned the relatively brief preliminary report. No timer. No evidence of an internal detonation device. *Remote-detonated.* The bomb had been remote-detonated by someone watching Nicole's car, Ian concluded. But why had they not waited until she was in the car?

"Call Kruger," he instructed Mildred. "I need a ride to D.C."

"Yes sir." Mildred turned back at the door. "I'll ask him to be ready within the hour."

"Good," Ian agreed.

"You think she'd go back to D.C.?" Martinez gingerly fingered the tightly taped bridge of his nose.

"Yes, I do."

"I'll drop you at the airport," Martinez offered. "That is if you don't mind me driving your car, mine's still in the shop."

"That's fine." Ian estimated that Victoria's private jet could have him in D.C. a good half hour before the earliest commercial flight on Nicole's schedule. He stood, mentally ticking off the items he would need to take with him. He would need to stop by his place and pick up another weapon and a change of clothes. Nicole probably left his Glock in the Explorer, but there was nothing he could do about that right now. He glanced at Martinez. "Let's go. I'll confirm the itinerary with Kruger en route."

"After I drop you off, I'll look for the Explorer," Martinez grumbled as they headed toward the elevators. "I can't believe she stole my brother's truck." Martinez shook his head disgustedly. "And, man, I've never had my butt kicked so badly. By a female at that.'' He flashed Ian a look of dismay. "I hope you're not going to tell anybody about that."

Ian stabbed the elevator call button, then shot the man next to him an amused look. "Don't worry, Martinez, your secret is safe with me."

"Mr. Michaels, wait!"

Ian paused before getting onto the elevator. Amy Wells, the newest member of the agency's clerical staff, hurried toward him, those long, coppery curls bouncing around her shoulders.

"Miss Wells," he greeted patiently, though impatience pounded through his veins. He had to get to D.C. before Nicole did.

"Mildred needs your signature before you leave since Mrs. Colby won't be back for another week." Amy indicated the report she held and offered him a pen. She blushed, clearly intimidated at having to speak to him much less request anything of him.

Ian produced a smile. "No problem." He quickly penned his official signature.

"Gosh, Martinez, what happened to you?" Amy asked abruptly, all wide-eyed innocence.

Before Martinez could come up with a suitable explanation, Ian leaned toward her and whispered, "It's a secret." He touched his lips with one finger in a gesture of silence and stepped inside the elevator. The doors closed, leaving Miss Wells staring in dismay after them. Martinez wasn't going to live this down anytime soon.

NICOLE PARKED her car down the street from her apartment building. Darkness shrouded the old neighborhood she had called home for five years now. Only forty minutes from her office, the small Virginia community boasted quiet living with all the conveniences of the city. Nicole sighed, then closed her eyes for a long moment. She was tired. Her trip to Chicago had been a fiasco, and a colossal waste of precious time. Nicole glanced at the digital clock on her dash. Only two hours until her flight to Atlanta. She had to get a move on. She had wasted enough time stopping to purchase something to wear besides Ian's sweats.

"Suck it up, Reed," she scolded herself as she scanned the deserted street once more. Walking into that building and then her dark apartment was not something she looked forward to—especially since the only other tenant was probably out of town as usual. But what choice did she have? She needed clothes and cash, and new ID. She had left her purse at Ian's. No way would she have chanced going back to get it. Her next flight was reserved under an alias. She certainly couldn't go anywhere broke and without clean ID. It would take lots of hard cash to do what she had to do. Replanting a witness wasn't cheap. Or easy. Not to mention the fact that she was doing this on her own. She knew better than to risk anyone at the agency finding out. And she definitely couldn't hang around D.C. long. It wouldn't take the man—or woman, she amended—long to track her back here. Ian wouldn't be far behind her. And he would be royally ticked off. Nicole decided she had better be gone when he arrived.

Her gaze sweeping left to right, then back, Nicole emerged from the car. She adjusted the baseball cap she had crammed her hair into, then rolled her head to loosen up her neck. God she was tense. Her right hand slid instinctively to her weapon she had retrieved from an airport locker. She tucked it more firmly into the waistband of her jeans at the small of her back. The denim jacket she wore concealed it well. She could have taken it to Chicago with her, but hadn't wanted to go through the hassle with airport authorities. So she had left the weapon and her bureau ID in a locker. She had left Ian's Glock in the Explorer back at O'Hare. He wouldn't be happy, but he would get over it. Martinez would find it when he picked up his brother's vehicle. Losing a weapon wasn't conducive to sleeping at night.

Nicole breathed a sigh of relief when she entered the well-lit courtyard that flanked the right side of her building. Only three stories, each floor of the old building housed just two apartments. The place was definitely small compared to the others in this neighborhood, but it was clean and well kept. And quiet. How could it be anything else? she mused. In the five years since she'd moved in, more than half the other apartments had always been vacant. Like now.

The sound of a dog barking on the next block reminded Nicole that she was wasting time. She glanced up at her unadorned, second-story balcony. On the first floor, the only other tenant's terrace contained an assortment of flowering and green plants. Nicole was never home long enough to care for plants or pets. She shrugged listlessly. People like her didn't have time for such distractions.

The pool shimmered like a tranquil lagoon in the full-moonlight as she hurried past it and around to the front entrance. A slight breeze whispered through the leaves of the surrounding trees. This lovely courtyard had been the main selling point for the place in Nicole's opinion. With one more look to either side of her, she slid the key into the lock and entered the deserted stairwell.

Nicole paused to listen for sound. The answering silence soothed her frazzled nerves. *Okay,* she assured herself, *everything is going to be fine.* She had done this plenty of times before. But no matter how she fought it, the memory of her car exploding right before her eyes kept replaying in her head. The connection could no longer be denied, she realized as more images reeled through her tired mind. The director's telephone exploding while he sat at his desk. The death-dealing explosion at Agent Daniels's house. The letter bomb that had exploded in her mail carrier's bag just before he reached her apartment building's mail station. The single shot she knew deep in her gut had been meant for her in that shopping-mall parking lot. Then her rental car. Nicole shook off the lingering images before her next memory could take form. She had to focus. Even without the warning letter she had received from Daniels two days after his unsolved murder, things were all too clear now.

Someone knew their secret.

Slowly, silently, Nicole climbed the two flights of stairs that seemed to go on forever. The white walls and absolute quiet allowed other images and voices she didn't want to hear or see to creep into her thoughts. Ian's cold, hard look when he had come face-to-face with her in Victoria Colby's office. The soft, sensual whispering of his voice as he made love to her. Nicole forced away the vivid memories. Fear gripped her heart when her errant mind replayed the scene outside Ian's town house when he had been shot. She thanked God again that he hadn't been hurt worse.

What a fool she was for seeking him out and dragging him into this mess. She would do this alone. She had thought it through. She could do it. And Ian would be safe. Last night had opened her eyes to the truth she had wanted to deny for three years now. No matter what happened to her, Nicole could not bear to take a chance on Ian getting hurt again—physically or emotionally.

Distraction was a dangerous risk. One neither of them could afford to take. Nicole would do her job to the best of her ability...alone. And Ian could live his life the way he deserved without her interference. He had a posh job, a great house. And probably lots of women, a little voice added. Nicole clenched her teeth and refused to consider Ian's social life. She was an even bigger fool for not stopping to think that he might even be seriously involved with someone. He was, after all, incredibly good-looking, and that voice...

Just thinking about the sound of his voice made her insides quiver. Nicole paused as she reached the landing outside her apartment. *Get a grip, Reed,* she chastised silently. *That line of thinking is hazardous to your health.*

She listened outside her nondescript gray door for what felt like half an eternity before she inserted her key into the lock. The only sound was her heart thudding in her chest. Willing herself to calm, she reached beneath her jacket for her weapon. Nicole pushed the door inward, spilling light into the dark foyer. She stepped inside, hit the switch for the overhead light, and with one foot eased the door closed behind her.

She scanned the darkness beyond the foyer for any movement, while listening intently past the hush of the central unit. Nothing. Relieved, she reached behind her and locked the door, then stepped soundlessly toward the living room. Every nerve ending on alert, she eased quietly into the room. Holding her breath, she leaned down and turned on the table lamp. A soft, golden glow lit the center of the room. The far edges remained in shadow.

Years of training not allowing her to relax her guard until she had checked every nook and cranny, Nicole moved cautiously around the perimeter of the room.

After giving her bedroom and bathroom the all clear, Nicole finally took a deep breath. She silently retraced her steps down the hall and slipped into the kitchen, caution still restraining her. The light from the hall glinted against the array of stainless-steel pots and pans hanging from the rack over the island bar. White cabinets and countertops reflected the minimal light reaching out to them.

Paranoia could be a good thing, she told that lingering sensation that made the hair on the back of her neck continue to stand on end. But enough was enough. There was no one here. The place was as quiet as a tomb.

"Poor choice in words, Reed," she muttered as she lowered her weapon. She was starved. Beyond starved. She frowned—she was so hungry she could actually smell food. Nicole closed her eyes and inhaled deeply of the scent her imagination had conjured. Chinese. Wouldn't it be nice if she could take time to drop by Won's on her way back to the airport? Her stomach rumbled in agreement.

"God, I'm starved," she said aloud then flipped on the overhead fluorescent.

"Eating is essential to survival, Nicole."

Nicole's pulse jumped, her heart rocketed into her throat. She whirled toward the sound of Ian's voice in the far corner of the kitchen, her weapon instinctively leveled on the target. She blinked twice to adjust to the bright light. Drinks and containers of Chinese takeout—Won's no less—sat in the middle of her kitchen table.

He'd remembered.

Nicole almost smiled as she lowered her weapon, and

relaxed her fire-ready stance. Her attention shifted to Ian's left hand as he pushed one container forward, then to his right where he held a weapon trained expertly on her. *Uh-oh.* Slowly, she lifted her reluctant gaze to his ever-unreadable one.

"I want answers, Nicole." He leaned back in his chair. "And I want them now."

Chapter Three

"Can't I eat first?" Nicole suggested, her gaze no longer riveted to the sleek silver barrel of Ian's weapon, but surveying the hard planes and angles of his handsome face. Her desire for food evaporated, replaced by a lingering desire of another sort that never seemed to go completely away in this man's presence.

"No."

Stalling, Nicole placed her weapon on the island, pulled off her cap and tossed it aside, then leaned casually against the counter. She was too tired to do this right now, and she sure didn't have any time to waste. But Ian would never let her off the hook this time. "Look, I—" she began.

He shook his head slowly from side to side, halting her attempted diversionary tactic. He placed his own weapon on the table's glass top, his fingers splayed on the grip. Ian wasn't going anywhere, she admitted reluctantly, he intended to wait her out. And time was the one thing she didn't have.

With a beleaguered sigh, Nicole crossed her arms over her middle and proceeded to give him the heavily varnished version. She kept her gaze carefully focused on the carryout box, even licked her lips for effect, but he ignored her not-so-subtle hints. "Three weeks ago my director stayed a little later than usual at the office. Everyone else was gone. Apparently his telephone rang and then exploded."

Nicole shrugged, then glanced beyond Ian's shoulder, giving the appearance of eye contact. "I'm sure you can fill in the resulting details." She had got the call from Daniels. Walked into that office and seen...

Nicole immediately suppressed the details she remembered far too vividly. Especially the image of Landon's devastated widow at the funeral. "A few days after that—"

"Look at me, Nicole."

She blinked, hesitated, then leveled her gaze on his. "Satisfied?"

He nodded, once.

She clenched her jaw to prevent the directions she wanted to give him on exactly where he could go. Why hadn't he just stayed in Chicago and let her do what had to be done? Why did he bother coming after her? Nicole plunged her fingers into her hair and massaged her aching skull. She would never understand the man. Blocking the emotion she knew would give her away, Nicole commanded her body to relax. She dropped her arms to her sides and continued. "Four days after Director Landon's death, Agent Daniels died in another explosion."

"What kind of explosion?"

"Gas leak. His house." Nicole struggled with the effort to keep her emotions at bay. Distance. She was a pro, she knew how to disengage emotionally. *Just do it,* she instructed silently. "There was hardly anything left to identify."

Nicole fell silent, unable to continue...unable to look away from Ian's penetrating, metallic gaze. Years of training weren't supposed to disintegrate like this. The realization that death was hot on her heels tugged at her composure. Ian's expression remained perfectly cool, unaffected. His damned black suit and shirt looked as if he'd just put them on. Nicole thought about her own disheveled appearance—unwashed jeans and T-shirt, her hair a mess. She almost laughed. But not Ian. Every perfect, dark hair was in place. The barest hint of five o'clock shadow darkened his rigid jaw, lending him an air of danger.

She had to get out of here. Nicole was out of time. The tangle of emotions she could no longer restrain gripped her with an intensity that shook her to the core. She drew in a harsh breath. How had things got so screwed up? Two people she knew personally, had worked with for years, were dead. She trembled inside, barely concealing the reaction. And now their killer intended to see that she stopped breathing too. This wasn't supposed to happen. They had taken every precaution.

"Go on," Ian instructed when she remained silent.

Nicole swallowed the tears of frustration that swelled into her throat and glared at him. "Two days after Daniels's murder, I received a letter from him, postmarked the day before he died." She paused. *Okay, girl, get a grip.* This would be the tricky part. Her attention focused inward, beyond the knot of feelings hovering way too close to the surface. She couldn't allow Ian to see the lie in her eyes. "Daniels said that he believed someone was trying to kill him. The same person who killed Director Landon. He warned me that if anything happened to him that I should consider myself next on the list."

Nicole gripped the counter, hard. "That's it," she finished, hoping like hell he would leave it at that.

Ian considered her last statement for a time. "Why?"

That tone. That damned irritatingly calm-in-the-face-of-disaster tone. "How should I know?" she snapped. Nicole resurrected the rage she had initially felt upon hearing of Landon's, then Daniels's death. She used that anger as camouflage now. "It's not like we're the blooming Red Cross." She flung her arms upward in frustration. "You know how this business works. You make enemies. Lots of them."

"Why?" he repeated, so annoyingly calm that Nicole jerked with tension.

"I don't know," she ground out.

His assessment took about three seconds. "You're lying."

Nicole stared at the tiled floor and bit the inside of her cheek. This was pointless. Ian read her too well. She turned and looked him square in the eye. "That information is sensitive. Shared on a need-to-know basis only."

His long fingers curled around the nine-millimeter's grip. "Right now, Nicole, you *need* to tell me the truth more than you've ever *needed* to do anything in your life."

Nicole rubbed her tired eyes with the heels of her hands. God, she wished this nightmare was over. "I don't have time for this, Ian." She blew out a breath of frustration. "Someone is trying to kill me and I have to get out of here."

"Where are you going?"

She shot him another deadly glare. She wanted to scream—to force him to react. "That's none of your business."

Ian stood. Nicole's tension escalated to a new level. Maybe she would get that reaction after all. His gaze never leaving her, he reached beneath his jacket and tucked his weapon away. She frowned. Why did he do that? Then he walked right up to her, sending her heart into a violent staccato. Ian placed one hand on the counter on either side of her, and leaned in close.

"I'm making it my business." His accented tone was so soft, yet so clearly lethal.

Nicole steeled herself against his nearness. His scent invaded her senses, making her weak. Making her want to tell him anything he wanted to hear. "Just let me get my things together and I swear I'll tell you on the way to the airport," she hedged.

"You'll tell me now."

Nicole moistened her lips. "Please, Ian, I can't miss that flight."

"*Now.*"

She closed her eyes and shook her head in defeat. This was a mistake. "Fine." Nicole opened her eyes and took a long look into Ian's cool, unsuspecting gaze. What would he do when she gave him that truth he wanted so badly? One thing was certain, helping her wouldn't be on his mind. Killing her, maybe. Despising her, definitely.

"All right. Three years ago, I was assigned the most sensitive, not to mention the most important, case of my career." She hesitated, dreading the metamorphosis she would see in those silver eyes. "Landon made the decision. He concluded that as long as the witness was alive, there was no way to ensure absolute safety."

Ian's gaze narrowed slightly. "There are never any guarantees. Witnesses know that going into the program."

Nicole cleared her throat, it didn't help. "This one was special."

"How special?" Ian asked cautiously.

"Special enough to warrant a blackout operation." She

leveled her gaze on his, hard as that proved. "Total blackout," she added.

A trace of denial flickered in his now-wary gaze.

"My assignment was to make sure the world thought this one was dead." Nicole watched the confusion, then outrage slowly replace the denial. "It was the only way to keep him safe. If anyone had suspected that he'd survived, his life wouldn't have been worth squat." She swallowed convulsively. "It was the only way, Ian."

"The forensics report was conclusive," he countered, his voice as cold as ice.

"Daniels took care of the explosion and a John-Doe body to keep forensics happy." Nicole reminded herself to breathe. She squeezed her eyes shut before meeting his relentless gaze once more. She would have given almost anything within her power not to have to answer the question she knew he would ask next.

"And what, precisely, were your instructions?" Icy, edged with steel, his words cut through her like a knife.

"It was my job to make sure you failed in yours."

He straightened. Nicole jerked in reaction to the abrupt move. His fists clenched at his sides, a muscle jumped in his jaw. "Why me?"

"You were the best," she admitted reluctantly, knowing she was only adding insult to injury. "Your reputation was widely known. The cartel would have expected us to use our best. We had to consider every contingency."

"You're telling me that Raymond Solomon is alive."

Nicole backed against the counter as far as she could to escape the arctic chill radiating from Ian. "Yes."

"You didn't request the assignment for the publicity of working a high-profile case as you told me? It had nothing to do with competition between the bureau and the marshal service? Nothing to do with getting yourself another promotion?''

Too sick with self-disgust to answer, Nicole slowly shook her head. What had seemed so right, so just at the time, now felt devious and twisted.

Something dark and forbidding surfaced in his eyes, the angles and lines of his handsome face turned to granite. ''You played my backup—had *sex* with me—just to make sure I was properly distracted?''

This was the reaction she had expected, dreaded. Nothing she could say would make him believe that she hadn't meant things to go so far. That their lovemaking—

''Answer me,'' he demanded, that softly accented voice uncharacteristically harsh.

''I did my job.'' Nicole pleaded with him to understand with her eyes. ''But I swear, Ian, sleeping with you wasn't part of it.''

He smiled. It wasn't pleasant. ''Just a little something extra thrown in for good measure, huh?''

Nicole trembled visibly, as much from the anger mounting inside her as the pain constricting her chest, making if difficult to breathe. ''I did what I had to do to keep Raymond Solomon safe. The job I was sworn to do. What happened between the two of us was personal.''

He glared at her with so much disgust that Nicole felt sick with the fallout. ''You're damned right it was personal,'' he said bitterly. ''You allowed me to believe for three years that my negligence had cost a man his life.''

The air raced out of her lungs on a shudder. ''Yes, I did,'' she admitted. Nicole dragged in a harsh breath. ''And I'd do it again if it meant keeping that witness alive.'' She laughed then, a short, brittle sound. ''The hell of it is, Michaels, you would have done the same thing, and you know it.''

Three long beats passed, the tension thickening with each. Then he released a heavy breath. "Yes. I would have."

Weak with relief, Nicole watched his features slowly relax, his eyes return to that calm, translucent silver. He might not ever forgive her, but at least maybe he understood. That was something "So." Nicole straightened, then tucked her hands into her back pockets and went for a subject change. "Are you going to let me eat or what? I told you I'm on a tight schedule here."

To his surprise, as swiftly as it had risen, Ian's rage receded. He stepped back so Nicole could move. He watched her slip into a chair at the table, pulling one foot beneath her. She opened a container and quickly lifted a forkful of rice to her mouth. She closed her eyes and moaned her pleasure. Ian looked away. His emotions were far too raw now to even look at her.

Relief suddenly washed over him as the realization that Solomon was alive sank in. He had lived with the weight of guilt for so long that he felt lightheaded without it. His instincts had been right all along. The cover story of why Nicole had been assigned to work with him on that case had never really fit, in his opinion. The whole thing had felt wrong from the beginning.

Nicole had betrayed him. Ian had fully expected a different reaction when he finally got the truth. He definitely hadn't anticipated this complete deflation of his darker emotions. But somehow he just couldn't manage the wounded warrior bit. The fact that she was following orders cast a slightly different light on things.

But betrayal was betrayal, he reminded himself. He frowned. Nothing. No incensed outrage, no roaring desire to retaliate. He shook his head. He, apparently, wasn't ready to exact his pound of flesh from Nicole. He glanced at the woman who had wreaked such havoc with his world. But it would take time for him to come to terms with the reality of what had taken place between them three years ago. Maybe he never would. Understanding was one thing, forgiveness entirely another.

But right now, he had a more pressing problem. Someone was running a game. And she seemed to think it had something to do with the Solomon case. Ian crossed the room and sat down at the table with Nicole. Though he might never forgive her for what she had done, he couldn't live with himself if he allowed anything to happen to her. Nicole Reed presented a facade that was tough as nails, but she had limits just like anyone else. And right now she was very close to exceeding those limits. She needed his help. He would give her the help she needed because he couldn't do otherwise, but then it would be over. He would walk away.

His decision made, Ian watched her devour the sesame chicken for a while before he interrupted. He smiled to himself when he recalled how frequently Nicole actually forgot to eat. But she always made up for any missed meals when she remembered.

"Who gave Landon the order to take charge?"

Nicole looked thoughtful for a moment. "I don't know. Daniels and I were given our orders and we didn't ask questions."

"You're certain the threat to your life has something to do with Solomon?" Ian pressed.

She nodded adamantly, then swallowed. "Daniels thought the same thing. He said so in his letter." She took a quick drink of cola. "There were three of us directly involved in the operation." Her eyes grew somber. "Two are dead." She stared at the food in front of her as if she had suddenly lost her appetite.

"All three of you knew Solomon's final location?" Ian took Nicole's fork and stabbed a nugget of spiced chicken, then popped it into his mouth.

"No. Daniels had nothing to do with that part." She frowned in thought. "In fact, I'm the only one who knew exactly where Solomon ended up."

Ian considered that statement. "What do you mean where he ended up?" He laid the fork aside.

"About six months after his highly publicized demise, Solomon contacted me." She made a disgusted sound in her throat. "After all we'd been through to plant him safely. I gave him considerable hell for taking such a risk."

Ian suppressed a grin. "I can imagine." Nicole smiled warmly, and something inside Ian softened. He immediately checked the reaction.

"Solomon was convinced that someone was on to him." She shrugged. "So I replanted him and told him I'd kick his—well, that he'd better not rear his ugly head again."

Nicole pulled one knee up and propped her elbow on it, then plowed her fingers through her long hair. Ian clenched his fingers into fists to prevent the almost involuntary reaction to reach out and touch those long, silky tresses.

"I've even considered that it might be Solomon himself trying to kill me," Nicole said doubtfully. "That way there would be no possibility of a future leak. But I really can't see that weasel engineering all this." She massaged her temples. "I guess there's always the possibility that he contacted someone from his former life."

"Whoever it is," Ian assured her, "he isn't trying to kill you."

Her startled gaze connected with Ian's. "Have you been

listening at all? You saw my rental car explode. The ambush outside your place—''

''If he intended to kill you, you'd be dead now.''

She searched his gaze, the wheels turning inside that pretty head with this new, unexpected information. ''Your basis for that conclusion?''

''The explosive device in your car was remote-detonated.'' Ian leaned back in the chair and stretched his legs in front of him. Exhaustion clawed at him, but he ignored it. ''He had to be watching. If he wanted you dead, he would have waited until you were in the car, or at least closer.''

Realization dawned in those sky blue eyes. ''You've seen the lab report already?''

''The preliminary,'' he clarified.

Nicole shook her head. ''I don't get it.''

''And any shooter worth his salt would have taken you out sometime during the ninety or so seconds you fiddled with Martinez's keys before you got into his vehicle.'' The memory still sent fear rushing through Ian's veins.

''Yeah,'' she agreed. She stabbed another piece of chicken, but paused before putting it into her mouth. ''That was kind of a stupid thing to do.'' Those full lips dipped into a worried frown. ''If he isn't trying to kill me, then what is going on?'' She dropped the fork and untouched chicken back into the box.

''By the way.'' Ignoring her question, Ian cocked a brow and shot her a look. ''Martinez is quite upset with you about his brother's truck.''

Nicole scrubbed a hand over her face, her body language giving away the depth of her own exhaustion. ''Sorry,'' she offered with feigned humility.

''I would avoid him in the near future.''

Nicole's forehead creased with her deepening frown. "Just because I borrowed his truck?"

Ian sighed loudly. "Well, you did break his nose."

"What can I say?" She flared her palms. "The guy had a gun. Old habits are hard to break."

Ian settled a serious gaze on hers. "Just try and remember which ones are the good guys in the future."

Nicole sent him a mock salute. "Yes, sir."

"Now," Ian began, turning his attention back to business. "What's our plan?"

"*Our* plan?"

"That's right," he told her bluntly, his tone brooking no argument. "And this time there will be no secrets."

"You still want to help me?" The look of genuine surprise mixed with hopefulness in her eyes sucked at something deep inside him. "In spite of what I just told you?"

"Yes."

Nicole blew out a relieved breath. She was no fool. She knew she needed his help. "All right. I say we stash Solomon some place safe until we can get a handle on what's going on."

"Wrong."

Irritation stole across her delicate features, enhancing the lines of fatigue around her blue eyes. "What's wrong about that? Do you have a better idea?"

"No."

She rolled her eyes. "Then what's your point?"

"The point is that you would be doing exactly what they want you to do."

"Oh, really? And how might I be doing that?" she snapped.

Ian draped his arm over the empty chair next to him and studied her for a long moment. She was tired, she wasn't thinking clearly. "If you make live contact with Solomon, you'll be leading the shooter right to the mark. You said yourself that no one knows where he is but you."

She shook her head, sending that blond mane into action. "Daniels thought maybe someone was already on to Solomon's location. Besides, I know how to lose a tail."

"Some are more difficult to shake than others." Ian shrugged. "And if Solomon's location had already been compromised, why bother coming after you with all these elaborate death threats? Why waste the time or the effort? The shooter could just go straight to the mark."

"You're right." The reality of what she had almost done hit Nicole hard. "Why didn't I see that?"

Ian caught himself before he covered her hand with his own. The only way he could help Nicole was to keep his distance. Their relationship had to be maintained on a strictly professional level, for more reasons than one. "You've been through a lot in the past three weeks with no backup. Emotion and instinct have gotten all tangled up."

Nicole sat bolt upright. "I have to get word to Solomon to sit tight. If I don't show tonight without letting him know, he might get spooked."

"Don't worry. I'll have Martinez show up in your place to hold Solomon's hand."

"Good idea," Nicole murmured distractedly. "Solomon might do something lame." Nicole's questioning gaze landed on Ian's. "What do you think we should do next?"

It was Ian's turn to be surprised. Nicole usually preferred doing things her own way. "We sit tight and let the shooter come to us," he suggested.

"You think he'll do that considering I've hooked up with you now?"

Ian studied her concerned expression. Nicole was willing to risk her life by going it alone in order to protect Solomon. Ian wondered sometimes if the people they protected deserved such selfless sacrifice.

"If he wants Solomon, he won't have a choice," Ian assured her.

Glass shattered in the living room, followed by a thunderous whoosh. Ian shot to his feet, automatically reaching for his weapon. "Stay in here," he ordered curtly.

Before Nicole could protest, he moved cautiously into the hall. A distinct chemical odor filled his nostrils. A quick survey of the living room confirmed his suspicions. The east side of the room, including the front door, was already engulfed in flames. This was no simple Molotov cocktail. Ian gritted his teeth. He pivoted to find Nicole standing right behind him.

She swore. "We have to get out of here," she murmured distractedly as she considered the ravenous flames. The walls seemed to melt wherever the flames reached.

"The balcony," Ian agreed, grabbing her arm and ushering her in that direction.

Nicole shook her head, still staring at the mushrooming devastation. "Why is he doing this?"

"Hurry, Nicole," he ground out as he ushered her away from the threat.

Ian jerked the French doors open and dragged a hesitant Nicole out onto the balcony. He glanced over the balcony's railing at the pool below, then assessed the rapidly growing destruction behind them.

Nicole took one last glance at her home which was swiftly going up in smoke. "We have to get out of here," she repeated distractedly.

"You do swim, don't you?" Ian asked slowly.

She glared at him as if he'd lost complete control of his senses. "What? Yes!"

"Good, because we need to jump *now*."

Realization suddenly dawned in Nicole's eyes. "Have you lost your mind?"

"Probably," he agreed, his full attention on the inferno edging ever closer to their location. He wondered briefly if there were any other tenants in the building. He would have to see that everyone got out. Ian took another look over the railing. "Ladies first," he suggested, trying to sound optimistic.

Nicole balked. "Who knows if we'll even hit the pool. There's no way I'm jumping off this balcony, Michaels. We'll just have to figure out an alternative."

"Is that your final decision?" His gaze darted back to the flames now licking their way up the curtains of the balcony's French doors.

"Damn straight," she retorted, still assessing the situation.

Ian tossed his weapon into a small Dumpster two stories below and to the right. Then, before Nicole fully comprehended his intent, he picked her up and pitched her over the side.

He followed—hoping like hell he hadn't underestimated the required trajectory for a splash landing.

Chapter Four

Gasping for breath, Nicole dragged herself out of the deep end of the pool. She shoved the wet hair from her face and glared at the man emerging from the chilly water next to her.

"We're lucky we didn't break our necks," she complained crossly. "You could have killed us both."

Looking dark, wet and insanely wicked, Ian smiled. "But I didn't. In fact—" he swiped the dark hair from his eyes "—I saved your life."

Nicole got to her feet. The wet cotton T-shirt lay plastered to her chest like a second skin. At least she still had on her denim jacket. "Do me a favor," she groused, then shivered as the cold seeped into her skin.

Ian got to his feet, water puddling around him. "What?"

"Next time you want to save my life, just shoot me."

"Don't tempt me." He flashed Nicole a look that could have meant any number of things, none of which she wanted to consider at the moment. "We need to make sure your neighbors got out safely," he suggested, turning his attention to the building they had so hastily exited in such an unorthodox manner.

Nicole inhaled sharply as the roar of flames and the

distinctive crackle of destruction drew her attention back up to the balcony. Damn. They had got out just in time. She swallowed the lump of emotion rising in her throat. Agent Daniels hadn't been so lucky when his house went up in flames. How long would her luck hold out?

"We're okay," Ian assured her softly.

Nicole's gaze moved back to his. A frown tugged at her mouth. She must look pretty shaken if he was showing this much concern. Nicole watched, feeling oddly displaced, as Ian straightened his dripping wet jacket and strode to the nearby Dumpster. She scrubbed away the rivulets of water streaming down her face with the back of her hand. She wondered briefly how the man could look so good soaking wet and digging through a trash container. Nicole shivered again, whether from the cool night air or from simply looking at Ian, she couldn't be sure. She almost laughed out loud. What was wrong with her? Her apartment building was going up in flames and she was standing there ogling the only man she could trust to help her. And who, she reminded herself, had every reason to walk away without looking back.

When Ian found his gun, he tucked it into his waistband and turned in Nicole's direction. That silvery gaze connected with hers, and Nicole's knees went weak. She was losing it. That much was clear. Too much stress, not enough sleep…

"Stay behind me," he ordered.

Too tired and disgusted with herself to argue, Nicole obeyed. She stuck close behind Ian as he stole to the front corner of the building. Several tense seconds passed while he surveyed the street and sidewalk for any recognizable threat. No matter what she had done to him in the past, Ian would not walk away. He intended to protect her at all costs, and that bothered Nicole. But wasn't that what she wanted? She studied his intent features. She didn't want any of this to hurt Ian. And she definitely didn't want to fall in love with him again. Her heart couldn't take that kind of abuse a second time.

But she needed him. There was no one else.

"Let's go," he instructed quietly.

Half running to keep up with his long strides, Nicole followed Ian to the front entrance of her building. A crowd from the neighboring apartment complexes was already gathering in the street. Their murmuring grew louder as she and Ian took the front steps two at a time into the burning building. Nicole hesitated long enough to glance up at her apartment one last time. Flames shot out of the living-room window and licked upward, charring everything in their path. Panic tightened her chest when she allowed herself to briefly consider that she had just lost all her worldly possessions. Anger rushed through her veins then, quickly replacing the lesser emotion. Pushing aside the sudden and almost overwhelming urge for revenge, Nicole hurried after Ian. A voice from the crowd shouted an unnecessary reminder that the building was on fire as she disappeared inside.

"Which apartments are occupied?" Ian demanded the moment she cleared the door. Smoke drifted and curled down the stairs like eerie black fog.

"That's the only one besides mine." Nicole pointed to the door of the first-floor apartment on Ian's right. "The guy lives alone and he's out of town most of the time." Nicole resisted the urge to hold her breath. She blinked rapidly to fight the burn in her eyes.

"Let's hope he's not home now." Ian moved closer to the door, checked to see if it was locked, then kicked it hard near the knob. One more solid kick and the door flew inward. Ian surveyed the now-useless lock as he entered the apartment. "He really should have a dead bolt installed. Anyone could just walk right in."

Nicole rolled her eyes at his macho display. "You couldn't just do the thing with the credit card?" she chastised as she followed Ian inside.

"There's no time." Ian paused a beat at the sound of distant sirens. "Check the kitchen, I'll get the bedroom and bathroom," he said, already halfway across the room.

Less than a minute later, they met in the living room once more. "All clear," Nicole reported. The screaming sirens sounded much closer now.

"Good. We should go." Ian snagged Nicole's hand and moved quickly out the apartment door and through the thickening smoke in the stairwell. Nicole covered her nose and mouth with her free arm until she emerged into the fresh night air. A police cruiser careened around the corner at the end of the block, followed by two fire trucks. Ian pulled Nicole in the opposite direction, using the crowd of spectators as cover. No one paid them any real heed now that the red and blue lights had captured their collective attention. Shattering glass echoed through the night as windows exploded from the intensifying heat.

Once on the other side of the street, Ian unlocked and opened the driver's side door of a black sedan. "Get in," he commanded brusquely.

Unable to prevent one last look back at her former home, Nicole trembled with aftereffects. When would this end? She hugged her arms around her cold, wet middle. And, more important, how would it end?

"Nicole," Ian urged softly.

Nicole turned away from the devastating sight, then blinked away the lingering images. She had no place to go now. She had no home. And she definitely couldn't go back to her office.

Nicole swallowed tightly.

Ian's hand pressed gently against the small of her back. "Get in the car, Nicole," he murmured close to her ear.

Ian. At least she still had Ian.

But once he'd had time to really think about all that she had told him, would he turn his back on her?

"WE NEED a room for one night," Ian stated with as much charm and a smile as persuasive as anything the current James Bond had ever managed on the silver screen.

The expression on the hotel receptionist's face was priceless. Nicole could just imagine what must be going through the woman's mind. Ian stood before her counter as handsome as sin, and looking for all the world as if he had just been baptized, Armani suit included.

"Of…of course, sir." The receptionist blinked, obviously having just realized that she was staring. Blush stained her cheeks. "Smoking or nonsmoking?"

Ian removed his wallet and placed a damp credit card on her counter. "Nonsmoking, downstairs and facing the parking lot, please," he answered with another smile that made the woman's eyes widen in appreciation.

"Certainly, sir," she purred. "Is there anything else I could help you with?"

Ian leaned over the counter a bit. "Would you happen to know an all-night dry cleaner, *Jean?*" he inquired smoothly, using the name emblazoned in gold letters across her name tag.

The receptionist's eyes sparkled with glee. "I'm sure I can arrange that."

Nicole resisted the urge to kick Ian. She supposed that he couldn't help it if charm literally oozed from his magnificent body. The sound of his voice alone was enough to make most women's hearts beat a little faster. Deep, velvety, lightly accented in that unusual European blend. And he was so devilishly handsome. Nicole released a heavy sigh. She was wet, tired, homeless, and at this point, even beyond being affected by Ian's many fascinating attributes. Watching him focus that mesmerizing charm on another woman was about as far from entertaining as could be, in Nicole's opinion.

When the paperwork was finished and the receptionist properly dazzled, Ian led the way to the ground-floor room. He unlocked the door and stepped aside for Nicole to enter. A bed had never looked better, Nicole thought with overwhelming relief. She peeled off her jacket and kicked off her shoes. She shuddered as the air-conditioned temperature of the room penetrated her wet clothing.

"Take a hot shower," Ian told her as he locked the door and checked the window. He turned then, and stared at her with too much concern. "Leave your clothes and a towel outside the door."

Nicole nodded. She pivoted and hurried into the bathroom. After locking the door behind her, she removed her FBI identification and placed it on the back of the toilet tank, then stripped off her wet clothes. She opened the door only as far as necessary and deposited a towel and her soggy attire, sans her panties and bra, on the floor. She quickly removed the remaining towels from the towel bar and hung her underwear there. They would dry in no time at all and she had no intention of allowing Ian to touch them. That would just make putting them back on that much more difficult. Before she could stop it, the memory of their lovemaking only twenty-four hours ago loomed large in her mind. Ian could use his hands, his mouth, in ways that made her breath catch even now, just thinking about him. How would they ever spend the night together in this tiny room without wanting each other?

Wanting each other wouldn't be the problem, Nicole decided as she stepped into the hot spray of water. Not taking what the other had to offer would be the real test of self-discipline. Nicole closed her eyes and allowed the hot, heavenly liquid to flow freely over her face and down her body.

She had to remember that their time together couldn't be about what had happened between them three years ago, and it couldn't be about the lust that still lingered.

It had to be about one thing and one thing only, staying alive long enough to catch a killer who had already murdered at least two federal agents.

IAN GENEROUSLY TIPPED the hotel employee who showed up at the door to take the laundry bag containing their wet clothes. The guy looked more like a night custodian than a bellboy, but that didn't matter to Ian. He was quite certain that this particular service was not usually provided by the hotel, and he appreciated the effort. The helpful employee had also located a first-aid kit. Ian rotated his injured shoulder. It hurt like hell, and he'd had to remove the wet bandage. The wound would require another dressing.

Ian stepped over to the bed and tossed the first-aid kit next to his bag. He removed the shirt he had packed. He'd brought along only one change of clothes, so he and Nicole would have to share. Ian would wear the black slacks, Nicole would get the black button-up shirt.

Ian moved to the bathroom door and hesitated a moment before knocking. The sound of spraying water abruptly ceased and Ian moistened his lips as he imagined Nicole emerging from the shower amid a billowing cloud of steam, water droplets trickling down her bare, satiny skin. He closed his eyes and savored the vision of her slowly drying first her long blond hair, then her toned, slender body.

"What am I supposed to wear?"

The muffled demand snapped Ian from his erotic fantasy. He rubbed a hand over his chin and swore hotly under his breath. What was wrong with him? He could not allow this consuming desire for what he should not want to take control again. Nicole had betrayed him once already, he couldn't set himself up to allow it to happen again.

Ian hung the shirt on the knob. "It's on the door," he said tersely and turned away. He had a plan to lay out and arrangements to make. He didn't have time to lust after a woman, especially not Nicole.

Ian heard the door open then quickly close again. He gritted his teeth against the need welling inside him in spite of his renewed determination. Sharing quarters this close was going to be pure torture. Ian clenched his fists at his side and mentally reviewed all that had happened in the past thirty hours.

After three years, Nicole had come to him for help. His refusal had been short-lived. The rental car exploding with Nicole entirely too close had put a kind of fear in his heart that Ian had never before experienced. He still cared too much. And that was not a good thing. He had to stay focused and keep his distance. For Nicole's sake, and for his own. He would not permit himself to fall for her again, but he would see that she stayed safe. And, one way or another, he would get the bastard threatening her life. Ian remained convinced that these were only attempts intended to send Nicole rushing to relocate Solomon. But each incident was proving more haphazard with the kind

of high-risk variables that could easily get Nicole and anyone else who happened to be in the way killed.

Nicole seemed certain that this was the work of one
man, someone who knew about Solomon. That conclusion
didn't sit quite right with Ian. If their enemy was someone
inside the bureau, then what did he hope to gain by killing
Solomon? Would there be a payoff from the cartel? That
sounded the most reasonable and probable to Ian. Whoever was behind this scheme had strong motivation. Ian
frowned when he considered that a scumbag like Solomon
had warranted a blackout operation. Sure, the man was a
major witness in a high-profile federal case, but Ian had
seen plenty of others in his time. Solomon was the first
in Ian's experience to garner such special treatment. And
there was that little detail—the bureau had personally handled his case rather than inducting Solomon into the program through regular channels. Ian wasn't naive, though.
He knew that too often cases weren't handled by the book,
especially those over which the FBI wanted to retain absolute control. Perhaps it was a mere coincidence that
Landon worked this special operation, then wound up
dead, along with one of the only two other agents involved, but Ian doubted it. Coincidences of this nature
were rare.

With Landon and Daniels dead and Nicole on the run,
that meant that someone privy to Landon's original decision was behind this little game of cat and mouse. Ian's
frown deepened, setting off an ache in his temples. He
didn't like the sound of that at all. The only office with
the authority to give Landon the kind of leeway he had
taken was the attorney general's. Ian knew personally, or
at the very least by reputation, most of the people in that
office. He found it difficult to believe that one of them
would stoop to working for the cartel.

But it wasn't an impossibility, he admitted.

The bathroom door opened again and Ian stiffened. The scent of shampoo and soap quickly permeated every square inch of air in the suddenly too-small hotel room. Images flashed before Ian's eyes like scenes from a movie on fast-forward. Touching Nicole's skin. Kissing her full mouth. Licking, then suckling the dusky peaks of her breasts. Being inside her...

"Did you order any food?"

Ian grabbed back control and turned slowly to face her. She lingered near the bathroom door, keeping her distance. Her damp blond hair hung around her shoulders. The too-big shirt clung here and there to her warm, moist body where she had missed a spot or two with her towel. The black contrasted sharply with her porcelain skin. Ian swallowed hard as his gaze fell to those long, slender legs. She shifted under his perusal and his gaze shot up to meet her assessing blue eyes.

"Yes," he replied so calmly that he surprised himself. "Steak-Out. It should arrive soon." Ian turned back to the bed and picked up the small first-aid kit.

Before he realized she had moved, Nicole was right beside him, assessing the injury to his shoulder. Only Nicole could get this close to him undetected.

"Damn," she breathed. "I forgot about this." With warm, gentle fingers she touched his shoulder. She winced. "Let me see what's in that kit."

Nicole relieved Ian of the first-aid kit and ushered him to a chair. She placed the small plastic container on the nearby dresser and opened it. Lines of frustration creased Ian's brow as she picked through the limited options available. Nicole stood mere inches from him, her thigh against him. This close, he could see the outline of her breasts, the budded points of her nipples. His pulse reacted.

"I can take care of this myself," he protested, however belatedly.

"Don't be ridiculous, Ian," she argued while continuing to prowl through the kit.

Ian looked up at her, pinning her with his most intimidating glare. "I would prefer—"

"Be still," she ordered. Nicole edged even closer then as she turned her attention to his shoulder.

Ian tensed when those soft fingers touched his bare skin once more. First, she swabbed the wound with what he assumed to be an antibiotic cream or lotion. Ian gritted his teeth when pain speared through his arm. At least the pain drew his attention from those other thoughts. The ones he knew he shouldn't be thinking.

"I'm sorry," Nicole murmured, her face entirely too near to his. "I'm trying not to hurt you."

"I'm fine."

Nicole arranged then taped the gauze into place. Her delicate scent and the feel of her fingers on his skin tugged at Ian's senses. He wanted to turn toward her and pull her onto his lap. Onto the arousal already straining against his slacks. His hands tightened on the arms of his chair. Her thigh grazed his fingertips, fire shot through his veins, twisting the desire already knotted inside him.

"There," she announced as she stepped back to view her effort. "It's not my best work, but, considering what I had to work with, it'll do."

"It's fine." Ian stood and brushed past her.

"You're welcome," Nicole snapped.

Ian closed his bag and strode to the closet to store it. "Thank you," he allowed impatiently.

Nicole huffed a frustrated breath. "This isn't going to

work," she announced crossly. "We can't keep tiptoeing around each other like this."

Ian leaned against the wall next to the closet, using his good shoulder for support. "What do you propose we do?" he asked, sarcasm weighting his tone.

Her hands went to her hips and she advanced on him. "We can't work together if every time we look at each other or touch each other, we have flashbacks from the past."

"Agreed." Ian starred down into that irritated blue gaze. "We can go back to plan A."

"Plan A?" Nicole frowned.

"You holed up in a safe house with Martinez while I get to the bottom of what's going on."

Fury flashed in those baby blues. "No way."

"Then I would suggest that you keep your distance."

The anger in her eyes turned patronizing. "That's going to be a bit difficult considering there's only one bed, Mr. Charm-the-receptionist."

Ian stared at the bed. Why hadn't he thought of that? Every night he and Nicole had spent together had been spent in a shared bed. The notion of requesting two beds had not entered his mind. Ian swore silently. His gaze connected with her now-triumphant one. "It's a big bed, Nicole. I don't have a problem, do you?"

"Absolutely not." She smiled knowingly. "But then, how would you know if I did?" One brow arched in challenge. "And we both know *you* can't always hide what you're feeling."

Ian felt that muscle in his jaw begin to tic. "I'm beginning to agree with you, Nicole. Perhaps this isn't going to work."

She blinked, twice. Ian almost smiled. Now he had her attention.

"Do you want to hear plan B or not?" he inquired, satisfied that he had won that round.

Nicole dropped wearily onto the end of the bed. "You know I do," she said disgustedly.

"Good." Ian turned his back on her and strode to the chair he had been sitting in minutes before. He remained silent a full minute for good measure. Nicole squirmed visibly. He smiled then, just a little.

"Solomon is the most probable target," he began. "I would hazard a guess that the cartel is willing to pay a handsome sum for his termination."

"That's my theory." Nicole shoved a handful of hair behind her ear. "Since the only case of this caliber that Landon, Daniels and I have in common is Solomon's, I would say that's a safe assumption."

Ian thought for a moment, recalling the most prominent personnel in the AG's office. "Landon never once mentioned the name of the person who coordinated Solomon's case on the attorney-general's end?"

Nicole shook her head. "No." She shrugged. "And I didn't ask. You know the drill—need-to-know basis only."

Ian nodded. He knew the drill all right. But someone had to give that order. Ian would just have to tweak his old contacts and see what he could shake loose.

"There was one thing," Nicole said suddenly as if just remembering a significant piece of the puzzle.

"What's that?"

"Landon said that the order came from the highest level." Nicole chewed her lower lip. "Do you think that means what it sounds like it means?"

That would mean the attorney general himself, in Ian's opinion. Ian had known Blake Edwards half a lifetime. Blake had been something of a legend in the U.S. Marshal

Service as far back as when Ian had first signed on. There had never once been even the vaguest of accusations against the man. He was squeaky clean. Always had been.

Ian scrubbed a hand over his face noting in some distant part of his consciousness that he needed a shave. "Anything is possible." He resisted the urge to protest. No one was immune to falling prey to the lure of money. And this was most certainly about money.

"If it goes that high, how do we get the guy's attention? He could be a G-man or he could be a hired gun."

"He's on the inside," Ian insisted. "He knows too much." Ian didn't buy the hired-gun theory at all. This guy was a pro, and he knew far too much about Nicole's every move to be working on the outside. "If we go with the scenario that it's all about Solomon and someone's desire to find him," Ian began. "Then all we have to do is set a trap and wait for the bait to be taken."

Nicole settled a determined gaze on Ian. "To make the trap work you have to have the right kind of bait."

Ian shook his head slowly from side to side. "We're not going there, Nicole. Don't even think about it." He knew exactly what she had in mind. No way would he allow her to be the bait. He would find another way.

Nicole stood, placed her hands on her hips again and glared at him with the kind of determination that Ian knew wouldn't be easily swayed. "Landon was my director and Daniels was my fellow agent. Solomon is *my* witness. I will do this."

"No." Ian allowed his eyes to convey his own determination.

Nicole cocked her head and pinned him with a look that spoke of having an ace up her sleeve. "Since I'm the only one who knows Solomon's location, then I don't see that you have a choice."

Ian's lips twitched with the need to smile, but he suppressed the gesture. Nicole was good...too good. "I suppose you have a point there."

"You're darn right I do." Nicole plopped back onto the end of the bed. "Now, let's talk about that trap."

"Remember I'm sending Martinez to keep Solomon company so he doesn't panic," Ian reminded her. "All I need is the location. Then we need some out-of-the-way place to hole up for a few days."

Nicole's expression brightened. "I know just the place," she said quickly. "My cousin has a cabin in the southern part of the state. It's secluded, but not too far from civilization."

"Then we leave first thing in the morning," Ian concluded.

"We'll leave a trail any fool could follow," Nicole added, the plan already taking shape in her head. "And with Labor Day weekend starting tomorrow, maybe our guy will think we took a little vacation."

Ian did smile then. "Or a lover's tryst," he offered.

Nicole looked startled. "What are you suggesting?" she asked hesitantly, but Ian didn't miss the flicker of something like desire in her eyes.

Ian shrugged his one good shoulder. "If the guy knows our history, which he likely does, then falling back into each other's arms would be within the realm of predictability. If he thinks we're caught up in our lust, maybe he'll feel a little braver and make a bolder move out in the open."

Nicole's smile returned full wattage. "You're a genius, Michaels. Let's call Martinez now."

Now if only Ian could pretend his suggestion wasn't so close to the truth.

Chapter Five

Awareness came in slow, languid degrees for Ian. It was a creeping, swelling warmth that excited and weakened him at the same time. The next level of consciousness to filter through the cloak of sleep heightened his senses. The feel of smooth, satiny skin against his, the pleasant swell of firm breast in his palm, and the moist heat scorching his thigh. Ian inhaled deeply, savoring the subtle essence of Nicole before he released the breath. Slowly, very slowly, Ian opened his eyes. The exquisite detail of Nicole's perfect profile, the delicately carved bone structure, her full, lush mouth zoomed into focus. The fragile curve of her throat was so very near to his lips. He ached to touch her there with his mouth, to taste that elegant column with the tip of his tongue. The desire to move against her was a pleasure-pain in his loins.

While he lay there watching her, the blood thudding in his ears, Nicole's eyes drifted open. She blinked rapidly, her mind likely sorting and analyzing the flood of sensations washing over her senses as her own awareness kicked in. Nicole tensed, her responsive body no longer pliant beneath his. Ian was fully and painfully erect. With his arousal pressed against her belly, her sudden tension sent another stab of desire through him. Nicole's warning that Ian could not always hide what he felt echoed harshly inside his head. Instantly, irritation absorbed all else. Ian rolled away from her, sat up, then pushed to his feet without pause. He would not give her any additional satisfaction.

"Good morning," he tossed over his shoulder as he strode into the bathroom. Ian closed the door without waiting for her response. He swore hotly, repeatedly, something he rarely did. He plowed his fingers through his hair and forced himself to relax enough to take care of business. Maybe he couldn't always hide how he responded to Nicole. But one thing was certain, his condition this morning could just as easily be attributed to other biological urges. Except, Ian amended reluctantly, for the accelerated beating of his heart.

Long minutes passed before Ian regained complete control. No one but Nicole had ever wielded this much power over him. Somehow he had to find a way to numb himself to her presence.

Ian released a long, heavy breath. Remaining focused was the key. He had to keep his full attention on the matter at hand. Martinez was baby-sitting Solomon. Alexandra Preston, one of the Colby Agency's finest researchers, was pulling together updates on every member of the cartel Solomon's testimony had brought down or affected negatively. That left Ian and Nicole with the job of drawing out the hitman, hired gun or player, who seemed to have a penchant for blowing things up.

Ian stared at his reflection in the mirror. He needed a shower and a shave. And clothes. The hotel employee had assured him that their clothes would be ready first thing this morning. Maybe he should buzz the front desk and see if they were there waiting for delivery. Then, he and Nicole could be on their way. Composed now, Ian turned toward the door, but something in his peripheral vision brought him up short. His gaze shot back to the towel bar near the tub. Scant, lacy pink panties, and the matching frilly bra captured his full attention just long enough to suck the air completely out of his lungs.

A full ten minutes passed before Ian came back into the room. Nicole averted her gaze immediately, feigning interest in the channels she continued to surf. But the image of his bare chest, broad shoulders and taut abdomen were forever emblazoned on her memory. The way his dark hair curled around his neck. She shivered.

Ian paused at the bedside table, which was covered with the now-dry contents of his wallet, and picked up the telephone's receiver. Nicole used that opportunity to escape into the bathroom. She closed the door and sagged against it. She squeezed her eyes shut and exhaled a shaky breath. Even now her body hummed with the slowly retreating desire. Waking up with the feel of Ian's lean, hard body crushing into hers, his palm and long fingers cradling her breast, and his firm lips so frustratingly close to her sensitized skin, Nicole had almost burst into flames. Her whole body had been steaming hot, ready to absorb him right through her skin.

Nicole straightened and glanced at herself in the mirror. The telltale flush of sensual heat lingered on her skin. The expression in her eyes was nothing short of wild and needy. Nicole closed her eyes again and concentrated on calming the wanton beast still roaring inside her. The sound of Ian's voice, all tone and no words, reached her, touched her through the useless barrier of the wall and brought her blood back to an instant simmer. Nicole pivoted abruptly and paced the tiny room, three steps one way, and three steps back. Again and again she retraced her two-yard path. *Calm.* Reach for the calm, she commanded herself. She would control her reactions to Ian. Somehow. She had to.

She was homeless. A target running for her life and Solomon's. She had to think, reason, and take the necessary steps to ensure Solomon's safety, as well as her own. Her breath snagged in her throat at the abrupt memory of Ian's too-close encounter with a bullet. Nicole had to see that he stayed safe too. She had dragged him into this mess, and she would have to see that his insistence on helping her didn't get him killed. She shuddered at the thought, then quickly blocked it.

"Nicole."

She jumped, then turned to face the closed door. She had to pull herself together. "Yes," she managed as she threaded her fingers into her hair and massaged her tense scalp.

"I have your clothes. When you're finished in there I'd like to shower," he said, in that voice that melted her fledgling resolve not to be affected by him.

The unbidden image of Ian naked, with water sluicing over his powerful body rocked Nicole to the core. "Fine," she said curtly, then gritted her teeth so hard that her jaw ached. She knew too many techniques for maintaining control to allow this sort of distraction. It was past time she took charge. Whatever had once been between the two of them was no more. That fleeting connection had been under false pretense in the first place, and Nicole's subsequent betrayal had severed the bond forever. All that remained was physical attraction, lust borne of familiarity. Nothing else. When this was over, assuming either of them survived, she and Ian would go their separate ways.

End of story.

Forcing away any further thought of Ian, Nicole turned her attention to essential functions. She washed her hands and face, then rinsed her mouth with the complimentary small bottle of mouthwash. It wasn't quite the same as brushing her teeth, but it would have to do until she could purchase a few personal items. While she finger-combed her hair, Nicole made a mental list of items she would need to purchase for the weekend. Filing insurance claims, finding a new apartment and starting over from scratch would simply have to wait until later.

Much later.

Nicole frowned. She supposed that calling her office and checking in would be appropriate, though she was on approved leave. If any witnesses from last night's fire had described her to the police or the media, the guys at the office might get worried. Nicole would do that while Ian showered. Tamping down the images that thought immediately conjured, Nicole grabbed her dry lingerie and ID and tucked the items under her arm, then opened the door and breezed back into the room.

As Ian passed, his bag and freshly laundered suit in hand, he paused directly in front of Nicole. He offered the gun, butt-first, to her. "Don't open the door for anyone," he warned.

Nicole accepted the weapon without looking at him. As soon as he had closed the bathroom door behind him, Nicole laid the weapon aside and quickly stripped off Ian's shirt. She held the fabric close to her face and took a long deep breath. Ian's scent still lingered where his warm body had lain against her all night. Chastising herself, Nicole tossed the shirt aside and swiftly dressed. She felt a great deal less vulnerable wearing her own clothes. Wearing nothing but Ian's shirt had somehow made her more susceptible to him.

All she needed now was her own weapon and Nicole would be whole again.

•

THE COMMERCIAL FLIGHT into Charlottesville, Virginia, had proven decidedly uninteresting in Nicole's opinion. The hassle of obtaining approval to carry weapons on the flight had tried even the patience of the forever-unflappable Ian. Finally, all parties had agreed that, per the pilot's request, the weapons would be locked away in the cockpit until landing.

Taking the Colby Agency jet would have alleviated the entire situation, but the whole point was to leave a wide, easy path for their shadow to follow. If Nicole had ever been this careless with her travel plans, she had long since blocked the memory. First they had stopped by her office and picked up a weapon from her personal office safe. Her bureau ID was a little the worse for wear, but still usable. Nicole made sure all her co-workers knew that she planned to take a little weekend trip to her cousin's secluded mountain cabin. A few suggestive glances in Ian's direction and the whole office assumed she and Ian were lovers taking a little getaway.

After that, Nicole had led Ian on a whirlwind shopping trip in Georgetown. By lunchtime they had everything they would need for a long weekend in the wilderness, from the eyewear to the hiking boots. Their wardrobes looked straight off the pages of L.L. Bean. Ian always wore suits, his appearance nothing less than impeccable. That look was right for him; fit his personality to a T. Nicole blew out a disgusted breath and forced her attention to the passing fall landscape. Who would ever have suspected that he would look so hot in jeans and flannel? The man was six feet two inches of lean, hard muscle. Nicole blinked the image of his sculpted body from her mind. Don't go there, she warned that part of her that wanted so desperately to take whatever he would give during their short time together.

If that wasn't bad enough, Nicole had also got a glimpse of the kid in Ian when he'd selected the SUV at the rental agency. According to Ian it was exactly like the one he was currently considering purchasing. Black with tinted windows, four-wheel drive, fully loaded, the Range Rover was nice, Nicole had to agree. She stole a glance at its driver. But she could have gone the rest of her life without having to see his pleasure at how the vehicle handled, at how much he admired the interior. She didn't want to know the little things that pleased Ian. The more she knew about him, the more dangerous he was to her heart.

With only soft rock whispering from the speakers to break the silence, and two and one half hours of picture-perfect landscape behind them, the sign welcoming visitors to Town Creek was a truly welcome sight. Ian slowed to take in the view. Nestled between the gorgeous Appalachian Mountains, Town Creek and its Deep River proved a breathtaking sight no matter how many times Nicole saw it. Her cousin George, a psychiatrist in Richmond, was a diehard bass fisherman. In his opinion, there was no place on earth like the Deep River in Town Creek. He had been so impressed with the fishing as well as the friendly community that he had bought himself a vacation home here years ago. Nicole had visited a couple of times when George had had his thirtieth birthday or some milestone in his career he wanted to celebrate. The place was serenity exemplified. And George always left a key under the third rock from the front right corner of the cabin.

"Take the next right," Nicole said abruptly, almost forgetting that Ian didn't know the way. Her voice sounded strangely loud after the long drive without speaking.

Ian made the turn and began the winding journey that would take them high into the mountains and deep into the woods. Though the cabin was only ten or twelve miles from town, the narrow, winding road made the going slow. With the dense forest of soaring trees closing in around them, the dim light of dusk swiftly gave way to total darkness.

Thirty minutes later, Ian braked to a stop in front of the rustic one-story cabin. The place wasn't very large. There was a great room that served as a living room, dining room, and bedroom. A small kitchen and an even smaller bathroom lay beyond that. There was no telephone or cable television, but there was electricity and running water compliments of a heavy-duty generator and a deep well. George always restocked before he left. There would be canned goods in the cabinets and a full tank of gas in the generator, with additional fuel stored in the small outbuilding.

"You have a key?" Ian asked as he shut off the headlights and then the engine.

"No, but I know where he keeps it." Nicole reached into the back seat and retrieved the flashlight Ian had purchased with the rest of the gear.

Nicole tried to ignore Ian's brooding presence directly behind her as she made her way to the corner of the cabin, but it was impossible. She could feel the masculine warmth emanating from him in seductive waves. His heat pulled at her senses, made her want to turn and face him and then move into his arms. Giving herself a mental shake, Nicole crouched down and collected the key from beneath the rock. She dusted the dirt from it and strode purposefully toward the porch. Ian followed, saying nothing. But when Nicole inserted the key into the lock, he placed his hand on her arm.

"Let me go in first," he said, more of a quiet command than a suggestion.

Nicole shrugged off his touch. "Whatever." She stepped back out of his way. Let him play the big, tough protector. What did she care as long as the mission was accomplished?

Ian unlocked and opened the door. Nicole offered him the flashlight, knowing that would be his next request. At least if she handed it to him first, he wouldn't have to ask for it, and she wouldn't have to hear his voice unnecessarily. Nicole shook her head slowly in resignation. The situation was completely and utterly ridiculous.

The beam of the flashlight moved over the great room. Hewn and chinked log walls, four windows, three interior doors, wood floors embellished with braided rugs, and cathedral ceilings with huge wood support beams. George's taste in decorating was "bare and essential," but his housekeeping was immaculate. Though the furnishings were sparse, Nicole knew them to be comfortable. A round wood table with four chairs, an overstuffed sofa with matching arm chairs flanking it, one chest of drawers, a bookcase, and a huge king-size brass bed. The sight of the bed always caught Nicole off guard. Everything else in the place was wood, or plaid upholstery. But the bed—unfortunately singular—was shiny brass and covered with elegant linens.

"Lights?" The sound was hardly more than a whisper, but it glided along every nerve ending in Nicole's too-attentive body.

Nicole reached for a key on the hook by the front door. "We have to start up the generator," she said quickly. "It's around back. We can go through the kitchen and out the back door."

This time Ian led the way. He paused at the back door and surveyed the perimeter outside within the boundaries of the flashlight's beam. Satisfied that no one waited in the bushes, he descended the steps. Nicole followed.

The generator started a little sluggishly. Nicole supposed that it had been a while since her cousin's last visit. With him traveling around promoting his latest published work, she felt certain he was far too busy for fishing. But, knowing George, he would make up for it another time.

Nicole located the breaker box behind the kitchen door and flipped the breaker for the lights and the well pump. The cookstove and the hot-water heater were gas and only required that the pilot lights be lit. Ian insisted on lighting them, which suited Nicole just fine. She had been up close and personal with too much heat in the past couple of days as it was.

Once their gear was unpacked and stored away, Ian prowled the place like a caged animal. He adjusted the primitive country curtains to his liking, and examined the locks on the doors, twice. Bored with watching Ian's precise, methodical movements and trying to stay unaffected, Nicole pushed up from the comfortable sofa and strolled into the kitchen to do a little prowling of her own. She might as well inventory the supplies. They did have to eat for however long they would be here. That, at least, would occupy her restless mind.

One can of coffee, three cans of chili, six cans of beef stew, a twelve pack of canned sodas and several cans of juice. And wine. Nicole smiled. More than a dozen bottles of wine. Nicole searched through the remaining cabinets. Cleaning supplies, fire extinguisher, condoms. Nicole did a double take.

Condoms?

Under the sink?

She shook her head, closed the cabinet doors and stood. Now where would he hide the Godiva? George had a sweet tooth that only Godiva chocolate would assuage. Nicole shared in that little addiction. She rummaged through the cabinet drawers. It had to be here. George always kept a supply on hand.

"Hungry?"

Nicole snapped to attention and whirled around as if she had been caught with her hand in the cookie jar, her face flushed guiltily. "I was inventorying supplies," she said quickly. "We'll need a few provisions to carry us through the weekend," she added for good measure. Nicole moistened her lips and avoided that analyzing gray gaze. Ian probably didn't have even one bad habit. He was perfect.

Too perfect.

"If you'd like to rest, I'll take care of dinner," he offered in that smooth, liquid voice that made her quiver inside.

Nicole pushed away from the cabinet. "That's a good idea," she answered without looking at him. She paused long enough to take a look inside the fridge when she passed it. Nothing. The motor whined a bit, struggling to cool the warm interior now that electricity flowed again.

Standing in the middle of the great room, Nicole considered where George would hide his decadent treasure if not in the kitchen. *Dammit.* She wanted some chocolate, and she wanted it now. If she couldn't have Ian, at least she could have that.

Nicole resisted the urge to stamp her foot. What was wrong with her? Ian was off-limits. She glanced at the wide, inviting bed. And what were they going to do about that? Nicole released a big breath. Sure the bed was big, like the one at the hotel. But no matter how wide the bed, their bodies would draw each other like light to the dawn once sleep robbed them of conscious restraint.

Ian would just have to sleep on the couch.

With that decision behind her, Nicole resumed her search. She shuffled through the books and magazines in the bookcase. Her hands slowed as one title caught her eye. *Burn, Baby Burn.* Nicole's expression twisted into one of distaste. When she leafed through the publication, her suspicions were confirmed. Numerous sexual positions were described in graphic detail, pictures included. Aphrodisiacs of all kinds were enumerated. Nicole slapped the cover closed and shoved the magazine back into its original position, but not before she checked the address label on the back cover.

When had George started ordering such sexually explicit material? Several other shocking titles speared her attention. Nicole shrugged off the curiosity. Maybe he was working on a new medical journal. Sex and its many various and associated problems was often the subject of medical journals. After all, George was a shrink. He most likely had patients who needed counseling in that area.

Nicole moved on to the chest of drawers. Socks, underwear, pajamas. More condoms. Nicole frowned again. What the hell was George expecting? An orgy?

No chocolate there either.

Pacing back and forth as Ian had earlier, Nicole worried her bottom lip. Maybe George had depleted his supply the last time and had simply forgotten to bring more. Or perhaps he intended to replenish his stock the next time he visited.

The bathroom.

Nicole knew it was a long shot, but it was the only place she hadn't looked already. Aspirins, antibiotic ointment, alcohol, peroxide, the medicine cabinet contained them all, but no Godiva. The linen cabinet contained towels, washcloths, soap, feminine products. Nicole did another double take. Since when did George need feminine hygiene products? Okay, so maybe he brought his girl-friends here sometimes. Maybe one of his lady friends had left the intimate items. One brow lifted in skepticism when she eyed the array of scented bubble bath. Nicole closed the cabinet door and shuffled back into the great room. No chocolate. She looked up to find Ian pouring wine into stemmed glasses.

And damn if he didn't look good enough to eat. The perfect combination of elegance and danger.

She swallowed, hard.

"Have a seat, it's ready," he told her when she made no move to come closer. "Beef stew and a great red wine." He directed one of those rare ten-thousand-watt smiles in her direction.

Keeping her eyes on the hypnotic movements of his hands, Nicole slowly walked to the table and sat down. Ian settled into his own chair directly across from her and sipped his wine.

"Your cousin has outstanding taste," Ian commented, then licked the residue of wine from those full, firm lips.

Nicole blinked. What was Ian implying? Oh yeah, the wine. She grabbed her own glass. "Thank you," she said tightly. "I'll tell him you said so next time I see him." Nicole all but gulped the rich, red liquid. She had to get a hold of herself. The case. She had to concentrate on the case.

"How long has he owned this place?"

Nicole's head came up. "What?"

That silvery gaze connected fully with hers then. "You shouldn't worry so much, everything is going to be all right, Nicole."

Nicole's relief was palpable. He thought she was upset

about the case. "I know," she replied quietly, then quickly averted her gaze.

"You should eat and then get some rest. I'll take the first watch."

Why did he have to do that? Make her feel like she mattered more than anything else in the world to him? They were partners in solving this case. Nothing more.

That lie reverberated clear through to her bones.

Nicole took another big sip of her wine. Eat, Nicole, she ordered herself. The sooner you eat, the sooner you can leave the table. Three feet wasn't nearly enough space between them. Forcing herself to chew, then swallow, Nicole finished off her beef stew. She turned up her wineglass and emptied it as well.

"I'll take care of the next meal," she offered as she pushed back her chair and stood. "We can take turns." Nicole grabbed her plate and empty glass and headed to the kitchen without looking back. If Ian responded, she didn't hear him. Nicole rinsed her dishes and dried her hands. Now what? No TV. She supposed she could read. Several of the available titles flitted through her mind. Nope. That wouldn't do.

The chocolate. She had to find that chocolate. Nicole walked back into the great room and considered where else she could search. She had looked everywhere already. Hadn't she? Nicole frowned and scanned the big open space once more. Ian was busy clearing his dishes from the table. She ignored him.

A smile sent the corners of Nicole's mouth upward. The bed. She hadn't looked under the bed. Desperation driving her on, Nicole dashed across the room and dropped to her knees next to the bed. She lifted the spread and peered into the semi-darkness beneath the big brass bed. A few dust bunnies skittered across the floor. Nicole's smile widened to a triumphant grin. She tugged two large plastic containers clear of the bed. Through the translucent sides she could see that the boxes contained a variety of items. Godiva chocolate had to be in there somewhere. Nicole just knew it.

Nicole opened the first container and elation surged through her veins. Two large gold boxes were perched atop the other contents. The shiny gold winked beneath the light as Nicole quickly opened one package. A moan of pleasure escaped as she placed a small chunk of the heavenly chocolate in her mouth and closed her eyes in pure ecstasy.

"What's all this?"

Nicole's eyes popped open. Ian crouched right next to her. She had been so engrossed in finding her treasure that she hadn't even realized he'd moved. Pleasure exploded on her tongue and another tiny groan seeped out.

"Chocolate," she murmured with delight. "The very finest chocolate on earth. I adore it. George is absolutely addicted to the stuff."

"No, I don't mean the chocolate," Ian explained quietly. "I mean this."

Nicole stared down at the container as Ian moved aside the boxes of chocolate. Her eyes bulged in disbelief.

"It looks as if chocolate isn't Cousin George's only addiction."

The array of sex toys was far too comprehensive and—Nicole stared, agog, as Ian lifted the lid from the other container—too state-of-the-art to be called anything less than a very serious hobby.

"I take it the man likes to play games." Ian picked up a set of handcuffs and dangled them.

Nicole fingered a bottle of expensive-looking body oil. George into S and M? That couldn't be. He was much too straitlaced for that. The memory of the magazine with his name and address on the back cover flashed through her mind, along with a half dozen other titillating titles.

"Apparently," Nicole finally murmured. Images, sounds, erotic and forbidden, flickered through the private theater of her mind. She and Ian, touching, tasting, reaching...

Nicole blinked away the prohibited fantasies. She hurriedly placed the lids back on the containers and shoved them under the bed.

Out of sight, out of mind.

Right, Nicole thought with self-disgust. She pushed to her feet, chocolates in hand, strode back to the sofa and plopped down on it. She set the box of chocolate on the cushion beside her, then crossed her arms over her chest and stared at the far wall. What was she supposed to do for the next forty-eight hours in this secluded cabin with nothing to distract herself from disaster?

At precisely that moment, Ian settled himself at the other end of the couch. Nicole darted an uncharitable glance in his direction. *Burn, Baby Burn* snagged her attention. Ian had the magazine, reading it...looking at it...whatever.

One dark brow lifted speculatively. "Interesting," he noted aloud.

Nicole groaned inwardly. How would she ever survive this weekend surrounded by sex toys and "how to" guides for the sexually depraved?

Ian made a small sound of disbelief, then a slow, rich laugh drew Nicole's reluctant gaze back to the lights and shadows of his angular face.

She was doomed.

Chapter Six

Ian came instantly awake.

He held perfectly still as he listened for the sound again. A board creaked, then the distinct sound of a footstep just outside the front door. Ian withdrew his gun from beneath his pillow, threw back the blanket, and sat up on the couch. He listened again. The knob turned with a definitive click, once, twice. Ian stood and moved silently across the room. He was halfway to the door when the mattress shifting alerted him to Nicole's movement. His eyes already adjusted to the darkness, he saw her rise from the bed, weapon trained expertly on the threat. Ian waited until she moved closer to ensure that she understood when he indicated that she should move to the far side of the door. Soundlessly she glided into a position where the opening door would provide cover from immediate danger.

Anticipation pounding through his veins, Ian flattened against the wall at the same instant that the knob turned again and the door swung inward.

One quick sweep of Ian's right foot and the startled intruder lay facedown on the floor. In one fluid move, Ian had his knee pressed into the man's back, the barrel of his weapon nudged into the back of the man's skull.

"Don't move," Ian warned. He slipped the fingers of his free hand into the man's pocket to retrieve his wallet and check for identification.

The lights came on and Nicole crouched next to Ian as he pulled a driver's license from the wallet. "George?" she demanded in disbelief. "What the hell are you doing here?"

Ian glanced from the man pinned to the floor to the Virginia driver's license he held in his hand. *George Reed.* Ian scowled and shifted his weight from the man's back.

"I could ask you the same thing," George said, a bit shakily as he pushed to his knees.

Ian tucked his weapon into his waistband at the small of his back and offered his hand to assist George in getting up. George shot Ian a cross look, but accepted the assistance. So this was Dr. George Reed, Ian mused as he closed and locked the door. He looked to be several years older than Nicole. Same blond hair and blue eyes. Tall and lean. Ian suppressed a smile when he remembered the hidden treasure beneath the bed.

"Why didn't you tell me you were coming up?" George was asking as he dusted himself off. "I would have planned dinner with you or something," he added, casting another less-than-appreciative look in Ian's direction.

Ignoring George's dubious glances, Ian noticed for the first time since this little episode began what Nicole was wearing. A white T-shirt that hit mid-thigh. Ian swallowed hard as he imagined what color those lacy panties might be this time. Lavender? Red? His groin tightened. Red satin against Nicole's creamy skin. A slow, diffused excitement oozed forth and spread across his own skin. That same hot, tingly sensation exploded inside him, and Ian felt himself harden.

Ian gritted his teeth and forced away any thought of Nicole's body or her attire. "Were you followed up the mountain?"

"What?" Frowning, and still a bit unsteady, George pivoted to face Ian.

"We don't want anyone to know we're here," Nicole explained, drawing George's attention back to her.

"Why not?" he demanded to know. "Does this have something to do with your position at the bureau?"

Nicole said yes at the same time that Ian said no.

George looked from one to the other, his frown deepening. "Which is it, yes or no?"

Ian pinned Nicole with a warning look.

"Well," she began slowly. "Ian and I used to work together," she stammered. "So, it's sort of work-related."

George's expression did a complete turnaround. "I see," he said knowingly. "A little *internal affair.*"

Ian wasn't amused. "Did anyone follow you?" he asked again.

George hooked a thumb in Ian's direction. "Who is this guy, Nicole? He's even more serious than you."

Nicole cleared her throat. "Sorry," she offered. "George, this is Ian Michaels." Nicole gestured hesitantly, then shrugged. "We're former colleagues and we've been comparing notes on an old case that's still unsolved." She gave the men her back and strode across the room to place her weapon on the dining table.

George snagged Ian's hand and pumped it once, firmly. "Any friend of Nicole's is a friend of mine."

Ian held on with an insistent pressure when George would have pulled his hand away. "Did anyone follow you up the mountain?" he asked slowly and for the third time. Ian pressed him with a gaze that he hoped conveyed the full significance of his request.

George's amused expression wilted instantly. "No," he said quickly, pulling his hand away even more swiftly. "No one followed me. There was no traffic at all, in fact."

"Good."

"Well," Nicole chimed in with too much enthusiasm. "Why don't we have a cup of coffee and catch up?" She looked from George to Ian and back, uncertainty shimmering in her wide blue eyes.

"Will you be staying?" Ian asked of George. Nicole narrowed her gaze at Ian. He supposed he deserved that—after all, the cabin did belong to the man.

George shook his head adamantly, and held up his hands stop-sign fashion. "I don't want to intrude."

Nicole shot Ian the evil eye. "Don't be ridiculous, George," she argued sincerely. "It's 2:00 a.m., you have to stay. If you don't want to have coffee now, we can go back to bed for a few hours and then have coffee *together* when the sun is up."

"No, no, I can't do that," George countered with a bark of choked laughter. "I have a very pretty, and very impatient lady warming up in town at the lodge."

"I'm sure you don't want to keep her waiting," Ian suggested.

Nicole flashed her palms upward and adopted a look of feigned dismay. "You should have brought her with you. We could have had a party!"

Ian was definitely going to wring Nicole's lovely neck when George left...if he ever did.

"Another appealing offer," George considered aloud. "But Stephanie hates the woods. She won't come up here at all." He shook his head slowly from side to side. "She maintains that it makes her feel like she has the lead in a Friday the 13th sequel." He rubbed his chin. "I'm delving into her childhood to see if I can find the root of the problem.''

Nicole arched a speculative brow. "Stephanie is your patient?"

"Oh no," George rebutted quickly. One hand fluttered magnanimously. "I just can't help myself. I'm always evaluating my friends." George cocked his blond head in Nicole's direction. "And family," he added pointedly. "Unfortunately, it appears to be the nature of the beast."

Ian stared at the floor for a moment until the urge to laugh at Nicole's appalled expression subsided.

"I just dropped by to pick up a few things," George explained. "Stephanie absolutely adores chains," he added as he hurried to the bed.

Nicole's mouth dropped open. Ian chewed the inside of his cheek. He would never have guessed that Nicole would be so prudish when it came to sexual fantasy. Based on past experience, Ian found it difficult to fathom the result if Nicole abandoned all inhibitions and control. He responded instantly to the notion.

"I wanted to ask you about that, George," Nicole began as she moved slowly toward her cousin. George knelt and pulled the large plastic storage containers from beneath the bed. "You seem to have a new hobby."

"Just having some fun, cuz," he said while rummaging through one box. "You should try it. It's a real tension breaker. You and Ian feel free to use anything you'd like."

"Don't even think about taking the other box of Godiva," Nicole said abruptly. She snatched the remaining box from his hand. "I might be stuck here longer than I think."

George huffed an indignant breath. "Well, don't get all bent out of shape." He shoved the box, less the Godiva and chains, back under the sorely out-of-place brass bed. "I'm only too happy to share."

Nicole set her confiscated chocolate on the bed and dropped a quick kiss on George's cheek. "Thank you, George, you're a jewel among men." Nicole flicked a disdainful glare in Ian's direction.

Ian frowned. George, the sadomasochist, gets a kiss, and Ian gets a drop-dead look? Where was the justice in that?

Nicole walked George back to the door. "I wish we could meet for lunch or something," she was saying contritely.

George stole a final glance at Ian. "Your friend looks as if he plans to keep you all to himself."

Nicole sent Ian another glower. "Don't let his attitude fool you, George, Ian's nothing but a big teddy bear."

Ian felt one brow arch of its own accord. *Teddy Bear?* Ian didn't think so.

"Have a safe trip back into town, George," Ian offered politely.

"Love the accent," George remarked casually as he paused in the doorway. "It must thrill the ladies."

Ian's jaw tightened in an effort to refrain from comment.

"We may be in town tomorrow," Nicole told him as he pressed a farewell kiss to her cheek. "I'll call, maybe we can do lunch."

"Think about what I said. You need to relax!" George called over his shoulder as he trotted out to his Jeep Cherokee.

Ian watched until George was out of sight, then he closed and locked the door. He turned back to Nicole, and the sadness he saw in her eyes made something shift near his heart.

"Lunch isn't a good idea," he said quietly.

She folded her arms over her chest and sighed. "I know. I can't risk endangering George, or anyone else for that matter. Though I may be safe until this guy has Solomon's location, no one around me is." Nicole's worried gaze sought out Ian's. "That includes you, you know."

"I know how to take care of myself," Ian assured her. He wanted desperately to draw her into his arms and hold her until the sadness in her eyes went away.

"Daniels knew how to take care of himself, too," she returned, her voice lacking any inflection. "And he's dead anyway."

Ignoring the warnings his brain was already sending him, Ian took a step closer to her. "Daniels wasn't expecting the danger. I am. The element of surprise is everything. You know that as well as I do, Nicole."

She trembled visibly. Ian clenched his fists at his sides.

"Yeah, I know." She shook her head. Those big blue eyes looked suspiciously bright. "But dead is dead. Daniels was a highly trained and very skilled agent, and he's dead. Someone wants me dead as well." Her gaze connected fully with Ian's. "And you'll be dead if you get in his way."

Ian's resistance dissolved. He pulled Nicole into his arms and held her close. She smelled so good, like sweet, ripe peaches. She shuddered and his arms tightened around her. Ian closed his eyes then, and allowed himself to simply hold her. The case, their past, everything else ceased to matter. There was only Nicole and the way she needed him at the moment.

Beneath the thin cotton of her T-shirt, her nipples pebbled, creating an exquisite friction against his bare chest. The silk of her hair tantalized his hands. He wanted to thread his fingers into her hair and draw her head up for a long, steamy kiss.

But he didn't. Ian continued to hold her and nothing more.

"You should get some more sleep," he whispered against her ear. His eyes closed with the exquisite torture of continuing to hold her this close.

Nicole pulled back a little, her gaze directed at the floor. "You're right. We should both get back to sleep." She glanced up at him then, and Ian saw the flicker of desire that burned briefly in her eyes. "Good night, Ian." She broke free of his embrace and padded to the enormous bed.

"Good night," he murmured. He closed his eyes and sighed. No matter how tough she wanted to appear, Nicole was vulnerable right now. Almost fragile. And she was wrong, he added with mounting determination. He *would* keep her safe.

No matter what the cost.

NICOLE AWOKE to the delicious scent of fresh-brewed coffee and the calming sound of running water. She stretched languidly. *Ian.* The memory of how he had held her last night, so tenderly, so chastely, warmed her even now. Nicole sighed. Just when she was convinced that their relationship was about nothing more than sex, just when she thought she had figured the man out, he went and did something like that. Holding her as if he really cared, as if nothing else mattered.

She smiled when she considered George's visit in the wee hours of the morning. And his little secret. George was a great deal more adventurous than Nicole would ever have guessed. How could she have known him her entire life and not have gotten even an inkling that the man was into kinky sex? The image of Ian, handcuffed to the wide brass headboard, suddenly took center stage in Nicole's mind. A tiny barb of pleasure twisted low in her belly, followed by a slow warmth that gradually consumed her. She could see herself in the fantasy, on her hands and knees, moving over Ian's helpless but unbearably aroused body. She would take her time tasting him, licking here and there, then drawing mercilessly on all the right spots. He would beg her to take him inside her, plead for release, but Nicole would linger, making the pleasure last until the desire reached a frantic pitch.

Nicole pushed up to a sitting position, wrapped her arms around her legs, and rested her chin atop her knees. She blew out a disgusted breath. *Final warning, Reed. You've gone way beyond reason here,* she scolded harshly. Nicole closed her eyes and considered her predicament. Where was her willpower? Her self-discipline? Why couldn't she just look at Ian and pretend he was anybody else? A partner on a case? Someone she used to know in another life, when things were clearer and her job made much more sense? Someone *temporarily* back in her life?

Because it was impossible to describe Ian that simply. Everything about him and between them was complicated. Too complicated. And entirely too intense.

"Good morning."

Nicole opened her eyes to the subject of her worrisome reverie. Nicole blinked in surprise. He wore blue jeans that fit as if they were tailor-made for his long, lean body, and a gray cable-knit sweater that emphasized the breadth of his broad shoulders as well as the darker silver of his eyes. His dark hair was still slightly damp, and Nicole had the sudden almost overwhelming urge to run her fingers through it.

One side of his mouth lifted in a ghost of a smile. "Would you prefer your coffee in bed?"

No, she thought wickedly, *I'd prefer you in bed.* Nicole swallowed in an effort to halt the swell of need tightening her throat. "Good morning," she managed, her voice thick with sleep and the lust her fantasy had elicited. "I'll get my own coffee, thank you," she added with a tad more resolve.

"Fine." He turned and strode to the kitchen.

Nicole shivered. She could learn things about sensuality just by watching him walk across the room. He moved like a panther, slow, graceful, each step a fluid motion that encompassed his entire being. He appeared at once completely relaxed, yet poised for anything that might come his way. And his voice... Nicole hugged herself tighter. She tried to analyze the effect, tried to get used to it, but she was never fully prepared for the way it flowed over her, absorbed her in its essence.

A shower. She threw the covers back and bounded off the bed. After she'd showered and dressed they could drive into town for a few provisions. The trip would serve two purposes, a much-needed distraction and the opportunity to show themselves in public, to make sure the bait was taken. Nicole selected a pair of jeans and a red sweater. Red was always a definite eye-catcher. And today she needed something that stood out amid the earth-tone colors of autumn and the other diehard back-to-nature tourists. Nicole just hoped that their little excursion would garner the right attention. Dragging this weekend out any longer than necessary wouldn't be too smart.

Nicole hurried into the bathroom and quickly closed the door behind her. She needed distance. If she couldn't distance herself physically from Ian, which was impossible in the present scenario, she would simply have to distance herself emotionally from him. Her attempts had proven woefully inadequate thus far. But that was about to change. Nicole was finished playing around. It was time to get serious.

No one she cared about would be safe until this was over.

Especially Ian.

TOURISTS, attempting to make the most of summer's last holiday, had descended upon the tiny village of Town Creek. Ian closely monitored the knots of shoppers bustling up and down the sidewalks. Of course, the hitman following Nicole could be waiting behind any one of the pairs of designer sunglasses adorning the many faces around them. The clink of cheap dinnerware and the steady hum of conversation vibrated in the small, filled-to-capacity café as they had lunch. Unscuffed hiking boots and brand-new outdoorsy clothing separated the tourists—Ian and Nicole included—from the locals.

Ian watched Nicole pick at her chef's salad. She looked preoccupied, which, in this business, was a dangerous state of mind. Remaining alert at all times was top priority.

"How's your salad?" he inquired casually.

Nicole's gaze shot up to his. "Perfect," she responded quickly, flatly.

Ian studied her blank expression for a time. "Then why aren't you eating it?"

Nicole laid her fork aside and pushed her plate away. She leaned back into the padded vinyl upholstery of the wide booth and gave him a sardonic look. "I'm not hungry."

Ian fingered his sweating water glass. "Why?" he asked eventually.

"I don't have to have a reason, Michaels," she returned, an impatient edge in her voice.

Michaels. Ian understood now. She was closing him out. Building a wall around herself so he couldn't touch her. Preparing mentally for whatever fate lay in store for her. He supposed that was wise, the right thing to do even. But he didn't like it.

He looked straight into her eyes, and, to her credit, she didn't look away. "This may not turn out the way we've planned. He may not show at all," Ian suggested quietly.

"If he wants Solomon, he'll show." Steely insistence laced her tone, her gaze remained emotionless.

Ian dipped his head in acknowledgement. "*If* he wants Solomon," he agreed.

"He wants Solomon."

"You're certain of that?"

Nicole adopted a look that said she was bored with the subject. "We've been over this already."

Ian gestured for the passing waitress and then to his empty coffee cup. "Do you have a problem with going over it again?" He smiled his appreciation when the waitress filled his cup.

Nicole watched the woman walk away, then shifted her gaze back to Ian. "I'm bored with the subject."

"This could all be related to a different case," Ian suggested, choosing to ignore her comments.

"The only significant case Daniels and I had in common was Solomon's. Daniels thought the same thing, he said so in his note. That's proof enough for me." She sipped her lemonade and turned her attention to the pedestrians passing on the other side of the plate-glass window.

She was right. Not a single doubt existed in Ian's mind about that. The cartel never forgot, and they damn sure never forgave. If Solomon was found, he would die, slowly and painfully. The man playing with all the explosives knew that Nicole was the key—the only one left who could lead him to Solomon. Ian was certain that if Nicole made no move to lead the shooter to Solomon, he would eventually come after her to get what he wanted. Ian's gut clenched. That thought scared the hell out of him, but he knew it was the only way. They had put the ball in the other guy's court. He had the next move. Ian and Nicole only needed to wait for him to make that move. But waiting was proving nearly unbearable.

With Nicole still staring out the window, Ian took a moment to study her. She was beautiful. His chest constricted. And he wanted her again more than he had ever wanted anyone or anything in his life. But she was on the defensive now. She wanted this to be business, as it should be. Not allowing physical intimacy would make walking away easier. Ian had to remember that. Because he *would* walk away. He would not give Nicole the opportunity to hurt him again. He would protect her, but nothing more. Right now, Nicole was vulnerable and she needed him. When this was finished and she no longer needed his help, she would return to her life, and, just like before, she wouldn't look back. Not once.

This time Ian wouldn't be looking back either.

Ian swallowed hard. Somehow he would put aside all that drew him to Nicole. He had never met a woman like her. She was the *only* one who could hold her own with him…his match.

Let her erect her defensive barrier. She was only doing him a favor. Ian had a life to get back to as well. He enjoyed his work at the Colby Agency, and he liked living in Chicago. Nicole's home was in Washington. She lived for the bureau. When she'd had time to really consider all that had happened, she would only be more determined to remain loyal to her chosen profession.

"Are you ready?"

Nicole's sudden question jerked Ian back to the present. She was watching him, trying to discern his thoughts. "Yes," he answered. He placed the appropriate amount of cash on the table, then stood. Ian followed Nicole out the café door; the bell jingled, announcing their departure. The warm golden sun reigned supreme over the soft blue dome of the sky. Ian carefully surveyed the street and the dozen or so meters between them and the rented SUV. The packages from their earlier stops were already stowed in the back of the vehicle. Milk, eggs and cheese were stored in a cooler Ian had found in George's small storage building.

Ian suddenly found himself wondering if George and his girlfriend were all tied up in the lodge down the street. A smile teased his lips. The image of Nicole in leather that fit exactly like skin abruptly filled his head. Every muscle in his body contracted at the vivid visual stimulation. Ian's gaze immediately darted to Nicole's softly swaying hips. Her long, shapely legs were nicely defined by her body-hugging jeans. And then there was that silky veil of long, blond hair swinging against that sexy red sweater. Ian moistened his lips. The memory of waking up, their bodies entangled, aroused him further.

Nicole whirled around unexpectedly. She stepped back at the intensity she met in his eyes. "What's wrong? Why are you looking at me that way?"

Because he wanted to take her right then and there. Ian advanced the step she had retreated. She faltered back another tiny step, but the SUV stopped her.

"I've been thinking," Ian began, the idea gaining momentum even as he spoke. He leaned in closer, and placed one hand against the vehicle on either side of her. He inhaled her gentle fragrance—sweet, succulent peaches. A rush of renewed need made his next breath a chore. "If we want this to work, we have to make sure our guy believes it's for real."

Uncertainty flickered in those pretty blue eyes that exactly matched the day's perfect sky. "Agreed," she said hesitantly.

Ian leaned closer still. "Then we have to appear distracted," he whispered discreetly. "Distracted with each other."

She swallowed, the effort visible along the slender column of her throat. His fingers burned to trace that delicate terrain.

"I suppose so." Her words were barely a whisper.

The walls she had erected only this morning crumbled around her. Ian saw it in her eyes as a distant flame of desire kindled, and he felt it in her posture, she leaned forward, ever so slightly, without even realizing it.

"Then you agree," he suggested, his lips almost brushing hers, his gaze devouring every perfect, up-close detail of her lovely face, "that I should kiss you right now, just to be certain this looks authentic."

The tiny hitch in her breathing undid Ian completely. His mouth claimed hers. He kissed her, softly at first, absorbing the essence of citrus scent and hot, sweet Nicole. Desire pounded him brutally, and his kiss grew equally savage. He thrust his tongue into her mouth, pressed his arousal into her soft body. Fire surged through his veins, urging him on, compounding his need. His fingers splayed on the sun-warmed glass of the rear passenger window. His assault was relentless, until Nicole whimpered helplessly beneath his siege, then and only then did Ian pull back. His breath raged in and out of his lungs. Nicole's breathing was just as ragged. Her lips were pleasure-swollen, her eyes glazed with desire.

Enough, he ordered silently.

Ian opened the front passenger-side door. "Let's go," he ordered quietly, ignoring the look of disbelief swiftly claiming her features. He did another quick scan of the street as she climbed into the vehicle.

"You're a real bastard, do you know that, Michaels?" she hissed, daggers shooting from those piercing blue orbs.

Ian allowed her a half smile. "Yes."

He closed the door.

Chapter Seven

Nicole literally seethed. She donned her new sunglasses and glared out the tinted passenger-side window of the SUV as Ian slid behind the wheel. Damn him! All morning she had worked hard at distancing herself, setting boundaries. She knew what she had to do, and she had done it for the first time since laying eyes on the man. Forced herself to concentrate on anything but Ian and the heat that lingered between them. She snapped her seat belt into place with a little more force than was needed as the engine roared to life. What had he been trying to prove with that kiss?

…we have to make sure our guy believes it's for real.

But it wasn't for real. The emotions his every look, every touch evoked inside her weren't real. At least not for Ian. He was simply doing his job. Once he had decided to help her, that was a given. Ian Michaels never failed. He would do whatever it took to ensure her safety and catch the bad guy. If he personally enjoyed the kiss, that was just a perk. And why not? Nicole closed her eyes and shook her head grimly from side to side. She had done it to him, hadn't she? Ian would never forgive her for what had happened between them three years ago. What she had thought might be his lingering feelings for her were probably only his way of exacting his revenge. Well, she wasn't falling for it again. Ian Michaels had better keep his distance, because Nicole damn sure intended to maintain hers.

The chirping of Ian's cell phone jerked Nicole back to the present. Still in the parking slot, Ian shifted back into Park. She handed him the compact phone he'd asked her to carry in her purse.

"Yes," he answered, then listened for what seemed like an eternity.

Nicole studied his face carefully, looking for any subtle change in expression that might give the subject of the call away. But Ian was too good at masking his emotions. Nicole huffed a breath of exasperation. She hated being at anyone's mercy.

"Yes, that's sounds like the next logical step," Ian told the caller. Another long pause. "Keep me posted." He flipped the mouthpiece closed and turned to Nicole. "That was Alex Preston." Ian waited for Nicole to recognize the name of the other agent Victoria had recommended. "So far nothing has turned up on any of the cartel members. No one seems even remotely involved in what's happening to you. But," he qualified, "Alex has only scratched the surface at this point."

"What about Solomon?" Nicole kept her gaze steady on his, feeling more confident behind the concealing glasses.

"Martinez checked in this morning. Solomon is fine, a little testy about his accommodations, but otherwise fine."

"Good." Nicole directed her attention straight ahead. Unless Ian had additional new information, there was nothing else to discuss. She was still enormously annoyed with him about the kiss.

"Alex has decided to call in an outside source to obtain a more detailed report on the cartel."

Nicole stiffened. She wasn't sure she wanted anyone else brought in on this case. The fewer people who knew, the safer Solomon would be. "Who?"

"His name is Sloan. He's good."

Nicole considered the name. If it should ring a bell, it didn't. "What makes her think that this Sloan can get any closer to the cartel than she did?"

"Because Sloan plays as dirty as they do. He's a mercenary of sorts."

That got Nicole's undivided attention. She gave Ian a long, sideways assessment. "Since when does a firm like the Colby Agency deal with mercenaries?" Nicole couldn't picture Victoria Colby with a character resembling early Sylvester Stallone work in her elegant office. "Is she certain he can be trusted?"

"I don't know him personally, but if Victoria trusts him…" Ian offered, allowing the rest of his statement to trail off. A hint of a shrug lifted one broad shoulder. "That's all I need to know."

Victoria obviously lived up to the reputation that preceded her. Ian didn't trust easily. "I'd like to borrow your phone." Nicole held out her hand. "I want to make sure George made it back to his girlfriend last night," she explained when Ian hesitated.

He placed the phone in her open palm. "Make it brief."

Nicole rolled her eyes and punched in the telephone number she had memorized from the menu jacket in the café. Several local business logos were displayed on the plastic cover, including the River Lodge.

"Hello." The greeting was a breathless rush of syllables.

Nicole smiled. "George, just wanted to make sure you

didn't want to come have dinner with us this evening." Her brows furrowed as she listened intently in an effort to decipher the strange background noises accompanying George's heavy breathing. From the corner of her eye, Nicole saw Ian's fingers curl into a fist on his thigh. Two could play the game of pushing the other to the edge.

"Sorry, Nicole, but I'm a little busy at the moment." The pitch and intensity of the muffled sounds on the other end of the line increased. "How about we get together another time?" George suggested, his voice strained as if he were struggling.

"Okay. See you soon." Nicole closed the phone and offered it back to Ian. His glower was lethal.

"Don't play games with me, Nicole," he told her, in an equally lethal tone. "You know we have to do this alone."

Nicole shrugged innocently and dropped the phone she still held into her bag. "Who's playing games? I only wanted to make sure George was okay. I knew he wouldn't accept the offer." She faced forward again. "He was otherwise occupied."

"Look at me, Nicole."

The order was almost soft, but the skin on the back of her neck prickled with warning. Ian was deadly serious. Slowly, reluctantly, Nicole turned her head in his direction, her chin parallel with her shoulder. Resisting the urge to flinch, Nicole sat perfectly still as one long-fingered hand darted up to her face and plucked off her sunglasses. She blinked at the sudden brightness.

"Don't test my patience," he warned, pressing her with a gaze that reiterated his words.

Nicole sighed and faced forward again. "Whatever," she said flippantly as she grabbed back her eyewear. Ian would not tolerate her indifference well she knew. That thought pleased Nicole inordinately.

Several tense seconds passed before he shifted into reverse and, watching over his right shoulder, slowly backed from the parking slot. Nicole stared, not really seeing but looking through the tourists strolling past the quaint shops. She would never be, had never been like those people. Nicole had spent her entire adult life training or working for the bureau. The bureau was her life. Regret, abrupt and unbidden, trickled through her. She was twenty-nine years old. Wasn't there supposed to be something else? Ian's whispered words in that language she hadn't understood as he made love to her echoed through her mind.

She would never have that either.

Something familiar in someone in the crowd they passed grabbed her attention. Nicole frowned and spun around in her seat. "Wait!"

Ian braked to a stop in the middle of the street. "What's wrong?" A horn blasted behind them.

"Park," Nicole commanded as she unfastened her seat belt. By the time Ian had killed the engine in their new parking slot, Nicole was climbing out the door. "Over there." She pointed to the sporting goods shop on the corner across the street. "In the alley between the buildings."

Without question, Ian sprinted across the street, dodging traffic. Nicole followed, ignoring the irritated shouts and blaring horns. She concentrated hard on the image that had caught her eye. She had only seen the back of the man, but something about the way he moved seemed familiar. Instinct niggled at her even now. She knew him.

They reached the corner of the sporting goods shop. "He's wearing a navy blue jacket. Medium height and build, dark hair,'' she said quickly. "I know him,'' she added thoughtfully. Ian paused briefly to assess the situation and Nicole focused inward on the slow, deliberate walk of the man she had seen.

"Stay behind me,'' Ian commanded as he started forward.

Halfway down the alley, Ian reached beneath his sweater to the small of his back and withdrew his gun. Nicole's heart pounded with the anticipation flowing swiftly through her veins. Her fingers curled around the butt of the Beretta cradled in the back of her waistband. She withdrew her weapon and kept it pointed toward the ground as she trailed Ian through the shadowy, deserted alley. She turned around slowly from time to time to ensure they weren't being followed. Fear for Ian welled in her chest, suffocating her with its intensity.

They reached the end of the alley, and Ian waited, listening. Slowly he moved around the corner of the building.

Nothing.

Nicole swore hotly.

She shook her head, fury replacing the fear she had felt only moments before. "I know what I saw."

Ian studied the architecture of the buildings on either side of the alley as he spoke, "I don't doubt you, Nicole."

Ian's supportive response did nothing to slow Nicole's growing agitation. He was here. She saw him. Every instinct told her he was the one. Nicole followed Ian's gaze as he traced the landscape that rose sharply behind the buildings. The overgrown grass appeared undisturbed. To their left the alley abruptly dead-ended.

Ian started moving again. "This way," he said quietly.

Nicole followed, her hopes rising again. A door on the far end of the building to the right had captured Ian's attention. As they approached, Nicole could see that the door led into the sporting goods shop. Concealing his weapon once more beneath his sweater, Ian opened the door and entered the shop. Nicole did the same. The door led to what appeared to be the shipping and receiving section of the store. Another door, standing wide open and marked Employees Only, led into a short, narrow hallway which emptied into the large store.

"Stay right here," Ian instructed, before disappearing into the men's room.

Nicole leaned against the wall near the ladies' room door and watched the comings and goings at the end of the hall.

When Ian stepped back into the hall, he shook his head to indicate he had found nothing. "Check the ladies' room, just in case," he told her.

Nicole pushed the door inward and entered the bathroom. Two empty stalls, a sink and a short bench greeted her. No window, no other avenue of escape. She rejoined Ian in the hall and reported her findings.

Ian continued down the hall and drifted into the crowd of milling shoppers. Nicole scanned every face, every backside. He had to be in here. She stopped. A man with dark hair, wearing a navy blue jacket was rifling through a rack of golf shirts, his back turned to Nicole. Her heart rate kicked into overdrive. She blocked the steady murmur of conversation around her to focus solely on her target. Slowly, not taking her eyes off the man, Nicole approached him. Just when she would have reached out to him, a hand darted past her and grabbed the man by the shoulder. Ian whirled the guy around, his free hand already gripping his well-concealed weapon.

"What the—?" The man struggled to pull free of Ian's grip. He faltered back a step. "What's your problem?"

Nicole wilted. It wasn't him. Ian looked to her for confirmation. Nicole shook her head.

"Sorry," Ian offered. "I thought you were someone else."

The man muttered something under his breath and left the shop as fast as he could.

"You're sure?" Ian asked.

Nicole nodded. Though she hadn't actually seen the face of the man on the sidewalk, something in his manner spoke to her "The way this guy carried himself was wrong," she explained. Where could the man she had seen have gone?

Nicole followed Ian through the rest of the shop, but there was no one else with dark hair and wearing a solid-colored navy blue jacket. Doubt set in. Nicole began to wonder if she could have imagined the man. Maybe her eyes were playing tricks on her. Maybe she wanted this to be over so badly that she was conjuring up people who weren't there.

"If he was here, he's gone now," Ian said quietly. "We should be going."

If.

Nicole couldn't blame Ian for not believing her. She wasn't sure if she even believed herself anymore. As they walked back to the SUV, Nicole searched the pedestrians for any sign of a navy blue jacket. Ian appeared watchful as well. Still nothing. Nicole reached for the handle on the passenger-side door of their vehicle, but a paper fluttering beneath the windshield wiper caught her attention. A sales flyer. Henrietta's Florist and Gifts. Nicole frowned as she yanked the unwanted document free of the wiper. She tossed her bag and the flyer into the vehicle and climbed into her seat. Her temples pounded with frustration. He had to know they were here. She and Ian had left a trail a mile wide. He had to have followed.

Nicole stared out the window as Ian cruised down the street. In less than five minutes they had left the town behind and were halfway up the mountain road leading to George's private getaway. Images flickered in front of Nicole's eyes. The destruction in Landon's office. His bereaved widow weeping over his closed coffin at the cemetery. The absolute devastation at Daniels's house. The mysterious note from Daniels after his death. Her rental car exploding...the bullet crashing through the truck window and hitting Ian...her apartment going up in flames.

Nicole closed her eyes and forced the painful memories away. She summoned the figure she had seen for those few short seconds. She replayed the way he had moved. Nicole released a disgusted breath. Nothing. It was his body language that spoke to her and her mind just couldn't play it back precisely enough at the moment to capture the quality that she had recognized.

"Stop thinking about it, Nicole."

Ian's silky voice penetrated the layers of frustration shrouding her. She looked at him for a full minute before she replied. Did he have any idea how deeply she responded to the mere sound of his voice? "It was him," she murmured.

Ian regarded her briefly, those assessing gray eyes analyzing far too much and far too deeply for Nicole's comfort. "He'll be back," he assured her.

Nicole propped her elbow on the door and massaged her aching forehead. Yeah, he would be back. He wanted Solomon. And the only way he could get to Solomon was through Nicole.

Something crinkled beneath Nicole's boot when she shifted in her seat. The forgotten flyer had fallen onto the floor. Annoyed, she glared at the offending document and kicked it aside. Bold, bloodred letters drew her gaze back when she would have looked away.

I'm waiting for you, Nicole.

Her hand trembled as she reached for the wrinkled paper. She read it again when she had it in her hand. On the backside of the florist's advertisement, large printed letters spelled out the words. Her heart froze in her chest. Straining for a calm she didn't feel, Nicole forced herself to analyze the evidence she held. Identifying the block-style printing would be impossible even if they had a clue as to where to begin a comparison. Since there was no way to know how many people had handled the flyer, fingerprints would prove useless.

I'm waiting for you, Nicole.

It was a warning, plain and simple. He wanted her, Nicole knew. But he was waiting. Until she was alone. The thought shook her. Nicole glanced at the driver. Her heart kicked back into that rapid staccato.

Just her. He was waiting for her to be alone. And then he would make a move. Not before.

"What's that?"

Nicole jerked to attention. Ian had already parked in the driveway in front of George's cabin. She swallowed. "A message." Nicole handed the paper to Ian. "It was on the windshield after we came out of the sports shop. I thought it was just a local advertisement."

Ian studied the document for a time, then lifted his gaze to her. "He was watching us."

Nicole nodded.

"Good." Ian laid the paper on the console. "Lock the doors. Don't get out until I tell you it's safe to come inside. If anyone approaches this vehicle, drive away." Ian opened his door and stepped out, then turned back to

Nicole. "Move over here." He indicated the driver's seat, that silvery gaze intent and determined. "Drive away if you hear or see anything suspicious. Use the cell phone to call for help."

Nicole choked out a laugh. "Like hell."

"Do it, Nicole," he commanded harshly.

"All right," she relented, though there was no way she would ever drive away leaving Ian behind.

Ian pressed the lock button and closed the door. Nicole chewed on her lower lip as she watched him move cautiously around the cabin, his weapon readied. She held her breath until he appeared again from the other side. He studied the ground, and each window in the cabin as he passed it. He was looking for tracks or any other signs of entry, she knew. He crossed the porch and unlocked the door. Nicole's breath went still in her lungs as he disappeared once more, this time inside. Her gaze continuously swept the area around the cabin and the vehicle in which she sat, always moving back to the door, watching for Ian.

"This is nuts," Nicole muttered under her breath. She should be in there with Ian. Another minute ticked by. Making up her mind and steeling her resolve, Nicole withdrew her Beretta and opened the vehicle door. She was no untrained civilian. She knew the drill. Moving as swiftly and soundlessly as possible, Nicole stole across the yard. When she reached the porch steps, she relaxed a bit. Five seconds later she was at the door. Gripping the nine-millimeter with both hands she stepped across the threshold. She surveyed the room from left to right and back.

No Ian.

Adrenaline surged, stinging through her veins. Nicole stepped cautiously toward the kitchen, her gazed roved from side to side. She made a slow turn in the middle of the room to check the front door and the porch beyond it one more time.

"I told you to stay in the truck."

Nicole whipped toward the kitchen door. Ian loomed in the seemingly small opening, his expression fierce. Nicole relaxed her fire-ready stance. "I got lonely," she retorted as she tucked her weapon away.

After glaring at her a moment longer, Ian scanned the room. "I don't think anyone has been here."

"But he definitely knows we're here," Nicole countered.

"He knows."

She pushed a handful of hair over her shoulder. "He wants me alone," she remarked more to herself than to Ian.

Ian shot her a pointed look. "That's not going to happen," he said, a warning, not a reassurance.

Nicole moistened her lips. "What if he won't show with you hanging around?"

Ian cocked his head in that arrogant manner of his. "Then he won't show."

"So the point of this entire exercise is?" she demanded, her temper flaring as rapidly as her impatience.

Ian gazed steadily at her. "To keep you and Solomon alive."

"Gosh, I guess I forgot about that." Nicole pivoted and stormed toward the door.

Ian snagged her arm before she took two steps. "Think, Nicole," he urged softly. "When he gets desperate enough, then he'll come, despite my presence. He'll rethink his approach and make a move."

Nicole tried to shrug his hand off. "We need to unload the supplies."

Several more seconds passed before Ian released her. Without another word, he followed Nicole to the SUV. He unlocked and lifted the rear hatch, then picked up the cooler while Nicole collected the two small bags from the back seat. Her mind raced with possibilities. She searched her memory for something, anything that would trigger that feeling of recognition again.

Nothing came.

Nicole stole a glance at Ian as they carried the supplies into the cabin. She closed and locked the door, then joined him in the kitchen. Ian was right, she supposed. The guy eventually would make a move. He had to if he wanted Solomon. The problem was, how long would he wait? And how long would she and Ian survive living under the same small roof without making another heart-damaging mistake?

As if to validate her point, Nicole found herself suddenly and unavoidably mesmerized by Ian's precise, graceful movements. He reached to put a can of soup in the cupboard, placing it exactly in line with the other canned goods, the label facing outward. His lean, muscled frame made her want to feel his weight against her. He reached into the next bag and, one by one, removed the apples and oranges Nicole had selected in the market. Those long, artist's fingers closed around each fresh piece of fruit in a near-caressing manner.

Ian paused abruptly, a shiny red apple still in his hand. Seemingly in slow motion, he turned to find Nicole watching him so intently. The look that passed between them said more than any words could have. He smiled then, and brought that succulent piece of fruit to his full, firm mouth and took a bite, his eyes never leaving Nicole's. He chewed slowly, his lips moist with the luscious juice of the fresh fruit. And nothing would have pleased Nicole more than to lick that sweet stuff from those sensual lips.

Deep, deep inside Nicole, where nothing or no one else could touch her, something moved, and a kind of yearning she had never before experienced awoke and roared like a hungry beast. The need grew until her every sensory perception was focused inward to that one mushrooming sensation.

She would never survive another forty-eight hours alone with this man. He meant entirely too much to her.

Nicole needed a plan.

An *escape* plan.

Chapter Eight

By late afternoon on Sunday, Nicole felt ready to explode. Furious with herself as much as with Ian for feeling so helpless, she reached for the hand towel on the kitchen counter at the same time as he did. They glanced at each other briefly, but not briefly enough. Electricity zinged between them. Ian acquiesced with a barely perceptible nod, abandoning the towel to Nicole then turning his attention to the salad he was preparing. His long fingers poised on the tomato as he diced it with the skill of a master chef. Nicole dutifully dried the just-washed utensils, undeniably aware of Ian's every move. Disgusted, she tossed the towel aside and glanced at the battery-operated clock on the wall. Nicole quickly performed her second mental calculation of the day. Forty-three hours, twenty-seven minutes together, alone, in this growing-smaller-by-the-moment cabin. She bit back the urge to scream or break something.

The tension in the cubicle-sized kitchen was thick enough to cut with the knife Ian was currently using to chop the bell pepper. Taking a deep breath, Nicole decided to check on the pasta and sauce. Ian had insisted that, this being a holiday weekend, they should have some sort of celebratory meal. Nicole started toward the stove,

Ian turned in the direction of the sink and she barreled smack into his mile-wide chest.

"Sorry," he murmured.

Nicole jumped back, holding her palms out to ward off any further apology or moves in her direction. "It's fine."

While he watched contritely, Nicole stepped around him, maintaining a safe distance between their bodies. She stirred the pasta, then the sauce, staring into the thick, red concoction as if it held the answers to all her problems.

"Almost done, don't you think?"

Startled, Nicole jerked away from the sound of Ian's silky voice. Standing entirely too close to her for comfort, he regarded her for a long moment. Nicole's heart flip-flopped hard beneath her sternum. He hadn't bothered to shave this morning, and the day's beard growth only intensified his sexy aura. He looked dark and dangerous and absolutely delicious.

"Why are you so jumpy, Nicole?"

Nicole set the wooden spoon aside and placed the lid on the sauce. Ian didn't move, he hovered over her as if she needed his full attention. She pushed her suddenly damp palms over her jean-clad hips and lifted her chin defiantly. She glared at Ian to produce the full effect.

"I'm not jumpy," she snapped. "I'm just tired of bumping into you that's all." She folded her arms over her middle and retreated a step. "You're crowding me, Ian. Every time I turn around you're there."

He shrugged vaguely, his gaze carefully controlled. "It's difficult to stay out of each other's way in such close quarters," he said so calmly, so reasonably she wanted to slap him to see if his expression would change.

Irritation, desperation and a dozen other emotions whirled inside her. She had to get out of here. No one was coming as long as Ian shadowed her every move like this. Nicole had to find a way to ditch him. She would never get Landon's and Daniels's killer otherwise. The note had been specific. He had been waiting for *her*. Sure, he might eventually show with Ian here, as Ian had suggested, but Nicole was out of time. She could not tolerate another hour alone with Ian. And even if she could, staying only put Ian at risk.

Decision made, she took another step back, edging toward the kitchen door. "I think I'll take a bath," she announced out of the blue.

Ian frowned. "What about dinner?"

"I'm not hungry." She gave him her back. "Don't wait for me," she added as she stalked toward the bathroom. Once inside, she closed the door and pressed her forehead against it. God, she needed her head examined. She knew her time with Ian was only temporary. She knew that he would only break her heart…just like last time. Though last time hadn't really been his fault. Duty bound or not, she had no one else to blame but herself for that one. But how could she still want him so very desperately? How could she long for him with such need that simply looking at him propelled her toward orgasm? Because she admired and respected everything about him, she admitted. Ian was the one man who drew her on every conscious level. Could she risk his being in any further danger?

Nicole had to find a way to slip away from him. She had tried leaving late last night while Ian was sleeping, but he had awakened instantly the moment she rose from the bed. Nicole had pretended she needed to use the bathroom. He had waited until she was safely back into bed before relaxing again. Ian was too smart to fool that easily, too fast to outrun, and too damned good to trap.

Unless…

A wide smile suddenly spread across Nicole's face. Ian

wasn't immune to the physical attraction between them. He felt it too. He wanted her as much as she wanted him. Nicole moistened her lips and tried to recall the array of items George had stashed under the bed. She made a mental list of the erotic and kinky toys available. The handcuffs and body oil would do very nicely, she decided with a little too much glee.

Acting quickly before she lost her nerve, Nicole knelt in front of the cabinet beneath the bathroom sink. She dug through the items stored there until she found what she was looking for, a half-dozen bath scents. Ian loved apples. She picked up the one called Enchanted Apple and closed the cabinet doors. Nicole adjusted the tap until the water flowing into the tub was to her liking, then she added the bubble bath. She closed her eyes and inhaled the steamy scent. Good enough to eat, she thought with a wicked grin.

Oh yes, this would do nicely.

In record time Nicole stripped off her clothes and dropped them onto the floor, ensuring that her panties and bra lay atop the pile. She pinned her hair up and reached for a towel. On second thought, she opted to forego the towel. That would be her excuse. Nicole stepped gingerly into the welcoming warmth of the softly scented water. She slowly sank beneath its surface with a moan of pure pleasure.

Relax, Nicole, she ordered. *For it will take every ounce of willpower and persuasion you have to do what has to be done.*

Ian would never know what hit him.

IAN GLANCED at the still-closed bathroom door and frowned. Why had Nicole been in there so long? The salad was in the fridge, the bread, pasta and sauce in the oven keeping warm, and the wine, open and ready to serve, stood on the table. The only holdup was Nicole. She had said not to wait, but Ian waited anyway. He massaged his unshaven chin and considered her behavior since their arrival here, especially the last twenty-four hours. Maybe the note had shaken her more deeply than he had first thought. She was certainly jumpy enough. Then, maybe it was simply a matter of cabin fever.

No. Ian released a heavy breath. It was none of those things. Nicole was suffering from the same ailment that plagued him, sexual frustration.

He wanted Nicole. He wanted her so badly that it was a bone-deep ache. The thought of touching her had been there all day, prowling in the deepest, darkest recesses of his mind, like an enemy preparing to close in. If something didn't happen soon, one or both of them would lose control. Today had been the most difficult. Absolute silence surrounded them. It was as if even the birds knew it was Sunday and they should rest from their twittering and chirping. The sky was a magnificent canvas of blue with the occasional fluffy white cloud here and there like the smudges of a careless painter's brush. A slight breeze whispered through the trees from time to time, momentarily disrupting the utter silence.

Inside, the mouth-watering aroma of garlic and tomato sauce filled the air. He should be hungry, but like Nicole, he wasn't. Ian's gaze flitted across the room. The big brass bed stood waiting, beckoning to him like a buoy in deep waters. Ian knew that if he didn't do something soon he would drown of suffocating need. A desire that never completely went away smoldered just beneath the surface of his own flimsy hold on control.

He needed a walk. A very long walk. And before he came back inside he would have this fire under control once more. Ian stepped to the bathroom door and knocked once.

"Nicole, I'm going outside to check the generator," he said flatly, then turned to make good on his announcement, but her tentative voice stopped him.

"Ian?"

The sound of his name on her lips drew him back to the door, closer than he had been before, his face pressed against the smooth wooden surface. "Yes," he answered stiffly.

"I'm sorry to bother you," a pause accompanied by the splash of water, "but I failed to get a towel before I got into the tub. Now I can't get one without dripping all over the place. Would you," another agonizing pause, "come hand me a towel?"

The image of Nicole in that tub, surrounded by frothy water, bloomed before Ian's eyes. He could smell the clean, sweet fragrance of the scented water. Want speared through him, immediate and fierce. Ian braced his hands against the doorframe and summoned his crumbling resolve. The taste of her lips, the smell of her skin, how it felt to hold her in his arms kept playing through his mind. If he hadn't kissed her yesterday, maybe the need wouldn't be quite so savage. But he *had* kissed her. And he wanted to kiss her again.

"Ian?"

Soft, sultry, her voice tugged at him, destroyed the last of his defenses. "Yes," he rasped. His hand moved to the knob, gripped hard, ready to turn it and remove the one tangible barrier between them.

"The water's getting a little cold."

Ian turned the knob and pushed the door open. The warm, moist air enveloped him with that irresistible fragrance he couldn't quite name as he stepped into the small room. His gaze riveted on Nicole reclining against the end of the tub in water just deep enough to conceal her breasts. Mounds of bubbles floated around her. She smiled lazily up at Ian, those blue eyes liquid with feminine heat. All that silky hair was haphazardly pinned on top of her head, several strands had fallen free and now clung to her damp neck.

Forcing his gaze away from temptation, Ian took a towel from the linen closet. He swallowed with major difficulty, his body growing harder with each passing second, and turned back to her. Something in his peripheral vision drew him up short, pulling his attention to the floor. Nicole's discarded clothing lay at the foot of the tub, a ruby-red bra with matching panties topped the pile like a ripe cherry. Instantly, the vision of Nicole wearing those wicked undergarments played before his eyes. Full, rock-hard arousal tightened his loins.

Nicole suddenly sat up and wrapped her arms around her bent knees, but not before Ian got a gut-wrenching view of her breasts, water and bubbles sliding over their fullness. His hardened length twitched with urgency. Nicole nodded toward the washcloth hanging on the side of the tub.

"Would you mind washing my back?" She laid her cheek against her knees and closed her eyes.

Ian's hungry gaze roved every delicious rise and hollow. The firm curves of her legs; the swell of her breast where it was pressed against her thigh; the exquisite detail of her spine; the lovely length of her neck.

"Please," she urged when Ian didn't move fast enough.

Unable to dredge up a verbal response, he knelt next to the tub and picked up the damp washcloth with his left hand. He dipped it into the warm water and then slowly caressed the smooth skin of her back. His right hand fisted into the soft terry cloth of the towel.

"Hmmmmm," she moaned, "that feels nice."

Fire flashed through Ian's veins, heating him from the inside out. He couldn't take much more of this. Again and again he traced that soft, creamy terrain until he felt ready to explode. Nicole straightened and looked directly into his eyes. Ian saw the same need in those azure pools as was roaring through him. A muscle jerked in his tense jaw when his gaze traveled down to her nearly exposed breasts, then back. He wanted to kiss her...to touch her, but it would never stop there. Ian was well past holding back.

"Thank you," she murmured, her gaze examining his lips before moving back to his eyes.

"You're welcome," he said tightly.

"The towel?"

Ian lifted the towel he still clutched in his right hand toward her. Before he realized what she intended, Nicole took the towel from him and stood. Ian blinked, twice. He pushed to his feet, trying his level best to ignore her naked body as she smoothed the towel over her skin.

"Anything else?" he asked, his control a single frayed thread away from snapping.

"Actually, there is one thing." Nicole wrapped the towel around her, tucking the end between her breasts. She stepped out onto the polished wood floor directly in front of Ian.

Ian waited, his body pulsing with need.

She smiled sweetly. "Would you pour me a glass of wine? I'm suddenly very thirsty."

Ian looked away and licked his parched lips. "Sure."

Nicole closed her eyes until Ian had disappeared from her line of vision. She shivered with the need vibrating inside her. How would she ever be able to see this through? She gave herself a mental shake. She had to do it. One way or another, she had to get out from under Ian's watchful gaze. The bastard she wanted would never show with Ian so close. And if he did, Ian's life would be in serious jeopardy. Firming her resolve, Nicole dropped the towel to the floor and quickly pulled on her red undies. The realization of just how much she affected Ian made her giddy with excitement. But there was no time to dwell on that right now. She had to move swiftly. If Ian suspected her motives for one instant, the game would be over before it began. Nicole shouldered into one of Ian's flannel, button-up shirts. She left the top three buttons undone and squared her shoulders, then smiled. This would do just fine.

After checking her reflection in the mirror, Nicole padded into the great room. Ian filled the second of two glasses and placed the wine bottle on the table. He turned to greet her, glass of wine in hand. Nicole almost sighed out loud. She could spend the rest of her life just looking at him like this. His gaze so intent on her, a smoldering fire turning those silvery orbs to a darker gunmetal gray. The scene almost made her falter. Sharing a glass of wine after a long day at work. Making love until an exhausted sleep overtook them. A yearning so fierce rose in Nicole that her breath caught.

This, she reminded that silly part of her that wanted to dream, was all she and Ian would ever share. A few days alone before they took down the hitman stalking her, or, she admitted, before he took one or both of them down. Nothing with Ian was permanent. They had no future. Nicole blinked back the tears that burned behind her lids. She sucked in a harsh breath and forced her feet to take her all the way to his side.

"Thank you," she managed without her voice quaking. Nicole sipped the sweet wine, then emptied the glass. "Another, please."

Ian frowned a bit, but didn't argue. Those incredible hands merely set to the task, the long fingers of one hand cradling the bottle of wine, the other holding the slender stem of Nicole's glass. Her gaze made a path up his arm to his broad shoulders, then to the face that stole the breath she had only just regained. Ian Michaels was devastatingly handsome, completely honorable and totally selfless.

And Nicole would never, ever recover from the destruction to her heart.

She accepted the refilled glass and walked to the bed. She placed her drink on the night table and crouched down to pull one of the plastic containers from beneath the bed. She angled the chocolates on the table in front of her wine, then prowled through the container until she found what she was looking for. She hid the item she would need most behind the chocolates, then reached back into the container for the body oil. Strawberries and champagne. Nicole smiled when she considered that Ian was likely watching her every move. She pushed the box of wicked toys out of the way and climbed onto the bed. With painstaking slowness and thoroughness, Nicole massaged the scented oil into her skin. Her right leg was first, her foot included. Nicole stretched it this way and that until she had given full attention to every square inch. Then she gave the same treatment to the left.

When Nicole stole a glance in Ian's direction from beneath her lids, he was standing stock-still by the table, his empty glass still clutched in his hand. Time to turn up the heat, she decided. Nicole dropped her feet back onto the floor and stood, her back to Ian. She unbuttoned the shirt and shrugged it off, allowing it to drop to the floor. With the same ambition, she rubbed the oil on first one arm and then the other. The scent was fabulous. Nicole closed her eyes and inhaled deeply. She moaned her approval. How could anyone resist this tantalizing fragrance?

"What are you doing, Nicole?"

Nicole shivered. He was right behind her. Her eyes opened. She bit back a little smile of triumph. "I'm bored, Ian," she said languidly. She turned to face him. His eyes immediately moved over her body, heating her skin as if he were touching her. "There's nothing else to do but talk and I don't want to talk," she added nonchalantly. His analyzing gaze riveted to hers, Nicole took the opportunity to smooth her oil-covered hand over her chest, then the part of her breasts exposed above the red satin. His gaze traced her every move. Nicole inhaled deeply and released it on an exaggerated sigh of contentment. "This feels really nice. Would you like to try it?"

"Don't play games with me," Ian warned in a distinctly tight voice.

Nicole allowed him a teasing smile. "Games can be fun, Ian." She thrust the oil into his hand and climbed back onto the bed. "Here," she instructed from her prone position, "do my back." Several tense seconds clicked by while Ian's gaze traveled the length of her. From her vantage point, there was no way to miss just how she was affecting Ian. The thick bulge of his arousal made her feminine muscles tighten, sending a tingle through her.

Ian's gaze connected with hers and Nicole's heart thudded in her chest at the sheer heat she saw there. But she didn't miss the rhythmic flexing of the tiny muscle in his tense jaw. He was fighting rather than yielding to the desire so obviously burning inside him.

Nicole scrambled to her knees then and moved to the

edge of the bed, within easy reach of him. She hadn't gone this far to give up without a fight of her own. She reached up and undid her hair, allowing it to slip down around her shoulders. Nicole pitched the pins in the general direction of the bedside table. She snagged Ian's hand in hers and tugged. He resisted at first, but then allowed her to pull him a step closer to the bed. Nicole moistened her lips in one long, languid stroke, then pressed a tiny kiss to his lips. "Don't make me beg, Ian," she murmured, her eyes searching his, urging him to react.

Surrender flared in those silvery depths, the oil dropped to the floor. Ian cupped her face in his hands and pulled her mouth up to his. His kiss was brutal, relentless and unmercifully hot. Too many feelings to name rushed through Nicole, all focusing on her center, making her wet and hot and needy. Her hands went to his chest and found their way under his sweater. The feel of his muscled body beneath her fingers almost undid her completely. Nicole drew back, but Ian stole another taste of her mouth before she escaped his reach. She tugged his sweater up and over his head, then tossed it to the floor. She couldn't prevent the smile of approval when she surveyed his tousled hair and amazing chest. He no longer wore the bandage on his shoulder. The wound was healing nicely. A reminder of how close she had come to losing him. She would make sure that didn't happen again. Nicole encircled his waist, removed his gun, and placed it in the container on the floor next to the bedside table.

Ian pulled her hard against him and lowered her to the bed. His weight covered her, making her weak with want. Not until he had trapped her fully between his powerful thighs did Ian lower his mouth to hers once more. His taste filled her, tempted her beyond all reason. Nicole fought to hold onto her sanity. Slowly, thoroughly, he kissed her as no one else ever had, and it went on forever. Taking a moment to catch his breath, he nibbled her lower lip. Nicole whimpered as he moved lower still, down the column of her throat. Each tender kiss took him closer and closer to the pebbled peaks begging for his attention. He exposed one taut nipple. Nicole's fingers fisted in the smooth sheets beneath her. Ian's wine-kissed breath rushed over her breast, sending another wave of intense desire to her core. He licked and taunted with the tip of his tongue, again and again, before he took that wanting peak into his mouth and sucked. Nicole writhed beneath him, the feel of denim against her skin only adding to the delicious friction.

She had to stop him, regain control before she lost it completely. Nicole placed the heels of her hands against his shoulders and forced his tempting mouth from her body. His breath ragged, his eyes fierce, he looked to Nicole for an explanation of why he had to stop. She summoned her most alluring smile. "I want to be on top," she whispered, then rubbed her knee along the inside of his thigh. Ian rolled over, pulling her onto his waist. Nicole pressed her heat against his arousal to show her approval. Ian groaned and closed his eyes with the same agony she felt.

Nicole blinked away the image of how he looked beneath her. Dark, dangerous and completely at her mercy. She had to get a grip on the situation. Ensuring that her body grazed his, she reached for the oil, then settled astride his lean hips. Nicole pulled his hands from her thighs and placed them above his head. She leaned down to nip at his lips, allowing that dark stubble to tease her skin. He tried to capture her mouth, but she was too fast for him.

"Hold on right here," she murmured as she guided his

hands to the spindles of the brass headboard. When he obeyed her command, Nicole rewarded him with several long, undulating strokes of her heat along the length of his arousal. Each languid move propelled her closer and closer to release. She squeezed him with her thighs, making him groan savagely with pleasure. Nicole massaged the scented oil onto his chest, tasting every now and then, paying particular attention to the ruddy peaks of his male nipples. Ian lifted against her, and Nicole closed her eyes to fight the almost overwhelming need to take him inside her. Her feminine muscles clenched and throbbed. She was so wet, the thin panel of silk between her thighs was drenched with the evidence of her desire. She had to finish this now, or she would never be able to stop. Nicole planted a trail of slow, hot kisses to his navel. She hesitated there, laving that part of his body with special attention. Ian stiffened, then relaxed. He was on the verge. Any second now, he would be beyond stopping. He would simply roll Nicole over and bury himself inside her, and she would be too far gone to stop him. She wanted him…badly.

When Nicole unbuttoned his fly and flicked her tongue there, he jerked. She slowly slid his zipper down, then pushed her hands between the denim and smooth silk of his navy blue boxers. He made a strained sound and his hands tightened on the brass spindles. His muscles flexed, making Nicole's heart flutter beneath her sternum. She tamped down the urge to reach up and glide her hands over all that taunt muscle. She eased back, pushed his jeans off his hips as he obediently lifted them from the bed. Nicole removed his shoes and socks, tossed them aside, then tugged his jeans the rest of the way off. They landed on the floor atop his shoes.

He was very hard. The thick ridge of his arousal be-

neath the dark silk made Nicole ache with the need to be
filled by him. She crawled on her hands and knees up the
length of his body, pausing to torment his sensitive navel
once more. She was pushing him ever closer to the edge,
she knew, but she just couldn't stop herself. Ian's hands
went around her arms and he pulled her up to him. Nicole's heart froze. Too late. His breath was hot on her
lips. His eyes were frantic.

"This is your last chance to stop, Nicole," he rasped,
that soft accent thick with his desire. "If you're having
second thoughts..." His eyes searched hers as his words
trailed off.

Nicole swallowed, then essayed a mischievous smile.
"This is my show, Michaels." She pulled free of his
grasp and pushed his hands back above his head. "We
do this my way." Nicole closed her eyes in ecstasy as she
ground the throbbing heat between her thighs into his
arousal one more time for good measure. With nothing
but the thin layers of silk between them, pleasure
screamed through her. "I promise it will be like nothing
you've ever experienced," she said tautly.

Ian's answering groan was all that Nicole needed to
hear. She opened her eyes to find his closed tight. His
hips moved restlessly beneath her. He was ready, she decided. Leaning down to suck hard on his right nipple,
Nicole used the distraction to reach behind the chocolates
and retrieve the item she had hidden there. She moved to
the left nipple, nibbling with her teeth, then sucking hard.
Before the movements of her hands penetrated Ian's haze
of lust, Nicole had the handcuffs around his left wrist and
one metal spindle about midway on the headboard, effectively shackling him to the bed. Frowning, Ian reached for
her with his free hand. Nicole scrambled backwards out
of his reach.

Fury flashed in his eyes, devouring all signs of desire. He jerked against his restraint. "Give me the key," he said in a tone just shy of lethal.

Nicole flipped her hair over her shoulders. "All right, all right. Don't get all bent out of shape, Ian, it was just a thought. I'll find the key." Nicole climbed off the bed. Her heart pounding so hard she felt certain he could hear it, she knelt by the box and dug for the key. When she had it in her hands, she shoved the container, Ian's gun still in it, beneath the bed. She stood quickly, and took two steps back.

Ian sat up straighter in the bed. He shook his head slowly from side to side. Nicole felt certain that she had never seen, nor would she ever again see, a look quite that dark, that intent. She swallowed. Ian just might not forgive her for this. Just one more thing for him to hold against her. But she had to do it.

She backed all the way to the dining table. "I'll leave the key right here," she told him with as much bravado as possible. "I'm doing the right thing, Ian," she said when he didn't respond. "It's the only way. Nicole jerked on a pair of jeans and the discarded shirt as swiftly as possible, her gaze darting back to Ian every few seconds. He said nothing, he simply stared at her with a kind of disappointment and disapproval that stabbed at her heart. She tugged on her socks and boots, and made quick work of tying them. Nicole tucked her Beretta into her waistband at the small of her back and shouldered into her denim jacket. She snatched up the keys to the Range Rover and turned back to Ian. He hadn't said a word.

"It'll be better if I do this alone," she told him. "He's not going to approach me as long as you're around." Nicole closed her eyes for a moment to dispel the image of him sprawled across the bed, almost naked, and completely at her mercy. Finally, she opened her eyes and faced the inevitable. "I'm sorry," she stammered. "It's the only way." Nicole whirled and rushed toward the door.

"Nicole."

She turned around slowly, reluctantly. She winced inside when she met the arctic chill in his eyes. She lifted her chin and held that icy gaze. "Yeah?" she asked.

"It will take me approximately fifteen minutes to dismantle this bed, drag the headboard across the room and reach the key." His tone was stone-cold. "Five minutes after that I'll be out the door. I'll find you within twenty-four hours, and then," he paused, giving her time to absorb the impact of his words, "you will regret this."

Nicole grabbed her purse and rushed out the door without looking back. She had twenty minutes. She climbed behind the wheel of the SUV and started the engine. She had to get out of here.

Ian Michaels never made idle threats.

Chapter Nine

Removing the first rail from the headboard proved the most awkward. Once that was accomplished, the rest was easy. Ian pushed the mattress and box spring away from the headboard as far as he could with the other rail still in place. A couple of minutes later the headboard was completely disconnected from the rest of the bed. He didn't take time to analyze the fact that he had once again permitted Nicole to get the upper hand while he was lost in the lust he should never have allowed in the first place. He could kick himself for that later. Right now he had to catch up with Nicole. He clenched his jaw to hold back the string of curses poised on the tip of his tongue. That would do no good, he didn't have time to waste stewing over his mistake.

He had to find Nicole.

Before anyone else did.

Ian snatched the key to the handcuffs off the table and liberated his hand from the brass spindle. He tossed the key onto the table and shook his head at his own gullibility. He was a first-class fool. And now Nicole was in danger and she was too damned hardheaded to see her error. His fury growing with each step, Ian carried the headboard back to the bed and pitched it, rattling handcuff and all, onto the mattress. If George dropped by unexpectedly this evening, he probably wouldn't be too pleased about the mess. Nicole could explain the circumstances to him...

If she didn't get herself killed first.

Ian jerked on his jeans, adjusted the throbbing arousal she'd left him with, then pulled on his sweater. Her scent lingered on his skin, making him ache for her all the more. Gritting his teeth against the desire still humming in his body, he fished his gun from beneath the crippled bed. He tugged on his hiking boots and quickly laced them. Combing the fingers of his right hand through his hair, he glanced at his watch. Fifteen minutes. A hint of a smile twitched his lips. Five minutes earlier than he had anticipated. Ian pulled on his jacket on his way out the door. It was nearing dusk now. The sky was clear and the moon was full, that was good. If he hurried and maintained a steady pace, he would reach town in an hour, an hour and fifteen minutes tops. He needed a telephone. His cell phone was in Nicole's bag. Another mistake. He never suffered those kinds of lapses in judgment.

Only with Nicole.

When he reached town, it would take only one call to Alex and Nicole wouldn't get far in the SUV. The state police would stop her before she got across the line. But, knowing Nicole, Ian thought ruefully as he jogged down the driveway and out onto the paved road, she would dump the SUV somewhere in town and rent—or *borrow*—another vehicle to make her escape clean.

The thought that she might not make it into town tightened the knot of dread growing in his gut. If they were being watched as Ian suspected, the predator would already be tailing his prey, moving in for the kill.

Unfortunately, that was exactly what Nicole wanted.

She intended to force the issue—force a confrontation. And to keep him out of it. Ian swore as he scanned the darkness falling swiftly around him, then the low-hung moon.

He hoped he wasn't too late already.

NICOLE DROVE as fast as she dared down the curvy mountain road. A plan had already formed in her mind. She would ditch the SUV near the sporting goods store and check into a room at the lodge where George was staying. Ian would think she had hitched a ride out of town. To increase the odds in her favor, maybe Nicole would give George a call and tell him that she had found a ride back to Charlottesville and that she intended to fly back to D.C. Ian would no doubt contact George the moment he made it into town. That little ploy would throw Ian off track and keep him busy for a few hours at least. In the meantime, Nicole would hang out in the local diner or the pub and see if she could attract herself a guy with a *dynamite* personality.

The vehicle suddenly jerked as if the engine might die. Nicole frowned and quickly checked the gauges. All registered normal—except the gas gauge.

Empty.

Nicole swore under her breath.

Another jerk, sputter, and the engine died completely. The steeply inclining road was all that kept the vehicle moving then. Nicole wrestled with the steering wheel until she had navigated the next curve and could pull the SUV off the road onto a stretch of narrow shoulder that looked the least treacherous.

"Damn," she muttered shakily. She needed to get a grip here. She forced the image of Ian and his final words out of her mind. Nicole tried the ignition again, just in case the gauge was wrong. It wouldn't start. She banged her fist against the steering wheel and surveyed the dense woods on either side of her. Several more miles of deserted road cut through the terrain before her, curving like a snake between the thick woods and flowing ever downward. This was a hell of a mess, she mused with a disgusted huff of resignation. Her fail-safe plan hadn't been so safe after all. Ian would laugh his head off when he found her stranded halfway down the mountain. Well, he might laugh after he had finished with her. Revenge would be his first order of business. Why hadn't she noticed the gauges when she started the damned vehicle in the first place? When had they got fuel last? Not since that first day, she remembered. Ian had filled the tank the day they arrived in Town Creek. But they hadn't gone anywhere, except into town that once. Surely they hadn't used an entire tank....

The tiny hairs on the back of Nicole's neck suddenly stood on end. They definitely had not used that much gas. No way. She surveyed her seemingly deserted surroundings once more.

He was here.

If not in the immediate vicinity, nearby. Anticipation mushroomed inside her, making her heart beat faster. She had to get out of the open. Nicole slammed the side of her fist hard against the dome light to break the bulb, then opened the car door. She emerged from the vehicle slowly, her gaze scanning constantly. She closed the door behind her with one hip. The burn of adrenaline heightened her senses, made her more alert. It was almost completely dark now, except for the brilliant moon that hung just over the treetops.

The way Nicole saw it, she had two options. She could head back toward the cabin and risk leading the bad guy right to Ian, not to mention she would likely meet Ian on his way down. Nicole shook her head at that thought. Ian was supremely annoyed. She definitely didn't want to see him again until he'd had some time to cool off—maybe not even in this century. On the other hand, she could head into town.

Town, she decided when the vivid mental picture of Ian's furious gaze flashed through her mind. Besides, she wanted the man in the navy blue jacket whose movements tripped some sort of vague memory for her. She wanted him badly. She wanted him to pay for what he had done.

Nicole adjusted the weapon at the small of her back and turned herself in the direction of town. What was five or six miles? she mused. For cover, Nicole decided to walk along the edge of the woods. No point in making herself an easy target. If Ian's theory was true, she would be safe until she gave up Solomon's location, but why take the risk?

She jumped across the narrow, sloping ditch and started for the woods, but a sound behind Nicole froze her in her tracks. She whirled around, instinctively going for her weapon, drawing it, and assuming a fire-ready stance. Another burst of adrenaline shot through her. Nicole strained to make out the dark figure standing near the passenger side of the SUV. In some recess of her brain she reminded herself she hadn't gained the woods just yet, leaving her almost as open a target as the guy standing on the side of the road.

Almost...

...but not quite. The outline of the trees still shadowed her presence.

"Take one more step and you're a dead man," Nicole warned in a loud, firm voice.

"You can't kill a man who's already dead, Agent Reed."

An eerie stillness fell over Nicole. *That voice.* Her heart froze in her chest, but somehow continued to beat, pushing pure ice through her veins. *It couldn't be.* Her mouth opened, worked, but the words she needed would not form on her tongue.

Daniels.

"A little slow on the uptake on this one, huh, Reed?" He moved closer, out of the concealing blackness of the SUV.

"Forensics was conclusive," she heard herself say in a tone so emotionless, so dead calm she barely recognized it as her own.

He laughed, a dry, humorless sound that grated along her nerve endings. "What's one more missing John Doe body? It won't be the first time we've borrowed something no one will ever miss, right, Agent Reed?"

The memory of the conversation she'd had with Ian on this very subject back in her D.C. apartment echoed through her stunned mind. Of course, forensics would be muddled in a case like Daniels's, there was hardly anything left to identify. Hadn't Daniels done the very same thing in Solomon's case? Landon had given the order, Nicole and Daniels had simply carried it out…to the letter.

"Sorry about your apartment," he offered contritely as he took another step down the steep bank. "But you didn't leave me much choice. I had to turn up the heat to prod you into action. But then you came here and holed up with lover boy. I need Solomon, Nicole."

His words snapped Nicole from her disturbing reverie. "What do you want with Solomon?" she demanded, easing back a step. She maintained a steady bead on Daniels.

She had to keep reminding herself that this was real. Daniels was alive and the man was trying to get to Solomon—through her.

Another of those cynical laughs shattered the otherwise silence. "Let's just say he has something I want. That's all you need to know."

Ire flowed through Nicole at the implication of his statement. "I can't believe you would stoop to working for the cartel, Daniels. Which one of the scumbags hired you?" she ground out. "Did they pay you extra for taking Landon out, or did you do that one just for the fun of blowing someone up?"

Another couple of feet of tall grass disappeared between them. "Who said anything about the cartel?" Daniels smiled, a sinister gesture that made Nicole shudder inside. "Oh, I see." He ran a hand over his balding head, then down to massage his chin as he studied her with those beady black eyes. "Don't worry, Nicole, you'll be pleased to know that this has nothing at all to do with the cartel."

That habitual movement—stroking his chin. That was part of the mannerism that had caught Nicole's attention in town the day before. Though he'd had his back turned, some small part of her had recognized his body language.

A new kind of calm settled over Nicole as all the pieces fell into place. Daniels knew everything—except the final location of Solomon. He had access to her every move, to Landon. He was one of the best explosives experts in the country. He knew all the tricks of the trade. Cloak-and-dagger games were his favorite kind, she remembered as he moved closer still.

"Stop right there, Daniels," she commanded, warning bells going off inside her head. He was too close. She needed to think. There was no way she was letting Daniels get away with this. No way. But could she shoot a fellow agent, rogue or not, without him drawing his weapon? She tightened her grip on the Beretta and leveled her gaze firmly on his. "I'm taking you in," she told him bluntly. The blood was pounding in her ears, urging the adrenaline through her veins.

Daniels reached behind him and drew his own weapon. The oxygen evaporated in Nicole's lungs. Her finger snugged against the trigger of her weapon. The desire to fire now was a palpable force pounding away at her consciousness. Nicole gritted her teeth against it, resisted the urge. If she killed Daniels now and Ian was right about there being someone else working with him, Nicole might never be completely safe again. Solomon sure as hell wouldn't be. And justice would never be served.

"All I want is Solomon, nothing else," Daniels assured her, holding his palms up in a magnanimous manner. His weapon hung loosely from the fingertips of his right hand in a non-threatening manner, as if he had no intention at all of using it.

Nicole licked her lips and retreated a few more inches. "What does Solomon have that you want?" Daniels wanted something big. Big enough to make him throw away his career at the bureau only five years from his pension, not to mention his complete identity since he was considered dead. She vaguely remembered someone commenting after his supposed death that he'd never been married, had no children. There had been no one left to ask questions, or even to grieve. He had nothing to lose, Nicole realized. Alarm slid down her spine. And everything to gain. Solomon had been the cartel's accountant, which meant he handled their money. He could have even stashed some away for his own future use. He had to know that WITSEC wouldn't support him forever. A little here, a little there, and pretty soon he would have accumulated himself a really nice nest egg. Unless or until he got caught, then he would end up dead.

Or under WITSEC's umbrella in the witness protection program.

Daniels smiled as if he knew Nicole had just realized his motivation. "Enough of the small talk," he announced impatiently. "Let's go, Nicole. My car is only a hundred or so yards back up the road."

Nicole laughed, a choked sound. "I'm not going anywhere with you, you bastard." She moved back another half step.

Daniels shrugged, his weapon still dangling from his fingertips. "Fine. I guess I'll just have to go back and get what I want out of lover boy."

Nicole tensed. Had Daniels gone into the cabin immediately after she had left to find Ian still helpless and unarmed? Before Nicole could shake off the horrifying possibility, Daniels charged at her. He knocked the Beretta from her hand, then slammed into Nicole with the full force of his heavy body. They rolled, Nicole kicked him hard in the shin while struggling to keep the barrel of his weapon away from her. His hot curses shattered the dark silence around them, his strong fingers went around her neck. Panic shot through Nicole but her instinct for survival was greater, she kneed Daniels hard in the groin, then pushed him off her. She scrambled, half crawling, half running in the direction of where her weapon had hit the ground. Daniels was still howling, trying to stagger to his feet. Nicole grabbed her weapon from the grass, rolled to her back and fired. If she killed the son of a bitch, so be it. Daniels hit the dirt low, crawling for cover of his own.

"Come back here, you bitch!" he screamed.

Nicole scrambled to her feet and lunged into the concealing woods before Daniels could get a good bead on her. A shot fired over her head. Damn. She moved faster, more deeply into the woods. She rushed up the steady grade of the mountain, tripping over exposed roots and fallen branches. Underbrush grabbed at her clothing and scratched at her face like gnarled, bony fingers. The steep incline fought her, but Nicole pressed on. She had to get as much distance as possible between the two of them. She forced the images of Landon's dead body, his grieving widow, from her mind. Daniels had done that. Nicole encouraged the anger, allowed it to diminish the lesser emotions clawing at her consciousness. She had to run fast. If Daniels caught her, she would be dead as soon as he extracted Solomon's location from her. Though she was prepared to die before giving up the information, there were ways to break even the toughest and most highly trained agent.

The covering of decay on the forest floor sank here and there beneath her scrambling feet, yanking her back precious inches instead of giving her purchase to propel herself forward. Fear and frustration swelled in her throat, choking her, but Nicole ignored it. Faster and faster she climbed, stumbling forward occasionally on the rugged, steep terrain. Nicole moved faster, the instinct for survival kicking into high gear. She was much younger than Daniels, more physically fit. Daniels called out to her twice before going silent. Her breath raging in and out of her lungs, Nicole dived behind a large boulder and flattened herself against its surface. She listened above the sound of her ragged breathing.

Daniels was good, she had to give him that, but she was better. When her respiration had slowed and she felt certain he was nowhere nearby, she slowly, quietly picked her way deeper into the woods. She couldn't let him catch her. She needed time to think what her next move should be.

If Daniels caught her now she would end up just as dead as Landon. She had to stay alive to protect Solomon, and to bring Daniels and whoever might be working with him to justice.

And she had to draw the danger away from Ian. She had hurt Ian too badly already. Nicole could not bear the thought of him enduring any further pain because of her.

She loved him too much.

Nicole stilled. Loved him? Yes, she did. But he would never love her. The sad part was, she couldn't really blame him.

IAN SKIDDED to a halt at the sound of gunfire. One shot, then another a few seconds later. His heart hammered wildly in his chest. *Nicole.* Fear, cold and brutal surged through him. Ian pushed forward, running harder. He had to reach her before it was too late. Judging by the sound of the shots, he was close, very close.

He slowed only long enough to see that the dark, nondescript sedan on the side of the road was abandoned, then he ran even harder. A hundred yards later he rounded a sharp curve in the road and spotted the Range Rover.

Ian slowed to a walk when he approached the deserted SUV. He scanned the surrounding darkness, but noticed no movement, heard no sound. Nothing appeared amiss. He hesitated near the Range Rover to look for anything out of place. The driver's door was ajar, the interior light smashed. Nicole had known she was being followed or suspected danger was close. But why stop here? Some sort of malfunction would be the most likely reason. But the vehicle had been running perfectly yesterday. Someone could have tampered with it during the night, he supposed. Ian swallowed back the fear clawing at his throat. He surveyed the woods that seemed to go on forever around him. She had to be here somewhere, but he didn't dare call out to her. If his presence had not been detected as of yet, that was all the better.

The distant sound of a voice, male and gruff, drew Ian's gaze to the woods. The disembodied voice called out Nicole's name a second time. Ian moved slowly in that direction. Nicole was out there, and hot on her heels was the man who had been sent to find Solomon. Somehow Ian had to get between them. Head off the danger. He focused on slowing his breathing and calming his heart rate while blocking all else from his mind. He had to concentrate, focus on his goal. Sound was his enemy now. The ground was covered with fallen and decaying leaves, twigs and branches. The brush was thick, making the going difficult. Slowly, silently, Ian stole his way through nature's maze. He paused to listen frequently, assessing even the vaguest of noises, watching for movement in the shadows.

Nicole couldn't be far, nor was her pursuer. That thought propelled Ian forward, pushing him faster, risking the possibility of making some attention-drawing sound. If he couldn't get between the two of them, his only option would be to draw the man's attention.

Anything to protect Nicole.

Chapter Ten

The minutes ticked by, each second punctuated by the beating of Ian's heart. The fear for Nicole's safety and the run from the cabin had caused Ian's fury with Nicole to abate. Later, when she was safely in his care once more, he would make good on his warning. For now, his every sensory perception was sharply focused on his surroundings. Each nocturnal sound was carefully analyzed and utilized either to avoid an area or to head in that direction. Ian moved steadily, discovering the occasional broken branch or disturbed cluster of leaves to indicate someone's passage shortly before him.

An hour crept by before Ian felt confident that Nicole had indeed outmaneuvered her pursuer. He smiled in spite of his irritation with her when he considered just how damned good Nicole was...in too many ways to list at the moment. And when he caught up with her, he was going to teach her a lesson she wouldn't forget. Ian blended into a stand of trees and paused to allow the sounds, however remote, to saturate his senses. With Nicole apparently safe, he intended to concentrate on overtaking her shadow. And when Ian got his hands on the bastard, he would regret every moment of anguish he had caused Nicole. Ian knew ways to inflict pain, physical as well as mental, that made even him cringe. He intended to use every single technique in his extensive repertoire.

A twig snapped, jerking Ian to full attention. Twenty-five or thirty yards to his right, he estimated. Slowly, making sure to keep himself camouflaged by the trees, Ian moved in that direction. He was close now. Very close. Anticipation flowed swiftly through him. Leaves rustled, slightly farther away. Nicole's shadow was moving back down the mountain. Had he given up so soon?

Ian frowned. Instinct warned that this was just another ploy of some sort. The man had been entirely too relentless, had taken too many extreme measures, to simply call it a night when he couldn't track Nicole down as quickly as he had hoped. No, Ian determined, the bastard was doubling back. Another smile tugged at Ian's mouth when realization dawned. The man knew Ian was here, and he had decided that he would take Ian if he couldn't have Nicole. Well, Ian mused, he would just see how good this guy was at cat and mouse.

Soundlessly, Ian moved in the direction of his pursuer. He waited and listened. The other guy moved more quickly now. Time to throw him off course. Ian picked up a piece of decaying wood about the size of a shoe and pitched it to his left as far as he could. It rustled a few leaves then plunked to the ground. Silence ruled for the next ten seconds. Then the brushing of a branch against nylon fabric, the crinkle of leaves beneath the weight of a footfall. He had taken the bait. Ian moved with great care and as much stealth as possible in that same direction. His pulse jerked into high speed. He could almost smell the confrontation.

Snap. Ian froze. A small twig hidden beneath the leaves had broken under his right foot. Another snap directly in front of him…only a few feet away. Ian raised his weapon into position. A glint of something shiny in the moonlight caught his eye a split second before he heard the distinct click of the safety being disengaged on a weapon. Nicole's Beretta was solid black, no chrome. His breath stilled in his chest and he remained absolutely still. Waiting for the next move.

Ian whipped to the right ten degrees and prepared to fire. The glittering chrome barrel of a nine-millimeter leveled a bead right between his eyes. The man stood no more than ten feet away. He was shorter and stockier than Ian. A swiftly receding hairline and dark eyes stared back at Ian from a pale complexion that looked even paler against the dark jacket he wore. He didn't look the least bit happy. And that fact gave Ian a great deal of pleasure. While Ian watched, the man moved two steps closer, into a small moonlit clearing. Ian moved into the clearing as well, his gaze never leaving the other man's.

"Well, well," the man said, irony in his tone, "looks like the night might not be a total loss after all."

Ian lifted a skeptical brow. "I don't know," he mused. "From where I'm standing, it looks as though you've lost out all the way around."

A sly grin slid across the man's pudgy features. "Oh, I think Nicole will be more than happy to do business with me now. She seems to have a soft spot when it comes to you. I'm sure she'll want you back in working order."

Ian tightened his grip on his weapon. "I'm relatively certain she doesn't have any tender feelings at all when it comes to you," he said offhandedly. "So you don't mind if we cut to the chase and I simply shoot you now, do you?"

Anger flashed in the man's wide gaze. The low-slung full moon provided ample light for Ian to watch the changing expressions on his indignant face. The man might be annoyed, but he understood the situation perfectly. Without Nicole, he would never find Solomon. Right now, Ian was the only bargaining chip he had. It was not likely that he would do anything foolish, such as shoot Ian where he stood.

"What's to keep me from killing you first?" he demanded heatedly. "You haven't got anything I need."

Ian cocked his head and eyed him speculatively. "Are you certain of that? Nicole and I have discussed a great many things in the past few days, including the Solomon case."

The man snickered. "Don't try to fool me, Marshal— or should I say ex-Marshal? Nicole wouldn't give you Solomon's location. She's only using you, Michaels, just like she did three years ago."

Ian's anger flared. He didn't need to be reminded of what Nicole had done. He knew all too well. He gritted his teeth against the almost overwhelming urge to kill the bastard where he stood. But he couldn't do that…not yet. "Perhaps," Ian allowed tightly. "But it was me she came to, and I haven't let her down yet."

Another disgusting chuckle. "But she gave you the slip, didn't she? Never let it be said that Nicole Reed is anything less than one fine piece of work. When I get the information I want from her, maybe I'll give her a go myself."

Ian suppressed the reaction that burned in his chest. He blinked to clear the desire to destroy from his eyes. The man was baiting him. But Ian would pick the time to retaliate and it wasn't now. "Your agenda is none of my concern," Ian said calmly. "I have my own plan."

Some of the cockiness drained from the man then. "What plan?" he snapped.

"I didn't get your name," Ian said, ignoring his question.

The man grinned widely. "Daniels," he offered as if the knowledge was a trophy. "Agent Daniels, formerly of the Federal Bureau of Investigations."

Daniels. So Ian had been right. It *was* an inside job. And Daniels had faked his own death to cover himself. "Bravo, Agent Daniels," Ian allowed without enthusiasm. "You're smarter than Nicole thought."

Daniels's grin died an instant death. "Too bad I can't say the same for you. You didn't have a clue that Nicole was working you like a puppet on a string."

Ian smiled. "Not a one," he agreed. "But who's working whom this time?" he suggested.

Daniels nodded as realization dawned. "Makes no difference to me what you two are up to, I just want Solomon."

"Take a number," Ian returned. "You're not the only one who wants Solomon."

Daniels shook his head slowly from side to side. "You don't know squat about Solomon, Mr. Fancy-pants-PI."

"You think I don't know about the money?" Ian was fishing now, though he was certain it was about money. The only thing he didn't know for sure was whose money and how Solomon had managed to get his hands on it.

A pallor slid over Daniels's features. "You can't know about that. Nobody knew about the money Solomon stole from the cartel but Landon. Not even Nicole knew about that," he argued hotly. "I saved Solomon's sorry ass, gave him a new start, the least he can do is pay up."

"Nicole knows more than you suspect, Daniels," Ian assured him. "Why do you think she replanted Solomon in the first place? She wanted him all to herself. In her mind, she was just as instrumental in saving his life as you.''

Daniels's face darkened, a sharp contrast to the previous paleness. He was irate now. ''That bitch had better keep her hands off my money. I didn't kill Landon and give up everything for nothing. We have plans for that money and nobody is going to take it away from us.''

Ian gave himself a mental pat on the back for scoring right on the mark. Daniels did have a partner. Now it would only be a matter of finding out who. ''I wouldn't be so sure about that, Nicole has a few plans of her own,'' Ian said evenly.

''Screw Nicole!'' Daniels roared. ''She gets nothing but a bullet between the eyes. If you're stupid enough to go along with her, you'll get the same thing.''

''Do I shoot first, or do you?'' Ian asked casually. He steadied his gaze down the length of his weapon's barrel. ''Nicole will get it all if we kill each other right now.''

Daniels glared at Ian from behind his own weapon for five long, tense seconds. ''We could strike a mutually satisfying deal,'' he proposed hesitantly.

''I'm listening,'' Ian replied as if he didn't care one way or the other.

''You give me Solomon's location, and I'll give you a third of the money.''

''Half,'' Ian countered.

His jaw clenched, Daniels shook with fury. ''I told you I'm not in this alone,'' he growled. ''Including you, there's three of us, we cut it three ways.''

Ian shrugged. ''I'll have to think about that.''

''You have ten seconds, then I shoot,'' Daniels warned.

Ian smiled. ''Why wait ten seconds?'' He angled his head slightly as if taking aim.

"Wait!" Daniels bellowed. "All right, all right! Fifty-fifty then."

"Think about it," Ian interjected. "Without Solomon you get nothing. I can produce Solomon."

"What about Nicole?" Daniels ground out.

"What about her?"

"She knows too much," Daniels clarified. "She'll never go along with this, she's a straight shooter."

"I'll take care of Nicole," Ian said coolly.

Daniels smiled again. "I guess you deserve that. After what she did to you, I don't blame you. I just want the pleasure of watching." His face twisted with the implication. "If it wasn't for her, I'd already have that money. She's been nothing but trouble."

"I'll contact you," Ian told him in a dismissing tone. "Call my office and leave a number."

"Don't try to double-cross me, Michaels," Daniels warned. "I'm not a patient man. You mess with me and I'll kill you." He smirked as if he had just remembered some significant point. "Remember, I'm dead. I've got nothing to lose."

"I'm sure your partner would appreciate your staying alive until he has his cut of the money," Ian reminded.

Daniels backed up a step, his weapon still carefully aimed on Ian's forehead. "My partner isn't worried," he said cryptically. "Can you say the same about yours?"

Ian silently watched as Daniels cautiously backed into the enveloping darkness of the dense forest. The man was one sick bastard. Ian had every intention of seeing that he got his, and his partner as well. Ian would follow Daniels, just to make sure he left as he had said he would. Only a fool would trust a man like Daniels to stick to his word. Once he had ensured that Daniels was out of here, then the real task would loom before him.

Ian had to convince Nicole to go along with this plan. She wouldn't like it. Nicole wanted Solomon, the scumbag, protected at all costs. But somehow Ian would convince her to ignore her instincts and trust him on this one.

But first he had to find her.

And when he did, this time he would have his revenge. Remembered desire stabbed at his groin, arousing him instantly to the point of pain. Ian backed into the shrouding darkness of the nearby trees, then slowly lowered his weapon and tucked it into his waistband at the small of his back.

Tonight Nicole would learn that for every action there was an equal reaction. For three years the need to settle this score had seethed inside him.

After tonight they would be even.

NICOLE RELEASED a long, slow breath. She closed her eyes and thanked God she had finally given Daniels the slip. It had been more than fifteen minutes since she had heard any sound behind her. He was obviously lost, or maybe he had given up. She pressed her forehead against the tree trunk next to her and forced away the too-vivid images of Landon and his office...of her rental car and her apartment building. She was tired and cold. For one long moment she wished she *had* killed Daniels, but her shot had been blind, an effort to divert attention from her mad dash into the woods. It had worked, just barely.

Ian.

She had no way of knowing if Ian was safe. Her stomach twisted into a thousand screaming knots of agony when she considered that if he were okay he would have been here by now. She had to make her way back down to the road, and then to the cabin. She had to know. He might need her help. Pain sliced clear through to her heart when she considered that he might be hurt or worse.

And it would be her fault.

She had left him totally defenseless. Stupid. Stupid. And for what? Sure, she knew who the bad guy was now—or at least who one of them was. But what price had she paid? Why hadn't she considered that she was putting Ian in danger with her stupid ploy? Why didn't she think? She had known that they were being watched. She should have been more careful.

Just like three years ago…she didn't think.

And look at the price she'd had to pay.

Ian would never forgive her.

The cold hard muzzle of a weapon suddenly nudged the back of her skull. Alarm surged through Nicole's body, she stiffened. Fear tightened around her neck like a noose. A hand closed around the grip of the weapon beneath her jacket, knuckles brushed her lower back as he withdrew the piece. Nicole shivered and cursed herself for being distracted. She should have heard his approach. She knew better than to let her guard down like this. There was no excuse. She blinked back the tears of frustration gathering in the corners of her eyes. She would not cry. Nicole set her jaw hard. Let the scumbag kill her. She would never give up Solomon's location. Whatever Solomon had that Daniels wanted, as far as Nicole was concerned, he would never get his hands on it. She heard her weapon hit the ground somewhere behind her and to her left.

The cold steel pressed harder into the base of her skull, igniting her fury. Reluctantly she raised her hands in surrender. Did he want her submissive?

"You can rot in hell, Daniels," she spat. "I'll never give up Solomon's location."

His continued silence rattled Nicole more than if he had ranted at her. He urged her forward against the tree. The bark felt rough against her face. The tip of the muzzle bored into her skull. Her heart slammed mercilessly, urging full-fledged panic. Her mind raced, grasping at fragments, but unable to hold on to anything long enough to form a coherent thought. She had to do something…had to run. Where was Ian? Her chest rose and fell with the breath storming in and out of her lungs. What would Daniels do with her now? Was he going to tie her up? Force her to his car?

"I'm not going to make this easy," she warned. Nicole could hear the fear in her voice. Dammit. She was trained better than this. Fight, she commanded. Her body froze, refused to respond. She was dead. He was going to kill her. She would never see Ian again. Nicole swallowed against the cold hard lump in her throat. A single tear slid down her cheek. And for what? A piece of garbage like Solomon. Her job…

Strong fingers fisted in the collar of her denim jacket and yanked it down and off her shoulders. Nicole jerked her hands free, frightened of being restrained in any manner. She shuddered inwardly. He probably intended to tie her hands with the jacket. She gritted her teeth when another tear fell. She hated to cry. Especially at the hands of a creep like Daniels. He reached around her, grabbed her shirtfront and ripped it open and down her shoulders. Buttons pinged through the air. Hysteria blurred Nicole's vision, made her head spin. *No!* She struggled, but he only pushed the weapon more firmly against her, a lethal reminder of what she had to lose.

"Don't do this," she choked out, the tears clogging her throat.

He moved closer, not quite touching her. Nicole licked

her lips and tried to control the tremors wracking her body. Just let him try what he had in mind, she resolved. It would be the biggest mistake of his screwed-up life. All it would take was one moment of distraction and she would make a move he would not soon forget.

She could feel his breath on her skin. His face was so close to her hair. The gun still firmly against her. She closed her eyes tightly and tried to draw away from him, but the tree stopped her, its bark rough against her bare skin.

"I swear," she managed, absolute hatred in her tone, "I'll kill you if you do this." Fear pumped through her veins so fast her heart felt ready to burst.

"Payback's a bitch, don't you think, Nicole?" he murmured against her ear in a softly accented voice that hummed with simmering anger.

Ian. Relief shuddered through Nicole, making her legs go boneless beneath her. The pressure from the cold steel muzzle eased instantly. Thank God. It was Ian. He had come to rescue her. He was safe.

And he was madder than hell.

Nicole tensed. "It was Daniels," she offered in hopes of disarming his temper. "It was him all along."

"I know, but I don't want to talk right now," he said furiously, his words clipped, rich with that European blend of accents.

Nicole swiped the moisture from her cheek with one shaky hand. Her skin was slightly chafed from the encounter with the tree bark. She drew in a steadying breath. He was really angry. And she deserved it.

"I thought it was the right thing to do," she murmured contritely. He would never believe her. Why should he? She had never done anything on the up and up where he was concerned.

"Turn around," he ordered tightly.

Nicole moistened her lips and slowly turned to face him. Savage determination glittered in those silvery depths. Nicole felt her heart start pumping wildly again. But this time it was different. The fear, the excitement was different...

"Remove your shoes."

His fierce gaze never deviated from hers. Nicole lifted one knee to her chest and unlaced her hiking boot, tugged it off, then repeated the process on the other foot. She rolled each sock off and tossed it onto the discarded boots. She stood then, waiting for his next instruction. The sliver of moonlight that cut through the canopy of branches cast a surreal glow over his handsome face, leaving devastating angles and shadows. She shivered visibly, then caught herself. She would not give him the satisfaction of knowing how deeply he affected her.

Not yet.

"Now the jeans," he instructed with just the right touch of danger and sensuality.

Nicole's breasts tingled beneath the satin encasing them. She could feel her nipples budding, yearning for his touch. Moisture pooled between her thighs. Need shuddered through her so fiercely that she thought she might not be able to stand long enough to take her jeans off. She released the button, then slowly eased the zipper down. Ian watched her every move, his gaze carefully controlled, giving nothing away. Nicole pushed the denim over her hips slowly, very slowly. Down her thighs, off one foot and then the other. The jeans joined the socks and shoes. She straightened, wearing nothing but those red panties and the matching red satin bra.

Ian surveyed her body thoroughly. Nicole's skin heated

wherever his gaze touched her. Warmth welled inside her when she saw that little muscle tic in his tense jaw.

Nicole waited until his gaze connected with hers again, then she licked her lips and asked, "What do you want me to do next?" Her voice was deeper than usual, sultry, sexy, she hardly recognized it as her own.

Ian stepped closer then. He shrugged off one shoulder of his jacket, placed his gun in the other hand and shouldered the rest of the way out of the jacket. He pitched it to the ground and turned his attention back to her. Desire zipped through Nicole as she anticipated his naked body. But her hopes were not to be realized.

One more step disappeared between them, her pulse reacted. "Put your hands above your head," he said quietly as if he had done nothing more than relate the time of day.

Nicole obediently placed her hands above her head. Her heart was racing now, her body literally throbbing with anticipation. Ian placed his weapon on the ground beside the discarded clothes. He picked up her shirt—his shirt actually. The one she had been wearing when she seduced him. The memory sent another barb of desire stinging through her. Ian stepped directly in front of her then, his body mere centimeters from hers. He reached up and swung the shirt around the tree and then tied it securely, trapping her hands between the soft material and the tree trunk. Nicole's breath caught in her throat when he looked down at her, his lips only an inch or two from hers. He stared at her mouth for what seemed like forever, then backed away. Nicole almost groaned with disappointment. She wanted to taste him, to feel his lips on hers. To feel his body against hers.

"Close your eyes," he commanded, the words nothing more than a whisper.

"Ian, I—" Her breath caught, stealing the rest of her thought. Trepidation tangled with the want twisting inside her. She wanted him in the worst way, but feared the intensity shimmering beneath that controlled exterior.

"Close your eyes," he repeated. His fists clenched at his sides, the only outward display of his own tension.

Nicole closed her eyes, surrendering to his complete domination. She no longer cared what he did to her as long as he made this mounting ache inside her go away.

The tip of one long finger touched her lips. Nicole trembled. He traced her jaw, then the length of her throat and along the strap of her bra until he reached the swell of her breast. He tugged the satin cup down to expose her taut nipple to the cool night air. He circled that peak, rolled it between his thumb and finger. Nicole moaned his name. His hot mouth covered her breast then. She shuddered with the sensations exploding all over her body. He laved her nipple with his tongue, then sucked her hard. She squirmed against her bonds. She wanted to touch him, to hold him against her. He nibbled, licked and kissed his way to her other breast, then gave it the same attention as he had the first. Slowly, methodically, until her whole body writhed beneath his assault, he tortured her.

"Ian," she cried. The rough texture of the bark against her skin heightened her senses, contrasting with the pleasure.

He moved lower, dropping to his knees. His hands worked a magic of their own on her bare skin, touching her in places, behind her knees, the swell of her bottom, making her tingle, making her sweat. His fingers found their way inside the waistband of her panties. Slowly, so very slowly, the wisp of silk slid down her thighs, all the way to her ankles. She lifted first one foot, then the other as he removed them. Nicole imagined the red silk landing on the nearby pile of clothing, but she kept her eyes closed tightly just as he had instructed.

His lips pressed against her mound and a cry wrenched from her throat. Her heart thundered in her chest, she felt certain Ian could hear it. If he didn't finish this soon, she would surely die. But his mouth just kept on moving against her. He spread her legs so far apart that Nicole felt more exposed than she ever had before. His tongue flicked along her feminine channel, once, twice. She shuddered uncontrollably. Deeper, harder, he thrust his hot, wicked tongue into her most intimate place. Nicole tugged harder at her bonds. She had to touch him. She had to see him, but something, some inner force kept her eyes tightly closed. She couldn't look. She could only feel. And every touch of his tongue, every squeeze of her thighs by those skilled fingers was intensified by her inability to see, or to return the touch.

The tightening began so far away that Nicole was sure she would go out of her mind before completion reached her. Ian slipped one long finger inside her, urging her toward that end, his thumb doing something insanely marvelous of its own. Tighter and tighter her muscles clenched around that part of him. He licked her bare skin near her belly button. His free hand squeezed her bottom again and again as that one finger slid in and out of her until that coil of tension quivered, ready to explode.

He stopped then.

Nicole cried out. She opened her eyes, searching frantically for his. He towered over her now, staring into her eyes, his own glowing with fiery desire. She struggled to free herself again, to touch him, to pull him to her. Her body was on fire, throbbing relentlessly for him. She was wet with his touch, and with her own desire.

"Please," she whimpered.

He didn't speak, he just reached up and released her. Her hands went immediately to his body. She pushed the sweater up, reveling in the feel of his muscled chest, but it wasn't enough. She needed him inside her. *Now.*

She wrenched open the button of his jeans. He stayed her frantic hands, choosing to lower the zipper himself over his hardened length. Nicole shoved his jeans and boxers just low enough to free him. He sprang forth, beautifully hard, deliciously male. Her body convulsed with need when she stroked him with her desperate fingers. He felt hot and alive. Ian's arms went around her and lifted her as if she weighed nothing at all. Nicole wrapped her legs around his waist and pressed into him. He groaned savagely as his arousal rubbed her tangle of damp curls. Somehow his mouth found hers and he kissed her brutally, sucking her tongue into his hungry mouth. He cradled her head with one hand and held her firmly against his mouth until he'd had his fill of tasting her, devouring her, taunting her with the flavor of her own heat.

Her body aching, Nicole rocked back and forth against him. His tip nudged her, then glided along her sensitized feminine channel. Nicole screamed her pleasure into his mouth. His kiss was relentless, drawing on her until she felt as if she were falling, becoming one with him. She lifted her bottom, and this time he guided that slick tip into her when she arched against him. One thick, hard inch at a time she took him. He stretched her, filled her completely. His fingers gripped her bottom and ushered her down to take that last inch or two. Climax crashed around her before she made another move. Wave after wave of pleasure, her feminine muscles clutched frantically around his hard shaft. Ian held her against his chest, crushing her tingling breasts against all that smooth muscle.

She knew he had moved, but the haze of lust was heavy, she wasn't sure when he moved. Ian had braced himself against the tree. His thick organ throbbed inside her, propelling her toward release again when she had barely recovered from the first one. He started then, moving her up and down along his length. Slowly, patiently, as if they had all night. His lips brushed hers. She opened her eyes to look into his, but they were closed, his face was intent with the exquisite friction happening between their connected bodies. Nicole threw her head back and took control of the dance then. She bucked against him, bearing down on him to the hilt, then rising slowly, pulling up to the tip. Ian groaned. His fingers clamped hard around her thighs in silent approval. Nicole increased the pace. She wanted to see him lose control. She resisted the urge to close her eyes when the waves of ecstasy pounded her again, harder than the last time, drawing on the lingering pulses of pleasure still rocking her. She moved faster, squeezed him inside her until he roared like a wild beast with his own climax. She slid slowly down him one last time, and she felt his body sigh.

His eyes drifted open and Nicole knew she was lost. Her heart thumped in her chest. Her arms went around his neck and she pressed her forehead to his. "You scared the hell out of me, Michaels, do you know that?" she whispered, trying to pretend she wasn't so devastated by what they had just shared.

"Yes."

She watched his lips as they formed that single word. The sound of his voice made her want to cry with some emotion she couldn't fully define. She drew back and stared into his beautiful face in the glimmering moonlight. How would she ever live without him?

One hand came up and he gently pushed a tendril of

hair from her cheek. The look of tenderness on his face undid her all the more. "Don't ever take a chance like that again," he murmured. His gaze searched her face. "You're lucky he didn't kill you."

Nicole swallowed the emotion that rose in her throat. She had to know the answer to one question. "Why do you care whether I live or die?" Her voice quavered, and she gritted her teeth to hold back a sob.

"It's what you hired me to do, isn't it?"

Chapter Eleven

Ian led the way back down to the road and the useless SUV. Nicole had said that it ran out of gas. She was certain that Daniels had somehow tampered with it. Ian agreed. Whatever the case, he had no intention of trying to get it back in working order. He would simply send for a replacement. Nicole followed silently behind him as he moved around to the other side of the vehicle. She hadn't said a single word since he'd answered her question. His response obviously had not been what she wanted to hear. But Ian refused to give her the satisfaction of knowing how much he cared for her. He blew out a breath of self-disgust and admitted the truth he had hidden from himself for three years—he cared too much. That fact changed nothing however. Nicole had hired him to do a job. He would do that job and then he would walk away. But the memory of touching her, tasting her, making love to her would burn in his brain for the rest of his life. No other woman would ever complete him the way Nicole did.

He retrieved his cell phone from the purse Nicole had abandoned on the passenger seat of the vehicle, then passed the purse to her. She slung the strap over her shoulder and folded her arms over her middle. The denim jacket was buttoned up from collar to hem. Beneath it she wore the ruined, buttonless flannel shirt. She looked like a recalcitrant child, pouting over her punishment. Ian swallowed the regret that rose instantly at the memory of how brutal he had been with her. He hadn't meant for it to be that way. His brows drew together in a frown. He hadn't planned on making love to her at all. He had simply intended to give her hell for what she had done. For the risk she had taken. And to clear the air once and for all. Instead he had only further muddied the waters. The moment his gaze had fallen upon her hovering in that cluster of small trees, a thousand emotions he had no control over whatsoever had flooded him, made him crazy. He wanted to frighten her, wanted to teach her a lesson...but, most of all, he wanted to tempt her until she melted into submission, then he wanted to take her for his own.

He had done that. He had crawled inside her skin, touched her in a way that changed him forever. Ian had no way of knowing if Nicole had been affected the same way, but he suspected she had—at least to some degree. Did it change anything? Ian didn't think so. Nicole was still bent on doing her job—at any cost. A renewed burst of anger swept through him when he considered that she had seduced him, shackled him to the bed, then left him to go do that job.

No. Nicole hadn't changed in three years. She might care about Ian, but her feelings were secondary to her loyalty to the bureau. He doubted she would ever change. Ian clenched his jaw and headed in the direction of the cabin. He couldn't change her mind, but he could protect her until they brought down Daniels and his partner.

And that was his job.

It was almost midnight before they reached the cabin. Neither had spoken. Tomorrow Ian would call the rental company to bring them a replacement vehicle. He unlocked the door, drew his weapon and entered the dimly lit cabin ahead of Nicole. When he was satisfied that all was as it should be, he tucked the gun back into his jeans.

Nicole groaned as she surveyed the partially dismantled bed. She pitched her purse onto the sofa and plowed her fingers through her hair. "George is going to kill me."

"At the rate you're going, he won't have to," Ian said flatly.

Her gaze snapped to his, those blue pools glittering with anger. "Oh, so we're back to that again," she said hotly. "I thought maybe I'd paid my penance for that one." The implication was scathing. "I'd almost forgotten your inability to let go of a grudge, Michaels."

Ian shouldered out of his jacket, then dropped it onto the back of the sofa. "What you did tonight," he began as he moved in her direction, "was very foolish, Nicole." He paused directly in front of her, leveling his unyielding gaze on hers. He was right, she was wrong. It was that simple. "Why can't you just admit that you always act before you think?"

Something, some emotion glimmered briefly in those crystal-blue eyes, but she blinked it away. "I accomplished what I set out to do," she said curtly. "I know what I'm up against now. It's always easier to do your job when you know your enemy."

Ian angled his head slightly and studied her. He winced inwardly when he considered her cheek where the tree bark had chafed it. That was his fault and he hated himself even more for it. "Sometimes your real enemy is yourself," he suggested quietly, pointedly.

"And you would know all about that, wouldn't you, Michaels?" she snapped. Nicole shook her head, her eyes suspiciously bright, and backed away from him, looking small and vulnerable in the big, buttoned-up jacket. ''I need a bath,'' she added as she pivoted and headed in that direction.

Ian squeezed his eyes shut and forced away the need to soothe her hurt feelings. He had to focus. This game had just moved to a new level, and he had to keep his head on straight. Daniels was no fool. Pulling a fast one on him would not be an easy task. It would take both Ian and Nicole's full attention, and combined skill. Money was a powerful motivator. Daniels had nothing to lose and everything to gain. And he wanted Nicole dead. She knew too much. That's what he had said. Daniels wanted to erase any clue that Solomon had survived that car bombing three years ago.

Daniels didn't just want Solomon's money. He wanted Solomon just as dead as he wanted Nicole. Daniels would do whatever it took to achieve that goal. He had even faked his own death to ensure the perfect alibi and to protect himself while he pursued his treasure. Daniels might be desperate to get what he wanted, but he had every intention of protecting himself at all costs. He was the sort of man who didn't really care about anything or anyone, only himself and what he set out to obtain.

But Ian had one thing that Daniels didn't have…the courage to die for what he believed in, for what he cared about. And he cared deeply about Nicole.

NICOLE AWOKE to the whispered tones of Ian's sensual voice. For one long moment she was deep in the woods again, her hands bound above her head, Ian's hands and mouth working her body into a sensual frenzy. Climax screaming down on her, then him stopping, looking at her as if he could eat her alive, but not touching her. Nicole groaned and curled into a ball. The tremendous ache she had felt at needing him, wanting him, and him standing back, just watching her, reverberated even now. Then he had set her free and she had taken control, or lost control, depending upon the way you looked at it.

Daniels. The lowlife. He was the one. Nicole dragged in a long, deep breath. How could she have been fooled by him? How could she have worked with him for years and not suspected that he was off-kilter? Daniels had killed Landon. The image of Landon's grieving widow flashed through Nicole's mind and she gritted her teeth. Daniels would pay. She would see to it. No matter what Ian said, Nicole would take Daniels down in her own way. And when this was over Ian would be out of her life…just as before, only this time it would be forever.

Nicole swallowed. She loved him. But there was no way she could tell him that. He would only consider it due punishment for the sins of her past. He would probably find it rather amusing. Nicole had ruined his career as a marshal, to a degree his life, actually, and in the process she had fallen hopelessly in love with him and was doomed to live alone and lonely for the rest of hers.

"You need to get dressed, we have to leave."

Nicole looked up to find Ian standing at the foot of the bed watching her. His silvery gaze was unreadable, as usual. His hands rested lightly against the brass footboard, his cell phone clasped in one. Who had he called? she wondered. Today he sported his preferred habit, black dress slacks, black shirt. And somewhere around here there would be a black suit jacket. Nicole sat up and shoved her tousled hair from her eyes.

"Where are we going?" she asked, her voice still rough with sleep, or perhaps the remembered events of last night. She kept her gaze on those long fingers, she didn't want him to read the emotions churning inside her even now. She wanted him to take her in his arms and tell her he felt the same way she did. She wanted him to kiss her the way he had kissed her last night. Then she wanted him to make love to her again, and then again after that. Her body warmed and softened in reaction to the mere thought of Ian's touch. The lingering discomfort of last night's hot, frantic sex did nothing to alleviate the need that surged so easily inside her this morning.

"We're going to Atlanta," he announced in that calm, controlled tone of his that irritated her beyond reason.

Nicole frowned. *Atlanta?* Solomon was in Atlanta. What was Ian plotting now? And without her input. She scrambled from the bed Ian had reassembled during her bath last night, and stalked over to where he stood watching her.

"What do you mean, we're going to Atlanta?" she demanded with as much challenge as she could garner, considering she was wearing nothing but a T-shirt and panties. She hugged her middle to shield her breasts. Her nipples were already hard from just looking at him.

His expression remained unchanged, he simply looked at her as if he felt nothing at all. "Alex is making the arrangements as we speak. The rental agency will have another car here within the hour."

Realization dawned with brutal clearness then. "You talked to Daniels last night."

"Yes."

Nicole swore. Things had happened so fast between them last night that she hadn't asked if he had run into Daniels. She had just assumed that Daniels had given up and retreated so that he could regroup. Fury, fierce and hot, rose in Nicole. She should have known better. There was no way Daniels would have gotten out of those woods without crossing Ian's path. *I know,* that's what Ian had said when she blurted Daniels's name. Ian had known even before she told him. Because he had talked to Daniels, reached some sort of compromise that didn't include Nicole.

She lifted her chin and glared at him defiantly. "Why are we going to Atlanta?" Nicole's pulse pounded in her ears. He intended to keep her in the dark. Well, she seethed, it wouldn't work.

Ian turned to face her more fully. Nicole resisted the urge to back up a step. That icy gray gaze connected with hers and Nicole knew that this was the old Ian, the one who had greeted her in Victoria Colby's office. Something that felt very much like regret filtered through her.

"I struck a deal with Daniels," Ian informed her. "I give him Solomon and he gives me half the money Solomon stole from the cartel three years ago."

Nicole shook her head slowly from side to side. "Daniels is too smart to believe that you would really cut him a deal," she countered, her emotions barely in check. She knew Ian too well—trusted him too completely—to believe for one second he was on the up-and-up about any such deal.

"Apparently Daniels believes that revenge is a strong motivation in this instance."

"I see." Nicole arched one brow knowingly. "Payback for what I did to you three years ago," she suggested. Tension radiated up her spine. This conversation was making her seriously uncomfortable. Ian's attitude wasn't helping.

"I can see where that would appear justified."

Nicole's jaws ached from clenching them so tightly. His perfectly controlled tone was driving her mad. "So you simply played along with his sadistic conclusions?"

"Something like that."

Rage boiled up in Nicole. She glared at Ian. "I won't take chances with Solomon's life," she warned, her voice barely maintained at a normal decibel. "And neither will you."

Their gazes were locked in a fierce battle of wills. "You will never be safe unless we get Daniels *and* his partner. I will do whatever it takes, Nicole," he countered darkly. "And so will you."

"Daniels has no idea where Solomon is," she argued evenly, despite the anger twisting in her chest, making her want to shudder. "Any place will do. We don't need to go to Atlanta. We don't need to be that close."

"Think, Nicole," Ian scolded, "Daniels knows you too well. He knows every alias you've ever used. Don't think he wasn't fully aware you were booked on a flight to Atlanta that last night in D.C. when your apartment went up in flames."

Nicole trembled at the memory and at the realization that she was losing this battle. "You can't be sure of that." Her argument was weaker this time. Ian had a point she couldn't really deny. And he knew it.

"No. I can't be certain, but I don't intend to risk tipping my hand either. We need him to lead us to his partner. If we screw up this opportunity, he won't make the same mistake twice. Alex has already instructed Daniels to go to Atlanta and wait at the Plaza Hotel for further instructions."

He was right. As much as she loathed to admit it. "And where do I fit into all this?"

Ian looked away. "I'm to contact him with Solomon's location," he said vaguely.

Nicole thought about that for a minute, and the answer hit her like a truck. "He doesn't know you know. He thinks you intend to seduce the information out of me,'' she said with a kind of choked laugh.

"That would be my guess." He still didn't look at her.

"And you allowed him to believe that," she fumed.

"Yes." He looked at her then, his gaze cool and distant. "I did."

Red swam before her eyes. She wanted to hit him. To demand some sort of retraction of his words. "What makes you think I'll go along with your little plan?" she said instead, bitterness dripping from her tone.

He stared down at her with that carefully constructed mask of control for two heart-stopping beats. "Because Martinez is with Solomon and I have your weapon, Nicole. From this moment, you can consider yourself in protective custody."

NICOLE CONTINUED her silent treatment the rest of the morning. Ian struggled with the need to make things right with her. But this was for the best. As long as this wall of anger remained between them, she would keep her distance. There was no room for error now. They would both need their full attention focused on the game as it played out, and the events to come as they unfolded. There was no room for anything else.

Ian stole a glance at Nicole's unyielding profile as the plane taxied to the airport gate in Atlanta. She didn't like being left out of the loop and Ian could understand that, but there was nothing to be done about it. This game had to be played by the rules Daniels set. Nicole knew that as well as Ian did. He had hoped she would come to see how well his plan would work, but that hadn't happened. Instead, she ignored him, continued to stew in silence.

The flight attendant gave the final instructions for disembarkation. Nicole released her lap restraint, keeping her gaze straight ahead. Ian pushed out of his seat and stepped to one side for Nicole to proceed him. He placed a hand against her arm, stopping her when she would have started down the aisle. Reluctantly, her gaze moved up to meet his.

"We'll have lunch here before we pick up our luggage," he told her. "Then we'll go to the hotel."

She shrugged off his hand. "Whatever." Nicole slung her purse over one shoulder and sauntered down the aisle.

Ian clenched his jaw against the irritation her indifference engendered in him. He followed her, working hard to ignore the way her hips, encased in some sort of dark blue knit that fit like a second skin, swayed so provocatively. The matching fuzzy sweater snuggled against her breasts and her slim rib cage. The effect was startlingly feminine, and undeniably sexy. Ian felt certain she had intended just that. But he wasn't buying in to her seductive ploy. This was one round she would simply have to play alone.

Ian signed for his weapon at the cockpit and tucked it beneath his jacket in the shoulder harness. He didn't like to wear the holster, but when traveling via commercial means and carrying a weapon, he usually did.

The airport was crowded. Ian stayed right behind Nicole, ensuring that she never got out of arm's reach, as they wove their way through the knots of people. He had a decidedly uneasy feeling about her attitude. Nicole Reed could be unpredictable, if not completely unmanageable when properly motivated by a situation.

"Will this place do?" she asked, stopping abruptly in front of a bar and grill. She appeared completely disinterested in his decision one way or another.

Ian surveyed the surrounding area. Gift shop, restaurant, rest rooms. No sign of Daniels. Ian fully expected the man to be waiting and watching at the airport. He would probably follow them when they left. Daniels would not wait for Ian's call. The man had every intention of setting the pace of this game, Ian was sure. If for some reason Daniels wasn't here, it was only because he hadn't managed an early enough flight.

"This place is fine," he replied, watching her reaction closely. He needed Nicole to work with him on this.

Nicole sighed dramatically and headed toward a table in that slow, graceful manner that looked more feline than human. She was purposely baiting him. What the hell did she expect to gain? Nothing she could do or say would change Ian's mind about how to proceed in this case.

She selected a relatively secluded table in the back corner, away from the passersby. A waiter appeared and offered menus as Ian sat down. Nicole thanked the guy with a wide smile, and an appreciative survey of his lean body. The waiter responded with an idiotic-looking grin. Ian tightened his jaw.

"May I get your drinks now?" the young man asked.

Another of those sultry smiles slid across Nicole's lips. "I'd like white wine, please," she said seductively.

Jealousy speared through Ian's chest. He almost flinched.

The waiter swallowed with obvious difficulty, then dragged his reluctant gaze to Ian. "And you, sir?"

Ian directed a lethal look at the waiter. "I'll have the same as my wife," he said quietly.

The color drained from the young man's eager face. His stupid grin drooped. "I'll get those right away, sir." He pivoted sharply and hurried away as if the hounds of hell were on his heels.

"You're such a comedian," Nicole said sarcastically,

then rolled her eyes. "I can just see you with a wife."
She gave her head a little shake and laughed softly.

"You find that hard to imagine?" he asked in a voice
heavy with implication.

That stopped Nicole cold. Her eyes widened slightly,
and her pretty mouth dropped open two full seconds before she spoke. "Let's just say it would take some stretching."

Ian lifted one shoulder in the barest of shrugs. "Not
really."

Nicole gave another of those sultry, utterly feminine
chuckles. "Next you'll be telling me you're even considering children."

Ian just looked at her then. Did she really believe him
that cold and untouchable? So heartless that no woman
would love him, would want to bear his children? That
thought cut to the bone.

"Here you go," the waiter announced as he cautiously
approached the table. He deposited their drinks in front
of them and stepped back slightly as if he feared Ian might
take off his head...or worse. "Are you ready to order
now?" he asked humbly.

Nicole was the first to recover. "Ham and cheese on
wheat," she said vacantly. She picked up her glass and
took a sip, feigning preoccupation with evaluating the
wine.

"The same," Ian answered without taking his gaze off
Nicole.

The waiter took their menus, made some vague comment and scurried away.

"There are a great many things I want, Nicole," Ian
said, something hard that he didn't quite understand in his
tone. "You have no idea."

"You're right," she said tightly. "I could say the same,

you know." She glared at him defiantly. "You have no idea what I want out of life, either."

"To replace your director," Ian said with unexpected malice. He blinked at the harshness of his own voice. The remark hit home. Nicole's surly attitude faltered. Hurt flickered in her eyes.

"You would think that," she muttered without looking at him.

He was out of line. Jealousy had driven him. Ian cursed himself for hurting her. He was supposed to be helping Nicole, not fighting with her over things that would never be.

Ian would never marry.

Never have children.

If he couldn't have Nicole—and he couldn't—he didn't want anyone else.

They ate in silence. The waiter whizzed by a couple of times, offering refills, which Ian declined. Nicole had a second glass of wine. She refused to look at Ian and that bothered him a great deal more than it should. He shouldn't care. He should simply concentrate on the risky business that lay ahead of them.

But he couldn't.

Ian dropped a few bills on the table and stood. "We should go," he announced.

Nicole drained her glass and hurried to her feet before he could do the gentlemanly thing and pull her chair back. He followed her back into the crowded corridor.

"Luggage pickup," he reminded.

Nicole glanced at the signs overhead and started in the direction indicated. They passed a bank of phones which reminded Ian that he should check in with Alex before they left the airport.

"Wait," he called after Nicole.

She turned around and walked back to where he waited. "What?" she demanded impatiently.

"I'm going to check in with Alex to see if Martinez has called before we go any further."

Nicole folded her arms over her chest and gave him her back. "Whatever," she mumbled.

God, he hated that word. He turned his back to the passing travelers, pulled out his cell phone and punched in the number. It wasn't really the word, he amended, it was the way she said it. It made him crazy. He wanted to shake her. Or kiss her…or something.

Ian swore.

As he waited for Alex to pick up her line, Ian shifted to his right to make sure Nicole hadn't wandered too far.

She was gone.

He whipped around, adrenaline charging through his veins, his gaze scanning the crowd. There she was. A sigh of relief hissed past his lips. He frowned. She was talking to a man in uniform. Airport security. What the hell? he wondered briefly.

"Ian, are you there?"

"I'll call you back," he said distractedly and closed the phone, then dropped it into his pocket. Never taking his eyes off Nicole, Ian started walking in her direction.

Nicole's gaze connected with his. Ian frowned. She had a sort of deer-caught-in-the-headlights expression. Ian ignored the glares he got from the people he cut in front of, and the shoulders that banged into him. He moved faster. She was up to something.

The security guard's head came up. He leveled his gaze on Ian. Nicole said something to him, her expression frantic now. The big, burly guard ushered her away. Nicole took one last look at Ian before darting for the escalator. Ian started after her.

"Stop right there, sir!"

Ian would have kept going, but he knew the guard was armed. So he stopped, held up his arms in classic surrender fashion and waited for the man to approach him. Nicole waved mischievously as she disappeared from view. Ian barely contained the mixture of anger, frustration and fear that boiled up inside him.

"Turn around real slow, friend," the guard ordered nervously.

Ian obeyed. He was surprised to find the guard's weapon drawn and aimed directly at his chest. What the hell had Nicole told him?

"The lady said you'd been harassing her," the guard said pointedly, his eyes studying Ian closely. Sweat beaded on his mahogany skin. "Trying to pick her up, she claimed."

Ian smiled as if he had been caught with his hand in the cookie jar. "I'm sorry—" he looked at the name tag pinned on the man's massive chest "—Mr. Winslow, I wasn't aware that there was anything illegal about hitting on a pretty lady."

Winslow didn't smile. "There isn't. But there is a law against carrying a concealed weapon in an airport." He nodded toward Ian's jacket. "The lady said you have a gun."

"May I?" Ian inquired, barely banking his fury.

"I'll do it," Winslow said. He moved closer, then lifted Ian's jacket with his free hand. He removed the weapon in Ian's holster. "I surely do hope you have a license for this, sir."

"Trust me, I do."

Winslow did smile then. "Oh, I think we'd better go on down to the security office and straighten this out, Mr..."

"Michaels," Ian told him. "Ian Michaels. And the lady you just assisted in flight was in my protective custody."

Winslow looked a little startled by that news. "Well, if that's the case, Mr. Michaels, I surely do apologize. But unless you can produce a badge, we still have to go to the office."

Ian waved his arms in defeat. "Fine." He started in the direction Winslow indicated, then hesitated. "You don't mind if I make a call on the way."

Winslow had put his own weapon away, but still held Ian's. He quickly patted Ian's pockets with his free hand, identifying the cell phone. "No problem, sir, be my guest."

Ian pulled out the phone and depressed the speed dial button for Alex. Two rings later she answered. The muscle in Ian's jaw was jumping in time with the pounding in his chest as he followed the guard toward the security office. "Call Martinez," Ian ordered curtly. "Tell him to move Solomon to the alternate location *now*. Nicole is probably on her way there." Ian ended the call and dropped the phone back into his pocket.

Nicole better have a hell of a good reason for her actions.

Chapter Twelve

The taxi driver made the trip across town in record time. For that, Ian tipped him generously. Ian was out of the car before it stopped rocking at the curb. He paused on the walk and surveyed the quiet neighborhood in one sweep. Before long, the yards would fill with children returning home from school, then their parents returning home from work. Solomon lived in a three-bedroom, red-brick, ranch-style house in a middle-class neighborhood that defined the word *average*. A dog barked from behind the fenced backyard at the house next door.

Solomon, with his cover as a retired NASA engineer, would never set foot in this quiet, average home again. When this was over, Nicole would have to replant him.

And that would be the end of this mission.

The end of their time together.

That was definitely for the best.

And all that depended upon whether Nicole, not Daniels, had got here before Ian. Dread pooled in Ian's stomach. He had to find her first. If for no other reason than to wring her lovely neck.

Daniels could have been waiting for them at the airport. He could have followed Nicole here.

The blinds were drawn, Ian noted, directing his atten-

tion back to what he had come here for. Nicole had had
a twenty-minute head start on him, but the cabbie had
regained some of that lost time. Ian moved cautiously up
the walk and to the front entrance. Pristine white, the
painted wooden door stood ajar. He glanced through the
narrow opening and saw nothing but beige wall. No
sound, no particular smells. Nothing.

Ian banished the thought that blood had a very distinct
odor. He wouldn't think about that. Moving to a higher
state of alert, he deadened his senses to all other distraction. She had to be here—or, at least, had to have been
here. Nicole had not been privy to the alternate location
Ian had arranged with Martinez. Nor did she know about
the preliminary measures Ian had insisted that Solomon
take once he was in Martinez's care. Nicole had no place
else but here to look for Solomon. Ian reached beneath
his jacket and withdrew his weapon. He flattened one
palm against the smooth painted surface of the door and
pushed it inward. The hinges groaned loudly, the sound
echoing across the deserted entry hall. Ian stepped onto
the polished oak floor, the leather soles of his shoes silent
as he moved toward the first door to his left. The living
room. An aging collection of value-priced furniture and a
couple of cheap paintings made up the decor of the dimly
lit space. He turned and started in the direction of the next
door, this one on his right. The dining room probably.

Table, four chairs, sideboard along the far wall. A bowl
of wax fruit as a centerpiece. Another painting.

No Nicole.

Anticipation rising steadily, Ian eased to the far end of
the hall. Silence hung around him like a dark cloud, dragging down his hopes, nudging at his emotions. She was
unarmed, defenseless. Anger and fear twisted inside Ian.
Where could she be? She had really crossed the line this

time. And this time, if she managed to come out of this unscathed, Ian intended to make sure she followed orders. Stashing her with Martinez would be the first order he initiated. She wouldn't like it, but that was too damned bad.

To Ian's left was a corridor that led to the bedrooms, he assumed, on the right another doorway. He readied his grip on his weapon and prepared to enter the kitchen.

The front door slammed shut.

Ian whirled toward it, his weapon leveled.

"You're losing your touch, Michaels." Nicole leaned casually against the closed door, pointed her finger at him as if it were a pistol and mouthed the word *pow*. "If I'd had a weapon, you'd be dead now."

A feeling Ian had never before experienced washed over him, something like rage, but stronger. Like relief, but more profound. The desire to lash out, strike something, was a pulsating need mushrooming in his chest.

"Is the house clean?" he asked calmly, despite the nuclear explosion of sensations erupting inside him.

"As a whistle," she said, angling her head a little to the side. "Martinez did a good job. I couldn't find one single piece of evidence that Solomon had ever even been here."

Ian essayed a ghost of a smile as he lowered his weapon, then placed it into the shoulder harness. "We're good at what we do at the Colby Agency," he returned, a tightness in his voice now.

Nicole straightened. The delicate features of her face hardened like stone. She walked slowly toward Ian. "This didn't happen in half an hour, Ian. Where is Solomon?" she demanded, uttering the words as if each were a separate statement from the other. She stopped right in front of Ian, glaring up at him, those blue eyes piercing points of smoky light.

"Martinez and I had anticipated this possibility. Solomon is safe." Ian leveled his gaze on hers. "Which is more than I can say about you, Nicole." He leaned his head a bit to one side and looked long and hard into her furious expression. "You're simply lucky, otherwise *you* would be dead now."

Her chin lifted in a graceful but defiant manner. "I'm not interested in a spitting contest, Michaels. I want to know where my witness is, and I want to know now."

Ian looked past her, at the door she had hidden behind. Only Nicole would think of such an obvious place. "We don't always get what we want, Nicole."

"You're interfering with the protection of a federal witness, that's a felony," she stated in a lethal tone. "Now, where is Solomon?"

Ian felt himself losing control. He clenched his jaw to hold back the irrational words he wanted to hurl at her. He curled his fingers into fists to prevent himself from grabbing her and shaking her. Nothing took precedence over her desire to prove she was the best the feds had to offer. Nothing else, not even her own life, mattered that much to her.

Ian's cell phone sounded, breaking the awkward, deafening silence.

His gaze still locked with hers, Ian pulled the phone from his pocket. "Yes." It was probably Alex confirming Martinez and Solomon's arrival at the alternative location.

"I've been waiting for your call."

Daniels.

Ian blinked, then averted his gaze from Nicole. His emotions immediately switched gears. "I'll call you when I'm ready."

"Thought maybe you'd run into a snag," Daniels suggested sarcastically. "Nicole's not giving you trouble, is she?" he asked knowingly.

"I have your number," Ian said flatly. "I'll contact you." He pressed the End button and pocketed the phone. Like hell Daniels had been waiting for a call. He had been waiting all right, waiting at the airport. Ian knew it as surely as he knew his own name. No doubt Nicole would confirm it.

"That was Daniels, wasn't it?" Nicole demanded, fury radiating from every inch of her.

With a reluctance that sapped his strength, Ian's gaze roved all the way down to her leather boots, then back to those fiery blue eyes. He wanted desperately to shake her, then to hold her. To prove to her that her career didn't have to be everything, that there was more to life than risking everything for scum like Solomon. But he couldn't risk opening himself up to that kind of rejection.

"It was, wasn't it?" she repeated.

"Yes," he admitted.

She shook her head determinedly. "This won't work, Ian. Daniels is too smart. He's playing you, just like he played me." Emotion glistened in her eyes then, ripping at Ian's already tattered defenses.

"And I'm playing him," Ian clarified. "The difference is that I'm not desperate. Daniels is. He wants that money."

Nicole flung her arms upward in frustration. "How can he be certain there is any money? Solomon could have blown it all by now!"

"That's not likely," Ian countered with complete confidence.

"Why not?" Her hands went to those luscious hips,

and he struggled with the impulse to allow his gaze to linger there. "It's been three years," she added.

"He wouldn't take the risk of spending too much too fast. Big spenders draw attention. Solomon would be very, very careful with his finances." Ian's brow quirked. "After all, he was an accountant. He would know all about making his money work for him without anyone ever knowing he had any."

Nicole swore as if an epiphany had just this minute dawned on her. "No wonder he was in such a big hurry to testify against his boss. He was probably close to being caught for embezzling. Solomon knew he was dead either way. Witness protection was his only hope."

"And somehow Daniels found out about the money and decided to blackmail Solomon," Ian added.

"But how could he know unless someone from the cartel leaked the information?"

"So far, Sloan agrees with Alex," Ian told her, recalling his conversation with Alex that morning. "He doesn't believe the cartel is involved." Ian shrugged halfheartedly. "Daniels outright denied any connection to the cartel."

Nicole settled her gaze on Ian's. "Enough stalling. You're not leaving me in the dark like this, Ian. Where is Solomon?" she asked again, her impatience as evident as her anger.

Ian held that infuriated gaze for a couple of beats before he answered. "The only way I'll give you that information is if you agree to stay out of sight with Martinez until this is over." She opened her mouth to rant at him, and Ian stopped her with a withering look. "But first, you will explain to me why you pulled that little stunt at the airport. Then I'll have your word that you will do exactly as I say from this moment on."

"Hell no," she growled in a raw, animal-like tone.

"Well, then," Ian said slowly. "We have a real problem, because I won't budge on the issue."

Nicole hesitated, her fiery resolve wavering beneath his unyielding glower. "You're not going to like it," she admitted cautiously.

"I already don't like it," Ian assured her in a low, lethal tone.

Nicole licked her lips, then shrugged. "Daniels was there. I saw him when you first stopped to make your call."

Ian swore hotly, his gaze boring relentlessly into hers. "You left the airport—unarmed—knowing that Daniels would follow you!" It wasn't really a question, Ian already knew the answer.

Nicole thought about his statement for a few seconds, then nodded. "Yeah, that's exactly what I did."

Ian rubbed at his forehead and the pounding, which abruptly started there. "You do realize how that sounds?" he returned, still not certain he believed her flippancy himself.

"I know Daniels," Nicole argued. "There was no way he was going to buy into the concept that I would give you Solomon's location without a fight. I had to make him believe that I was resisting the idea of giving up Solomon. Besides—" she shrugged nonchalantly "—one of us had to lose him."

Ian moved closer. "No more theatrics, Nicole," he ordered darkly. "I don't want you taking a risk like that again. In fact, I don't want you taking any risks at all."

Nicole squeezed her eyes shut and let go a ragged breath. "This is my responsibility, Ian," she countered. Vulnerability stared back at him when her eyes opened once more.

Ian encircled her arm with one hand and pulled her nearer. "We're in this together, Nicole. We're a team." His voice was taut with emotion now. "But I won't chance your safety."

Nicole turned her face into his throat and sagged against his chest. She sighed wearily and something shifted deep inside Ian. His arms went automatically around her, then tightened.

"I just want this to be over," she murmured.

"Soon," Ian promised. "For now Solomon is safe. And I will do whatever it takes to keep you safe." Her hair smelled like heaven and Ian wanted to hold her closer, make her believe that this would all magically work out. His body responded to hers much more than merely physically, it was as if their souls were somehow connected.

"Daniels and I worked the scene in Landon's office together," she said haltingly, her lips brushing his skin, making him ache for her. "How could I have worked with him, gone over and over the evidence and never suspected for one second that I was working side by side with the killer?" She trembled.

Ian tilted her face up and brushed the hair back from her cheeks. Tears glittered in her blue eyes. "You had no reason to suspect him. You can't blame yourself. This is not your fault, Nicole. You did the best job you could do."

She closed her eyes and sucked in a harsh breath. "I should have paid better attention. Things should never have got this far." She shook her head. "I bought Daniels's setup hook, line and sinker. I believed he was dead. I missed all the signs that are so clear now."

"Hindsight is twenty-twenty, Nicole," Ian pointed out, hoping to assuage her distress. "Things are always clearer when you're looking back."

Those wide, watery blue eyes searched his. "Daniels has gone over the edge. He's crazy. He'll kill you if he suspects for one second that you're setting a trap for him. I can't let you take that chance. This is between Daniels and me."

Ian stroked her soft cheek with his thumb, his fingers curled around her nape. He smiled, trying his best to soothe that fearful gaze. "You took this great risk because you were afraid for my life?"

She chewed her lower lip to prevent the smile that was already shining in her eyes. "Partly," she relented. "And partly because I was madder than hell at you for leaving me in the dark about your plans. But mainly because I knew that it was what Daniels would expect." She smiled, though a bit weakly. And Ian's heart felt oddly full.

"If anyone around here has a right to be angry, it's me," he corrected gently. "It took me fifteen minutes to persuade that security guard that I wasn't some pervert stalking beautiful, unsuspecting young women."

Nicole laughed, a soft, feminine sound that skittered along his nerve endings, making them tingle. "I thought that bit of improvisation was rather ingenious myself," she enthused. Her brows drew into a questioning V then. "You think I'm beautiful?" she asked almost shyly.

He sobered. "Yes."

"You rushed here to protect me?" she murmured, those wide blue eyes studying him too closely.

"You know I did." Ian's mood turned dark again. "You acted foolishly," he scolded softly. "What if Daniels had caught up with you?"

She frowned crossly, as if he should know better than that. "I didn't just wake up in this business yesterday, you know."

"No more, Nicole," he told her, his tone brooking no

argument. "We do this my way or you're out of the game. No more taking off on your own. No more arguments."

She looked far too hesitant for Ian's satisfaction.

"You said you trust me. You told Victoria there was no one else you could trust," he reminded. "Have you changed your mind so soon?"

Nicole sighed impatiently, then shook her head slowly from side to side.

"If you want to get Daniels," he began, "you'll do exactly as I say." He looked directly into her eyes, urging her to pay close attention. "Solomon is safe, that won't change. And I will bring down Daniels and his partner."

"You won't keep anything else from me?" she insisted.

Ian shook his head. "No."

"We're in this together. At no time will you try to leave me behind or in the dark?" she prodded.

It was Ian's turn to hesitate. He wasn't sure he could promise her that. Her safety was foremost in his mind. He couldn't risk her getting hurt in the final showdown. Ian wanted her nowhere around when he and Daniels met face-to-face again.

"Promise me, Ian," she demanded. "If you want me to cooperate with you, then you have to keep me in the loop. I won't do it any other way."

"All right," he finally agreed, against his better judgment. "On one condition."

She straightened. "What would that be?"

"That you do exactly as I say, no exceptions."

She sighed wearily. "Agreed."

NICOLE HUGGED herself more tightly beneath the scratchy blanket. Only two of Solomon's bedrooms had furniture, the one she was in and the one across the hall that Ian occupied. Nicole blew out a breath of frustration. Ian had not returned Daniels's call. Ian wanted to make him wait, to heighten the man's anxiety. Nicole agreed. Once that strategy was decided, Ian had suggested that it would be simpler for them to stay the night here and Nicole hadn't argued. What did it matter if they were in Solomon's house or a hotel? They were alone, and without any luggage. Ian had kindly offered his shirt for her to sleep in. Nicole was thankful. She had no desire to sleep in anything that belonged to Solomon.

When her gaze had connected with Daniels's today at the airport, Nicole had lost it completely. Fear that he would kill Ian had nearly paralyzed her. Without thought of her own safety or anything else, she had made use of the only tactic available to readily lose Ian. Then she had taken Daniels on a hell of a speedy chase. She had tipped the cab driver generously. Daniels didn't stand a chance against a guy who knew the city the way a good cabbie did. Nicole blew out a breath. Admittedly, she had been lucky. But her diversion had served its purpose. By the time Daniels could have made it back to the airport to try and latch on to Ian, Ian was long gone.

She had accomplished her mission of maintaining the integrity of Solomon's location while keeping Ian away from harm.

Ian.

Nicole flopped over onto her side and tried not to allow her thoughts to drift to the night before. It was no use. The scene in the woods kept right on playing through her mind. Ian loving her so intimately. The intensity in his eyes. How would she ever survive the rest of her life without him?

Enough, Reed, she chastised.

But what would happen tomorrow? There were so

many variables that would be out of her control. What if she or Ian lost their lives tomorrow as this game played out? She would have so many regrets. Not telling him how she really felt. Not making love with him one last time before…

Nicole stilled. It was true. She couldn't predict what would happen tomorrow. She clamped down hard on her lower lip to hold back the tears that instantly sprang to her eyes. Her whole life was out of control. She had realized that this afternoon. Ian must have thought she had gone off the deep end when she ditched him at the airport. But when he found her, rather than blow a gasket as she had fully expected, he had scolded her gently and then held her and assured her in that deep, sensual voice until she was thinking straight again. Nothing was right with her anymore. Her ability to do her job had obviously gone to hell. A killer had lurked right under her nose and she hadn't noticed. She had lost everything she owned when her apartment burned. When this was over, Ian would walk out of her life again.

This time forever.

What a mess.

She closed her eyes and banished the thoughts. She couldn't think about any of that right now, especially the part about Ian. It hurt too much. The conversation in the airport restaurant slammed into her heart with twisting force. Ian could see himself with a wife and children. He wanted those things.

Just not with her.

He didn't think of her as wife-and-mother material. She had never even thought of herself that way. But Ian made her want those things too.

Why was she torturing herself this way? Nicole threw off the covers and bounced out of the bed. She paced back and forth in the small room. She had known this day would come from the moment she'd walked into Victoria Colby's office and asked for Ian's help. Their time together would only be temporary. Why was she getting all weepy about it now?

Because she loved him.

Damn fate's twisted sense of irony, she mused.

That day in the Colby office she hadn't realized that significant fact just yet.

But now she knew.

And it didn't change a thing.

Ian would still leave her, just like before.

But what about tonight?

Could she make him feel the way he had made her feel last night? He had ripped the heart right from her chest. Left her mentally weak and physically satisfied. But was his motivation purely revenge? She had, after all, teased him ruthlessly before handcuffing him to the bed. But a part of her had wanted to make it real. Could she do that again? This time with the intent to follow through with what she started?

Her body warmed with anticipation.

Yes, she could.

Nicole walked to the door.

No, she couldn't do it. She pivoted and stalked back to the other side of the room.

The memory of his hands moving so expertly over her body sent an ache straight to her core. His mouth had tugged at her breasts. His fingers had played her like a finely tuned cello. Then he had possessed her so completely that her body shuddered toward release even now just recalling the mind-blowing moments.

She looked at the door once more. Just a few feet. That's all that separated them. They could make long, slow love tonight, then sleep the sleep of satiation in each other's arms.

Let tomorrow bring what it would.

Nicole retraced her steps, wrapped her fingers around the knob and turned. She opened the door and stepped into the dark hall. She could do this. They would have this one last night together. She shivered as chill bumps rushed over her bare skin. She would not live the rest of her life, however long or short it proved to be, regretting not having taken this one last moment with Ian.

Nicole paused at Ian's open door and whispered his name.

"What's wrong?" He sat up in bed.

Nicole could see his dark, tousled hair in the shaft of moonlight slipping in around the closed blinds. She moved closer to his bed…to him.

"I can't sleep," she whispered back.

Ian patted the covers beside him. "Sit down, we can talk until you're sleepy again."

Nicole crawled onto the bed beside him. Her arms went around his neck. "I don't want to talk," she whispered between the little kisses she planted along his throat.

Ian tensed. He encircled her arms with his long fingers. "Don't even think about it, Nicole," he warned.

Nicole realized her mistake then. She had said those same words to him before shackling him to the bed. She smiled against his jaw, his stubble sent currents of desire racing through her. "No," she clarified, then nipped his chin with her teeth. "I mean, I *really* don't want to talk."

Ian sat perfectly still for several moments, then he moved, pulling her down and rolling over so that she was beneath him. "You're sure about this?" he asked hoarsely.

Nicole didn't answer. Instead, she reached between

them and unfastened his slacks. When she cupped him with her hands, he was exquisitely hard already, pulsing actually. Nicole made a low sound of approval in her throat. She stroked his length, glorying in the feel of him, the smooth satiny texture of his male skin. He shuddered.

"Kiss me," he ordered tightly.

Nicole obeyed. She lifted her parted lips to his, thrusting her tongue into his welcoming mouth. She stroked his arousal again, sucked his tongue into her mouth, then lifted her hips against his. Need ripped through her, sending electrical bursts all along her too-hot skin. She was wet and throbbing already.

His hand found its way to her panties and two fingers dipped inside her, stretching, stroking. She gasped into his hungry mouth. He pulled back from the kiss and moved down to her breasts, taking each hard peak into his mouth through the thin material of the shirt. He sucked hard, then nibbled, torturing her endlessly. The shirt buttons opened beneath his efficient touch. He pushed the fabric off her arms, tugged it from under her, then tossed it to the floor. Sensation after sensation flooded her senses in anticipation of his next move. She writhed beneath him when he began again, his mouth loving one breast, his hand the other. Silently, her body speaking for her, she begged him to take her completely. He murmured soothing sounds while he continued his relentless, sensual assault. His weight on her was a delicious feeling of rightness, she tightened her arms around his lean waist and pulled him more firmly to her.

His own control ready to snap, Ian slid her panties down and off. He loomed over her again, then buried himself fully with one long stroke. Nicole cried out his name. He held very still then, their ragged breathing loud in the consuming silence. Slowly at first, his movements began. He drove harder, faster with each rhythmic thrust. She held on to his strong back, trying to make it last, but she couldn't. When he exploded inside her, filling her with his hot release, Nicole's body contracted around him, plunging her into that heart-stopping moment of pure physical pleasure.

For long minutes afterwards, they lay still, his forehead pressed to hers, neither speaking. Then he brushed his lips across hers and whispered something in that language she didn't understand, the sound exotic. Ian rolled to his side and pulled her against his chest, wrapped his strong arms around her.

"Sleep, Nicole," he whispered. "Tomorrow will be here too soon."

Something in his voice made the faintest flicker of uneasiness steal through Nicole. Ian knew their time together was drawing to an end the same as she did. Was he feeling the same urgency she was? Nicole snuggled closer to him, buried her face in the crook of his neck. Inhaled his unique masculine essence. Held him tighter than she ever had before...

...for the last time.

Chapter Thirteen

As darkness grayed into dawn Ian sat on the floor next to the bed and watched Nicole sleep. With the blinds partially opened, alternating slats of early-morning light and shadow fell across her prone form. His gaze traveled over the swell of her sheet-covered bottom, then up the smooth, bare skin of her back. Her arms were curled around the pillow, her right cheek snuggled against it. All that blond hair lay fanned across the pale blue sheets. She looked like an angel, all soft and vulnerable. Ian closed his eyes and summoned the vivid images that haunted him. The feel of her fingers on his skin, the taste of her lips. The tight, exquisitely hot feel of her body as he sank deeply into her. Those memories would have to last him a lifetime, because there would never be any more than this one moment between them.

He forced his eyes open and drank in the beauty of her one last time. Ian had been certain that he would never feel this way again. He had survived the devastation wreaked upon his heart once, but he would never get over her this time. She was the one and only woman for him…

…and the very one he couldn't have.

Ian blinked, then looked away. He did not possess the power to make Nicole happy. There was nothing he could offer her that would change the way this would all end. She would go back to D.C., back to the bureau. And Ian would go back to Chicago. He and Nicole shared just one thing—a kind of physical attraction that most people only dreamed about. Need welled inside at the mere thought of the intensity that drew them together. The kind that dwarfed all else. The fact that Ian loved her made no difference in the equation. The admission of his feelings to himself shook him a little. The realization that he couldn't have her shook him even harder.

But he could protect her.

Clearing his mind of the things he couldn't change, Ian dragged his gaze back to Nicole's sweet face. She was awake now, watching him, those wide blue eyes full of the same desire Ian could no longer conceal. She smiled, and something near his heart shifted.

"Good morning," she said sleepily. She glanced at the digital clock on the bedside table and frowned. "It's early." Her questioning gaze moved back to Ian as she raised up onto her elbows, the sheet now clutched to her bare breasts. "You're dressed." She studied him for a moment. "You weren't planning to cut out on me, were you?"

"No." Ian stood before she saw the truth in his eyes. Her statement had hit very close to the mark. He would very much like to leave her where she would be safe. "I'll get your clothes." He crossed to the door without looking back. He couldn't look at her one second longer without her seeing what he needed to hide, and without him wanting to take her again. That couldn't happen. He had to focus on the meeting with Daniels.

Nothing else.

"Do I have time for a shower?" she called after him.

"Sure," he returned offhandedly. Ian suppressed the

images that accompanied the thought of Nicole in the shower, but not before they made an impact. The water gliding over her soft skin. Her breasts jutting forward for his attention. He blew out a breath of frustration and forced the mental pictures away. He moved quickly about the other bedroom gathering Nicole's carelessly discarded clothes. The shirt he wore was slightly wrinkled this morning. Nicole's scent lingered on the fabric, distracting him, making his body harden. His jaw clenched when Nicole met him at the door wrapped in the pale blue sheet from the bed they had shared.

"Thanks," she offered as she accepted the wad of clothing. "I'll only be a few minutes."

"Take your time." Ian stepped around her, ensuring that their bodies didn't touch, and headed to the kitchen. There had to be coffee around here somewhere.

The glimpse of vulnerability Ian had seen in Nicole yesterday tugged at him sharply. No matter how tough Nicole wanted to seem, she was still a bit fragile deep inside. Ian dumped the grounds into the basket and poured the water into the reservoir. The past few weeks—especially finding out that Daniels was the killer—had been hard on Nicole. Daniels would pay for that too. Ian intended to see that the bastard paid for every moment of discomfort he had caused Nicole. The smell of fresh brewed coffee drifted from the machine, but it did nothing to lighten Ian's mood. He had to find a way to convince Nicole to stay out of the line of fire today.

Instinct told him that he would have more luck trying to convince Daniels to forget about the money.

Ian's cell phone chirped. He withdrew it from his pocket and accepted the call. "Yes." It was Alex.

"We're ready to proceed," he told her. "I'm going to call Daniels in ten minutes." Alex briefed him on the current status of Solomon and Martinez. The two were safely ensconced in a quiet suburb on the other side of the city. Ethan Delaney had arrived at the airport forty minutes ago in the agency's jet. He would arrive at Ian's location within fifteen minutes. Ian thanked Alex for the update and assured her that he would check in every couple of hours. She suggested again that he work a secondary backup plan with the local police, but Ian declined.

If this was going to work, it had to go down without a glitch. The more people involved, the greater the possibility of a breakdown in communications. And that meant a greater risk of someone getting trigger-happy.

"Smells good."

Ian turned to find Nicole, her hair still slightly damp, standing in the doorway. The blue slacks and sweater looked as good on her slender body today as they had yesterday.

"Have a cup," he offered, then smiled.

Nicole returned the smile with a bright one of her own. "Thanks."

The phone sounded again. This time it would be Daniels, Ian felt relatively certain. He took his time answering, his gaze on Nicole's every move as she poured the steaming coffee.

"Yes," he said finally.

"If this is your idea of a joke, Michaels, it's only going to blow up in your face," Daniels growled. "I've waited long enough for your call."

"I was just about to call you," Ian assured him.

Nicole's gaze met Ian's. He told her with his eyes that it was Daniels.

"When am I going to get Solomon?" he demanded.

"As soon as I meet your partner," Ian said bluntly.

"That wasn't part of the deal," Daniels screeched.

"This is between you and me. You got your fifty percent, what else do you want?"

"I just want to make sure your partner understands our agreement," Ian explained. "We meet, face-to-face, lay all our cards on the table, decide how we'll access the money, and then we pick up Solomon."

"I think you've forgotten just one thing," Daniels said in a cold, menacing tone. "I'm running this show, and I decide how this is going to go down."

"When you're feeling more cooperative, you know how to reach me." Ian ended the call and dropped the phone back into his pocket. Daniels would be calling back shortly. Patience was definitely not one of the man's virtues.

"What did he say?" Nicole asked, then sipped her coffee. She held the warm mug with both hands.

Ian reached for his cup. "He wasn't happy." He took a swallow of the hot liquid. "But he'll call back," he added at Nicole's distressed look.

Nicole nodded. "Okay." Her gaze locked on Ian's. "Daniels is on the edge, don't push him too far. He might do something crazy. We don't need crazy."

Ian set his cup back down. He readied himself for Nicole's blast of fury. "That's precisely why I want you to stay here today," Ian said slowly. Nicole's expression changed from relaxed to irate before he got the last word out.

Nicole slammed her cup down on the counter, coffee sloshing over the rim. "No way," she shot back. "You promised you wouldn't do this, Ian." Disappointment and hurt claimed her features. "I won't let you leave me out. We've been over and over this, until I'm sick of it. I'm not going to change my mind. Just forget it."

"I promised you that I wouldn't leave you out of the

loop,'' Ian said evenly. "I didn't say you would be going with me to meet Daniels."

Nicole shook her head adamantly. "Don't even think about it," she warned.

Ian closed the distance between them with slow, determined steps designed to intimidate. "You do realize that Daniels intends to kill you? You know too much, and you're still connected to the bureau. He won't allow you to walk away from this, Nicole."

She squared her shoulders. "I'll take my chances the same as you."

The doorbell sounded. She whirled toward the sound. She glared at Ian then, as if she knew full well who was at the door. Ian summoned the resolve it would take to do what had to be done. He strode to the front door, Nicole right behind him. This wasn't going to be easy. He had known it wouldn't be. After checking the viewfinder, Ian opened the door.

"Morning, Ian." Ethan sauntered into the entry hall and kicked the door closed behind him. He placed two rectangular cases on the floor. "Is that coffee I smell?"

Ethan looked nothing like the typical Colby Agency investigator. Ian doubted Victoria would tolerate the look from anyone else. His long brown hair was tied back with a thong. His jeans and shirt were worn, his boots scuffed.

But Ethan Delaney was one of a kind, and very, very good at surveillance. And there wasn't a better marksman alive.

Ian nodded his greeting. "Ethan Delaney, this is Nicole Reed."

An appreciative smile slid across Ethan's face as he offered Nicole his hand. "It's a pleasure to meet you, Miss Reed. A real pleasure."

Nicole glared first at Ethan's hand, then at Ian. "Tell

him to leave," she ground out, her eyes shooting enough sparks to burn the place down.

"You're prepared to die today, then?" Ian asked tersely. Irritation churned inside him. Why the hell wouldn't she listen to reason? "Because if you go with me today, that's what might very well happen."

"And I'm the only one?" she demanded. "You think Daniels is really going to give up half of what he's worked so hard for? That he'll follow through with this so-called deal? You can take the chance, but not me?"

"I'm willing to risk my life." Ian felt that muscle in his jaw begin to flex rhythmically. "But I'm not willing to risk yours."

Nicole huffed a breath of frustration and shook her head. "How heroic of you, Ian." She planted her hands firmly at her waist. "But this is my case and it's my decision. You're not going without me." She glanced at Ethan. "And don't think your friend here is going to stop me."

Ethan held up both hands, palms out. "Hey, lady, I heard all about what you did to Martinez." He grinned. "Believe me, I'm on your side."

Ian had known this was the way it would play out. Nicole was too damned stubborn for her own good. But he had to try. "All right," he relented. "But don't make one move—don't even breathe—unless I tell you to."

"I'll need a weapon," was her only reply.

Ian turned his attention to Ethan. "You have what we need?"

"Absolutely." Ethan picked up the two cases and looked to Ian for direction.

"This way," Ian told him, then led the way to the dining room.

Ethan set the cases on the dining table but opened only

one. "Your weapon of choice, I believe," he said as he offered Nicole a Beretta nine-millimeter.

She tested the weapon's weight, then checked the clip. "Thank you, Mr. Delaney. I always feel naked when I'm unarmed."

Ethan made a sound of approval in his throat. "I can definitely imagine that."

Ian shot him a warning look.

"You knew I wouldn't agree to staying behind," Nicole said, drawing Ian's attention back to her. "That's why you had him bring me a weapon."

"The thought did cross my mind."

Ethan slapped two fresh clips in Ian's hand. "You're a lucky man, Michaels."

"You think so?" Ian countered. He put a fresh clip into his weapon and pocketed the other. "She's determined to get herself killed, and maybe me as well, and you call that lucky?"

"Well now, that's why I'm here, isn't it?" Ethan pointed out good-naturedly. "The best plan is the one with good backup." He opened the second case, which held a disassembled high-powered rifle and related accessories.

"Well said," Ian agreed. If he couldn't keep Nicole out of the picture, at least he could make sure she was well covered from the best possible angles.

"I don't know about this," she said uncertainly. "If Daniels gets wind of a third party—"

Ian leveled his gaze on hers. "Daniels will never know Ethan is there."

NICOLE STUDIED Ian's handsome profile as they drove to the rendezvous point. She wanted to commit each detail to memory, so she could call upon it during all those long, lonely nights that lay ahead of her. She would remember every moment they had shared. And she would love him for the rest of her life. She prayed that she would somehow be able to protect Ian as this sting played out. If Daniels hurt him...

Nicole couldn't bear that thought. She had to do whatever it took to keep him safe. The agreed-upon meeting place was at an old rock quarry with nothing but trees around it. That would provide plenty of cover for Ethan. Daniels had been outraged when Ian would not allow him to pick the rendezvous location. But when Ian refused to budge on the point, Daniels caved. Another indication of his proximity to the edge. Nicole hoped like hell that Ethan was as good a shot as Ian implied. Both their lives might depend on it.

Ian turned right onto the gravel road that would lead down to the quarry. Nicole's heart pounded hard in her chest. Fear gripped her throat in a serious choke hold. What if Daniels showed up with half a dozen cohorts? His partner might be a whole damned committee. What if—

Stop it, Reed, she scolded. *Keep your focus. Put everything else out of your mind.* Nicole took a deep bolstering breath and rolled her shoulders one at a time. No way would she allow Ian to die in the next few minutes. She would protect him, she reaffirmed. She had dragged him into this mess and she would see that he made it safely out of it.

"Stash your weapon there." Ian gestured to the small storage compartment in the car door. Ethan had given them his rental, and he had driven the car parked in Solomon's garage.

Nicole frowned. "Why?"

"He'll pat you down and take your weapon," Ian explained. "Daniels considers you hostile."

"He'd better," Nicole said hotly.

"Do it, Nicole," Ian insisted as he braked the car to a stop near the abandoned quarry.

"This is not a good idea," she complained.

"When this is over," Ian said, his words staying her move to obey his order, "we need to talk."

Hope flickered in Nicole's heart, but the reality of the differences between them quickly dashed it. "Sure," she murmured. "We'll talk."

Turning away from him, Nicole placed her Beretta, butt up, in the compartment that was most likely designed for maps or tissues. She would not dwell on Ian's unexpected statement. Was it a promise or a threat? she wondered briefly, then put it out of her mind. Before Ian turned the engine off, she powered the window down for ready access to her weapon.

Daniels was here already. A dark sedan was parked some ten yards away from where Ian had stopped. The driver's-side door opened and Daniels emerged. Nicole suppressed the strong desire to destroy that rose immediately in her chest.

Ian placed a hand on her arm when she started to get out. "Slow and easy, Nicole," he warned.

Nicole nodded, then opened her door. She closed the door and leaned against it. Ian skirted the trunk, careful not to turn his back to the man sauntering toward them.

"Well, well, I didn't expect to see you again so soon," Daniels said disdainfully, his gaze traveling the length of Nicole, then back to her face.

"I guess I'm just lucky, that's all," Nicole spat.

"Maybe not," Daniels growled as he moved closer. He patted Nicole down, a little too thoroughly, too roughly.

"She's not carrying," Ian said pointedly.

Daniels turned and reached toward him.

Ian had the weapon in his hand and the muzzle pressed between Daniels's eyes before he knew Ian had moved. "You don't want to do that," Ian suggested in a dangerous voice that made even Nicole retreat farther against the car.

"Keep your weapon then," Daniels said quickly. "Just keep it holstered."

Ian took his time lowering his weapon, then putting it away. "Where's your partner?" he inquired, cutting to the chase. "I didn't come here today to see the sights. No partner, no Solomon."

"My partner is a little shy around strangers," Daniels said in an oily tone. "How about you and I take a little walk over to my car? We don't need Reed for this. She might make my partner nervous."

Nicole started to argue, but Ian stopped her with a look. She sagged against the car and crossed her arms in irritation. Daniels and Ian walked over to the other car. Nicole strained to listen to whatever was said. She wasn't about to miss a single word. She watched every move Daniels made. She felt fairly confident that Ian was safe as long as Daniels didn't have Solomon's location. But what about the partner? He was an unknown variable. He might go off half cocked and do something stupid. Nicole swallowed the metallic taste of fear rising in her throat. She cleared her mind and directed her full attention to the conversation taking place between the two men.

"You told me that she was being taken care of!" a female voice ranted angrily.

Nicole frowned. She didn't recognize the voice. Was Daniels's partner a woman? The passenger-side door of Daniels's car flung open and a petite redhead emerged.

Ice formed in Nicole's stomach. She shook her head in denial. It couldn't be...

Leonna Landon.

Director Landon's wife?

"I want her taken care of," Mrs. Landon demanded of Daniels. "She wasn't supposed to be here."

"All in good time," Daniels assured her. "All in good time."

"I was expecting a man," Ian said coolly, obviously to infuriate Leonna further.

Leonna laughed at him, her oversized purse swinging around her hips. "Get over it, Michaels, I am *the* man."

Ian turned to Daniels. "I'm not doing business with a middle *man*," he said curtly.

Before Daniels could respond, Leonna pushed between them, her hands on her thin hips. "I told you, I'm the one in charge here," she hissed.

"Convince me," Ian said evenly.

Leonna's rebuff involved a sexually explicit four-letter word and Ian.

"I don't think so." Ian gave them his back and strode deliberately in Nicole's direction.

The air evaporated in Nicole's lungs. He turned his back! He was an open target.

"Wait!" Daniels shouted.

Ian stopped. One side of his mouth lifted in a hint of a smile, for Nicole's eyes only. Then he slowly turned around.

Nicole dragged in a much-needed breath. The man was going to give her heart failure.

"Landon cut Solomon a deal," Daniels explained as Ian approached him once more. "That's why we operated outside the normal channels. Solomon bought himself special treatment. A total blackout operation. And the AG's office was none the wiser.''

That chunk of ice in Nicole's stomach shattered with the tension whipping through her body. Landon on the take? She wouldn't believe that. "You're lying," she charged angrily.

Ian cut her a warning glare.

Leonna appeared to get a cheap thrill from Nicole's distress. "Oh, yeah, Agent Reed, everybody's got their price." Leonna's red-red lips spread into a grin. "A cool million with more to come later was my dearly departed husband's. For one million dollars he gave the order for Solomon's special treatment. Then, when the time was right, there would be more money. A lot more.''

"Can we get down to business?" Ian said impatiently.

"Back off," Leonna snapped. "I want little Miss Goody-Two-shoes to know how it was.''

Nicole glared at the woman from across the short distance that separated them. Director Landon couldn't have been on the take. Nicole had respected him. She knew him. Defeat sucked at Nicole's composure. Landon had been... Oh, God, how could she have been so naive? Both Daniels and Landon had fooled her. Was she that gullible?

"Dear old Bobby was smart enough to take advantage of the prime opportunity Solomon offered," Leonna continued. "He just wasn't bright enough to keep me happy." She sniffed. "Stupid bastard thought he would keep the money hidden until he retired and moved away to some foreign country where no one would ever suspect where the money had come from. He was convinced he would get caught if he spent any of it.''

At least Landon had been right about that, Nicole mused. If he had suddenly begun to live above his means, suspicion would certainly have come his way.

Leonna patted her salon-styled hair. "I wasn't about to wait until I was too old to enjoy the money to spend it."

"That's where I come into the picture," Daniels interjected. "Leonna and I go back a long way," he said smugly. "When Leonna confided in me what Landon had done, well, I decided we had to do something about it."

"You're sick," Nicole said with disgust.

Another of those warning looks from Ian arrowed in her direction.

"If Landon already had the money, then why are we here?" Ian demanded.

Daniels smiled a sinister smile. "Because there's way more than just one million. The word the cartel put out after Solomon's highly publicized demise was twenty million."

"Why settle for one when you can have more?" Ian suggested. "And what about Solomon's cut?"

Daniels laughed. "Solomon isn't going to get squat. I plan to take the full twenty million."

"Ten," Ian reminded.

"As you put it so eloquently a few minutes ago," Daniels retorted, "I don't think so." The barrel of his weapon was in Ian's face before the last word stopped echoing around them. "Now," Daniels said in a self-satisfied tone, "where is Solomon?"

"Go to hell," Ian said, enunciating each word carefully so that there was no misunderstanding.

Nicole glanced at the woods between their position and the highway. Ethan was out there, but with Ian standing between Daniels and the woods Ethan would never get a clear shot. Nicole swallowed convulsively. She placed her hand on the car door. Slowly, one inch at a time, she reached toward her weapon.

"The deal is off," Ian said flatly.

Daniels's face contorted with rage, his knuckles whitened around the grip of his weapon. "And you're dead."

The bottom fell out of Nicole's stomach.

"We have to have Solomon," Leonna cried, staying Daniels's next move. "Without him we can't get the money! The money is in a joint foreign account. You have to have a special PIN to access it. Solomon supplied half the number, my husband the other half. It was a built-in safety net to make sure neither one tried to take the money without the other's knowledge."

"Landon is dead," Ian reminded.

"But I'm his widow," Leonna shot back. "What was his is mine. I have his half of the code." She turned to Daniels. "We have to have Solomon."

"Okay, Michaels," Daniels ground out. "Either tell me where he is or I'll kill you both."

"Then no one gets the money," Ian rationalized.

"I said tell me where Solomon is!" Daniels screamed.

One second turned to five. Nicole glanced at the woods again. Where the hell was Ethan? Her heart hammered in her chest. He probably still couldn't get a clean shot. Her fingers were almost to her weapon, but she couldn't make any sudden moves. Couldn't risk Daniels pulling that trigger.

"Fine," Daniels relented when Ian remained silent. He reached beneath Ian's jacket and took his weapon. "Then Reed dies."

Nicole stiffened. She saw Ian do the same. Her fingers tightened around the butt of her weapon. Could she draw it quickly enough and take out Daniels before he fired his weapon?

She didn't think so.

"I'll give you the choice." Daniels shifted his bead to Nicole. "Either you do it, or I will."

"No."

The single word, fierce and at the same time desperate, came from Ian.

Daniels turned his head, meeting Ian's gaze, without taking his expert aim off Nicole.

"I'll do it," Ian said quietly.

"Now that's more like it." Daniels thrust Ian's weapon at him at the same time that he focused his own weapon back on Ian. "Remember, if you miss, I won't. In fact, I'll enjoy killing her."

Ian turned to Nicole. That intense silvery gaze settled fully onto hers. Nicole's heart rushed up into her throat.

"If you can't do it, Michaels, I will," Daniels reminded.

"I'll do it," Ian repeated as he raised his weapon and took aim at Nicole.

Chapter Fourteen

Ian gazed down the barrel of his gun and into Nicole's eyes. *Trust me, Nicole,* he tried to relay with his own eyes. She stood there staring at him with one of those expressions of uncertainty and disbelief that is beyond describing with mere words. The urge for fight or flight stiffened her posture.

"Do it!" Daniels demanded harshly.

The blood roaring in his ears, Ian steadied his arm and fired just over Nicole's left shoulder. As if she had read Ian's mind and knew what to do, she dropped as if she had been hit. Ian pivoted and fired at Daniels, sending him diving for some kind of cover. Somewhere behind Ian the crack of a high-powered rifle sounded, and then the blast of a handgun from Leonna's direction. Leonna crumpled to the ground next to the dark sedan, a look of surprised dismay on her face. Ian kicked out of reach the thirty-two-caliber pistol Leonna had dropped onto the ground.

"I've been shot," Leonna wailed in disbelief.

One shot whizzed past Ian's head, then another. He dropped to the ground and rolled to cover near the car Daniels had driven. He crouched there and listened. Where was Nicole? He couldn't see her on the passenger side of their rental anymore. Where the hell was Ethan? He had taken care of Leonna and kept Daniels scrambling for cover, but where was he now?

Ethan's rifle sounded again, several shots, one right after the other. The crunch of gravel, then return fire, three shots, sounded next. Daniels again, or maybe Nicole. Definitely nine-millimeter. Ian moved around a groaning Leonna and to the front bumper of the sedan just in time to see Daniels duck for safety behind Ian's rental.

Ian's blood turned ice cold. His heart seemed to still in his chest. Daniels was going after Nicole. Keeping low just in case Daniels made any unexpected moves, Ian followed the same path he had taken. Ian waited, crouched at the front bumper of the car, until he had quieted his breathing.

Ian stole a quick look around the corner of the car. Daniels disappeared around the far end, near the trunk. Ian clenched his jaw, then eased in that direction, placing each step carefully so as not to disturb the gravel.

Voices then, but Ian didn't stop to listen. He kept moving cautiously in the direction Daniels had vanished.

"Tell me where Solomon is *now,*" Daniels threatened.

"Go to hell," Nicole rasped.

Her voice sounded strange, thin. Fear knotted in Ian's gut. Had Nicole been hit? Ian swallowed tightly, but controlled the urge to run to her. He couldn't risk alerting Daniels to his presence.

"Don't push me, Nicole, I swear I'll kill you," Daniels retorted, the desperation rising in his tone. "I want that money and I'm out of time."

"What good will the money do you, Daniels?" Nicole asked with blatant amusement, however faint. "You're dead, *you* just don't understand that yet."

Ian rounded the corner of the rear bumper just in time

to see Daniels press the muzzle of his weapon to Nicole's forehead. "Last chance," he snarled. "I'm going to pull this trigger in three seconds."

Every muscle in Ian's body tensed. Nicole lay against the bumper, her face extremely pale. Ian eased a step closer and put his gun to the back of Daniels's head. "That would be a costly mistake for you."

Daniels stiffened. Nicole's glassy-eyed gaze connected with Ian's. She smiled weakly. Fear exploded in Ian's chest. She *was* hit.

Daniels's weapon bored a little harder into Nicole's forehead, she blinked as if the movement took tremendous effort. "Go ahead, Michaels, shoot me. She'll die too."

"If that's your final word on the matter." Ian pressed his weapon harder into Daniels's skull. "Then we have nothing else to discuss."

"Shoot him," Nicole whispered.

Ian's heart thundered in his chest. She was getting weaker by the second.

"All I want is the money," Daniels said in an almost pleading tone.

"We all want something," Ian replied, his voice strangely calm. "The only question is how badly do you want the money? Are you willing to die for it? I assure you that if you don't lower your weapon *now,* you are going to die."

Daniels's hand shook. Everything inside Ian stilled as he waited for Daniels to concede defeat. Nicole appeared to have lost consciousness. But Ian couldn't take his eyes off Daniels long enough to see where she was hit.

Daniels blew out a ragged breath, then lowered his weapon. "You win, Michaels," he muttered.

Daniels pushed to his feet, Ian moved simultaneously. "Toss your weapon to your right."

"I hope she was worth it," Daniels said flippantly, still glaring down at Nicole.

"Toss the weapon," Ian repeated firmly.

Daniels abruptly spun around and his weapon leveled on Ian's chest. Ian shot him before he could squeeze off a round. The deadly hit echoed deafeningly around them for what felt like forever.

"We got a live one over here!" Ethan called from where Leonna had gone down. "I've called for help."

Ian knelt next to Nicole. His worst fears were realized when he found the wound leaking blood from her side. She roused a bit when he sat down beside her and pulled her onto his lap.

"Dammit, Michaels," Nicole fussed, her voice thready. "I know I told you that the next time you wanted to save my life you should just shoot me, but I didn't expect you to actually take a shot at me."

"You did well, you didn't move," he murmured, trying to smile for her benefit.

"I trust you. I knew you wouldn't shoot me." She frowned. "But then Daniels was about to come around behind you after Leonna went down. I couldn't let him shoot you either." She groaned. "It hurts like hell."

Ian pressed his hand harder over the wound to slow the bleeding. God, she had lost a lot of blood. "I'm sorry," he murmured. Ian was supposed to keep her safe. This wasn't supposed to happen. She had been trying to protect him. Nicole leaned heavily against him then, and he knew she had lost consciousness again. Ian stared down at her, then at the blood oozing between his fingers. He couldn't lose her. He shook his head. He wouldn't let her go. Tears stung his eyes.

There were things he needed to say to her.

He wouldn't let her go.

NICOLE WOKE gradually. Her mouth was painfully dry. Where was she? she wondered as focus slowly came to her. The room was white. Her head felt heavy, her brain like cotton. Something beeped near her head. She turned, the motion more a gradual falling to one side to look. Agony speared through her. Nicole groaned at the fierce stab of pain that seemed to come from all over her body at once. A collage of monitors and an IV bag hung near the bed. Two long clear tubes from two separate IV bags extended down to the bed and were taped to her arm.

She had been shot.

Nicole moaned with sensory overload as the images came flooding back to her. Was it over? Was Daniels dead? Leonna? She frowned. Nicole didn't want to think about Leonna and Director Landon. She had respected him, worked under his strong leadership for years, and never once suspected that he could be bought at any price. Nicole tightened her jaw, and blinked back the tears. She hoped like hell Daniels was dead. He deserved to die.

But all that really mattered to her was that Ian was safe. *Ian.*

Nicole cautiously moved her head to her left. He sat in a chair beside her bed, asleep. Nicole moistened her dry lips and smiled at how wonderful he looked. His jaw was covered in dark stubble, his suit was rumpled. But he looked like heaven on earth to Nicole. Had he been with her all this time? She frowned. She had no idea how long she had been in the hospital. She didn't even know what day it was. But Ian was here, and that made it all right.

"You're awake," that softly accented voice whispered.

Nicole's gaze connected with his as he stood and moved to her side. "How long have I been here?" she asked hoarsely. Her throat felt raw with thirst. "Could I have a drink, please?"

Ian quickly poured water into a small plastic cup and inserted a straw. He held it to her lips and Nicole drank long and deep.

"Not too much," he warned, then set the drink aside. "We came together in the ambulance yesterday just before noon. They took you to surgery immediately. You've been awake a few times since they moved you from recovery to this room but you may not remember."

"What time is it now?"

"Four-thirty in the morning."

"Have you been here all night?" Exhaustion was tugging at her ability to hold her eyes open. The bullet had hit her in the left side. She remembered lots of blood, savage pain.

"I'm fine," he told her in a tone that said he had no intention of leaving.

"Did they take anything out I might miss?" Nicole asked, her voice a bit wobbly. She went for a smile, but her lips wouldn't cooperate. Pain meds, she realized belatedly. She was fighting to stay awake, and they were working to drag her back into healing sleep.

Ian took her fingers in his and stroked her hand with his thumb. He kept his gaze carefully focused there when he answered. "The bullet snagged your intestines and grazed a kidney," he said quietly. His unreadable gaze moved back to hers then. "They repaired all that." He swallowed hard, the muscles along the tanned column of his throat struggled with the effort. "You'll be fine."

"Then why do you look so worried?" she whispered huskily.

He looked away then. "I swore I'd keep you safe. I failed," he murmured. "And I almost lost you."

Nicole's heart squeezed in her chest. "It wasn't your

fault. I was trying to distract Daniels.'' Her eyelids felt so heavy she could barely hold them open. "Is he dead?''

"Yes,'' Ian answered quietly. "And this time he won't be resurrecting himself.''

"Good,'' she said on a sigh.

"You should rest now, Nicole.'' She felt Ian's lips brush her forehead.

"You'll be here when I wake up?'' she heard herself ask as if from someplace very far away.

"Yes.''

The deep, rich sound of his voice followed her into unconsciousness.

WHEN NICOLE woke up again it was almost noon. Warm sunlight filtered in from the window on the far side of the room. The television flashed images across the screen, but the sound was muted. The clock on the wall showed two minutes before twelve. Nicole turned her head toward the chair Ian had occupied earlier. It was empty. Alarm fluttered through her.

Why had he left her?

Snatches of memories flitted across her still-groggy mind. Ian holding her hand, caressing her cheek, pressing a soothing, damp cloth to her face, murmuring soft words. He had been here all night and most of the day. Maybe he had taken a break to have lunch.

Nicole abruptly remembered his warning before the showdown with Daniels. *When this is over, we need to talk.* What did he mean by that? He probably wanted to say goodbye. Nicole closed her eyes and willed the tears to retreat. She didn't want to cry. She just wanted to go back to sleep and pretend it all away.

She had not told him that she loved him.

She had not thanked him for helping her bring down Daniels.

She had made a mistake.

And it was probably too late now to make it right.

Nicole loved Ian with all her heart, but there was no way that he would ever love her. He felt something for her, that was clear. But it wasn't enough. It wasn't the kind of love she felt for him. She had known from the beginning this day would come.

Nicole forced herself to relax. Sleep was what she needed right now.

She didn't need Ian.

She just wanted him more than she wanted anything else in the world, but she had to let him go. She was no good for him.

Later, when Nicole woke again, a huge bouquet of lush red roses stood on the table across the room. There had to be two dozen or more. It was the most beautiful floral arrangement she had ever seen.

A small white business card lay on the table beside her bed. She reached for it and grunted with the pain her movement generated. She read the name there. It was an agent from the local bureau office. Nicole's gaze moved back to the flowers. Could the flowers be from the bureau? Disappointment shuddered through her. She wanted them to be from Ian. They were too beautiful to be from her office.

The door suddenly swung inward and two nurses entered carrying two more large floral arrangements, but nothing as lovely as the roses. One from Nicole's office, and the other from Victoria Colby, one of the nurses explained.

"May I see the card from the bouquet of roses?" she asked before the two could get out of her room. The nurse closest to the table dug around in the flowers for several moments.

"There's no card with this one," she announced, frowning. "Anything else you need, Miss Reed?"

"No." Nicole felt downhearted. "Thank you," she managed. Where was Ian? Why had he left without even saying goodbye? She hurt like hell, and she was miserable.

The next time Nicole woke up, a nurse was there telling her she needed to try and eat something that looked terribly unappealing. Disgusted, sore and downright depressed, Nicole just looked at the tray before her. "Yuck," she muttered, when the nurse had scurried away.

"If you expect to get well, you have to eat, Nicole." Ian was sitting in the chair by her bed, watching her. He had showered and changed. The stubble no longer darkened his jaw.

Nicole couldn't prevent the relieved smiled that spread across her face. "Where did you go?"

"I had some loose ends to tie up," he said cryptically. "Leonna Landon is in a room down the hall under close watch. She's stable, and in a hell of a lot of trouble. The local police wanted a statement and I had to deal with your friends from the bureau. I didn't want them to disturb you."

"There's a card here from an Agent Turner," Nicole mentioned, and gestured to the table.

"A persistent fellow," Ian said crossly.

"Thank you." Nicole wasn't sure whether she was thanking him for taking care of the authorities, or for coming back. Both maybe. Nicole closed her eyes and silently thanked God Ian had returned. For whatever reason. She didn't want to be separated from him ever again. Her eyes popped open. But he would be leaving. Next time for

Chicago. And then, he wouldn't be coming back. A stab of pain that had nothing to do with her injury or the resulting surgery pierced her heart.

"Would you like me to help you? You should eat something." Ian was standing next to her bed now.

"The roses are beautiful," she commented, her gaze shifting to the huge bouquet. She didn't want Ian to see the emotion shining in her eyes. He had to go. She had to let him. "I wish I knew who sent them."

"I sent them," he said quietly.

Nicole's heart leapt, she smiled up at him. "Thank you, Ian, they're beautiful."

Ian looked away from her as if she had slapped him rather than thanked him. Long minutes of silence passed with him just standing there looking away, and Nicole thought she would scream if he didn't say something…anything.

Suddenly, he took her left hand in his. "We have to talk," he said finally, his gaze settling on hers.

This was it. Nicole felt her heart quiver in her chest. He was going to tell her he had to leave. That he wouldn't be back. That she should never come to him again for help or anything else.

And how could she blame him?

Every time Nicole showed up in Ian's life bad things happened. First he lost his career as a U.S. Marshal, then he risked his life to save hers. She must have been out of her mind to think he could feel about her the way she felt about him. This was for the best.

"All right, we'll talk," Nicole said in as firm a voice as she could manage. Might as well get it over with. Maybe she should just let him off the hook, make it easier on both of them. "I suppose you want to go first," she suggested, hoping he would do the gentlemanly thing and let her go first.

Ian smiled, or at least hinted at one. "Yes."

Nicole stared at the far wall then. She blew out a big breath. So much for ladies first. "Look, Ian," she blurted impatiently, "you don't have to say anything. I know it's over. I don't want you to apologize for anything that happened. Just because we were…together doesn't mean I expect some sort of commitment from you. I wanted what happened as much as you did." Nicole pulled her hand from his and fiddled with the sheet to distract herself. "Maybe more."

"Do you mind if I have my say before you push me out the door?"

"Goodbyes are hard enough without dragging them out," she argued, still not looking at him. "I never had any expectations about the future and us." Nicole swallowed the bitter taste that went with that lie. "We had a job to do, nothing else. So why don't you just say the words and let it go at that?"

"You think I want to leave?"

Nicole looked at him then. It was impossible to know exactly what he was thinking. "I can't blame you, you know," she murmured. "I betrayed you three years ago." She closed her eyes and shook her head. When she opened them again he was still watching her, waiting for her to continue. "And I've put you through hell this time. I can't think of a single reason you would want to stay." Her voice shook with the emotion clogging her throat. The pain of her injury was nothing compared with this. Her heart would never heal from the hurt of losing Ian.

"I can think of at least one," Ian countered in that soft, seductive tone that widened the crack in Nicole's heart.

"Sex doesn't count, Ian," she chided.

"Does being in love with you count?"

Nicole's gaze shot to his, she searched his face. Could he possibly mean that? "That would definitely count."

"There you have it then, the single reason," Ian concluded.

She had to hear him say the words...to her. "You're saying that...?" Nicole waited for him to finish the sentence.

"I'm in love with you and I can't imagine living the rest of my life without you." He took her hand in his once more. "There, I've said it."

Nicole couldn't speak for one long moment. She could only stare into those silvery eyes and rejoice in the knowledge that Ian loved her.

"Did you have anything you wanted to say to me?" he asked, a barely masked uncertainty in his voice.

Nicole swiped at a tear that slipped from the corner of her eye, threatening her flimsy hold on composure. "But we never see eye-to-eye on anything. You hate my ambition. Your cool-in-the-face-of-disaster drives me crazy. It will never work. So if you're just saying this to make me feel better because I was shot, then—"

Ian silenced her with his lips. He kissed her until she couldn't think straight. The feel of his firm lips against hers, the heat of his tongue as he invaded her mouth, melted Nicole's resolve. He squeezed her hand in his, then broke the kiss, tasting her one last time before drawing away.

"I never say anything I don't mean," he said matter-of-factly. "I love you. I've loved you for three years. And whatever our differences, we'll find a way to work them out."

Nicole's heart was pumping madly, the machine next to her bed tracked the speedy staccato. She smiled, her face a contradiction of emotions as the tears slid down her cheeks. Any minute now the nurses would come running. "Am I supposed to agree to your terms?" she asked teasingly. "Just because I'm in love with you too doesn't mean I'll cut you any slack."

"I wouldn't expect you to make it too easy for me," he returned in that tone that was equal parts elegance and danger. "That's half the attraction."

"So," Nicole lifted her chin in challenge. "What's the plan?"

"You get well, and when they release you I'll take you to my place in Chicago."

"Why your place?" she retorted.

Ian lifted one dark brow and gave her a look that said she should understand without his having to explain. "Well the last time I was at your place it was a bit hot for my liking."

Nicole frowned. "Oh, yeah, I'd forgotten that little detail."

"There's something else," Ian said solemnly, his gaze suddenly somber. "I was going to tell you earlier, but the doctor thought it would be better if I waited until you were—" he shrugged "—out of the woods."

A bone-deep chill settled over Nicole. She wasn't sure she could handle any more excitement—good or bad. She scrunched her toes and shifted her feet just to be sure. Everything seemed to be in working order. "You said I was going to be fine," she reminded him. Worry flickered in those silvery depths watching her so very intently. "It's not that simple, is it?"

"No." Ian brushed her cheek with his fingers. "There's more."

He paused, to give her time to brace herself, she supposed, but she would rather he get it over with. If she was never going to walk again, or if she had lost something she couldn't function properly without, she would just as soon know it now.

"When you arrived at the ER you had lost a great deal of blood. There was no time to waste. You were rushed into surgery, and numerous routine tests were run on the blood samples they took." His fingers tightened around hers. "Apparently, that first time we were together—" he glanced down at their joined hands, then back to her face "—you conceived. The trauma from the gunshot and the necessary surgery—"

"You're saying I'm pregnant?" Nicole interrupted, her thoughts whirling inside her head. Everything he said after *conceived* was lost to her. Surprise, then wonder claimed her. She felt cold, then hot, then frightened. A baby? Ian's baby?

"Yes, that's what I'm saying."

Nicole studied the pained expression on his face. What was he thinking? Was this why he had confessed his love for her? "Are they sure?" How could they know? It had only been a week. *Trauma.* The words echoed through her, but before she could say anything Ian spoke again.

"The blood test is conclusive within a few days of conception," he explained.

"Trauma," Nicole interjected before he could say anything else. "You said something about trauma."

"The trauma you sustained has put the pregnancy at risk." He inhaled a harsh breath. "There's a possibility that you'll lose the baby."

Nicole felt more vulnerable than she had ever felt in her entire life. A new kind of pain welled inside her. Her hand went instinctively, protectively to her belly. She closed her eyes against the mixture of joy and pain fighting for her attention. She was pregnant with Ian's baby, but the baby might not survive. A dozen emotions washed over her, intensifying with each wave. How could something she hadn't even known that she wanted feel suddenly as if it were all that mattered? The conversation in the airport restaurant abruptly flitted through her mind. Ian wanted children. He had said as much.

She opened her eyes and leveled her gaze on Ian's. "Is this why you've suddenly decided you're in love with me?"

Ian looked surprised by her question. "I love you, Nicole, and I'll love our baby, this one and however many others we choose to have." He pressed a tender kiss to her forehead, and whispered his next words close to her ear. "And if we lose this child and never have another, I'll still love you."

Nicole blinked back the renewed rush of tears. "Okay," she said, her voice a little shaky. "Which one of us is going to stay home with *her?*" she demanded, hoping to lighten the somber mood.

Ian smiled one of those genuinely charming smiles that stole her breath. "We'll take turns staying with *him.*"

"We'll need a bigger house," Nicole suggested.

"I know just the neighborhood," Ian agreed.

"A minivan and a nanny," she added for good measure.

Ian shrugged nonchalantly. "I can live with the minivan as long as I get to select the nanny," he offered generously.

"Forget it, Michaels," Nicole informed him. "You're going to be entirely too busy keeping me happy to concern yourself with a nanny." She grabbed his shirtfront and pulled him down for a kiss.

Ian brushed her lips with his own. "I look forward to the challenge." He sealed his words with a long, hot kiss.

Epilogue

"Do we have an update on the Richland case?" Victoria Colby asked as she scanned the report in her hand.

"Not yet," Ric Martinez told her as he shuffled through his stack of notes. "You know how Alex is, she calls in when she thinks about it, which isn't often. I don't have Ian's report either. He and Nicole went for their first ul-trasound this morning," he added. "The baby is terrific, and they're ninety percent sure it's a girl."

"Excellent," Victoria said with a smile. "Those two deserve the best." Victoria removed her reading glasses and studied Ric. He was still a little rough around the edges, but she was pleased with his progress. Ian had taught him well. "I'm sure Ian appreciates your handling this status meeting for him. With a new wife and a baby on the way, he's more than a little preoccupied these days."

Ric shot her one of those killer smiles that had every secretary in the building swooning. His Latin good looks only made the gesture more appealing.

"Yeah, well, Ian's a lucky man. That Nicole is a real heartbreaker." Ric rubbed the bridge of his nose. "When she's not breaking other things."

Victoria set the report and her glasses aside, and leaned

back in her chair. "I'm hoping to convince her to come to work for me if she decides not to go back to the bureau after her maternity leave."

"Nicole would be a definite asset," Ric agreed. He frowned then. "Speaking of assets, what's the deal with this Sloan guy?"

"Sloan?" Victoria couldn't hide the surprise in her voice. "Why do you ask?"

"Alex used him to gather some hard-to-come-by intel when Ian and Nicole were working the Solomon case. You were on vacation. Alex mentioned that Sloan once worked here. She called him some sort of legend."

Victoria almost smiled. It had been a very long time since she had thought of Sloan. She was surprised that he had agreed to help Alex. Maybe his circumstances had changed of late. Victoria would have to make it a point to give him a call. "He was with my husband from the agency's inception," she replied. "Sloan helped James to build the Colby Agency. And then he helped me keep it going after James's death."

"So he was second in command, like Ian," Ric suggested.

"Yes," Victoria told him, though that didn't begin to adequately describe Sloan. She wasn't sure she could properly relate in words the kind of man Sloan had been.

Ric shrugged one shoulder. "What was it that made him so special that Alex would refer to him as a legend?"

Victoria thought about that for a while before she answered. Sloan wasn't the kind of man who could be summed up in few words. "Sloan was the best tracker in the business. If you wanted to find someone no one else could, you called Sloan. He had this uncanny ability to read people even before he laid eyes on them. He studied their past, what they left behind, and he instinctively knew where to look to find them.''

''Sounds like a handy guy to have around in this business,'' Ric commented.

''He was the best,'' Victoria admitted, too many memories flashing across the private theater of her mind. ''The very best.''

''Why did he leave the agency?''

Victoria pulled her attention from the past and back to Ric. ''Things happened, he changed,'' she explained without really explaining at all. ''Sloan isn't the same man who worked for the Colby Agency all those years ago.''

''But the legend lives on,'' Ric offered.

''Yes,'' Victoria allowed. ''I suppose it does.''

* * * * *

Look for the
next installment of

THE COLBY AGENCY

series by Debra Webb
coming to you
in January 2002.

Only from Harlequin Intrigue.

Prologue

"I'll pay anything you ask," Rachel Larson insisted.

Victoria Colby regarded the woman across the wide expanse of her oak desk for a long moment before she responded. "Miss Larson, this is primarily an investigations agency. We accept clients who require personal protection on a case by case basis, and generally by referral only."

Disappointment shadowed Rachel's pale features. Dark circles beneath eyes that contained as much wariness as fear, and the ill fit of her clothing told Victoria that this young woman had not slept or eaten well in too many months. Her overall look of extreme fatigue signaled her proximity to the edge. The ability to size up a client had facilitated Victoria's climb to the top in this business. And right now, every instinct told her that this young woman was more than simply desperate.

"I'll need to know a great deal more before I can make a decision as to whether the Colby Agency will take your case," Victoria explained.

Rachel drew in a shaky breath and squared her shoulders. "Detective Clarence Taylor sent me. He was a police detective here in Chicago before moving to New Orleans."

Victoria considered the name for a moment. "Yes, I remember Detective Taylor. He left three or four years ago I believe."

Rachel nodded, hope kindled in those dark brown eyes. "That's right. He knows that I've exhausted every other possibility, including the police." Rachel leaned forward and clutched Victoria's desk like a lifeline against the violent waters churning her obviously troubled soul. "You have to help me, Mrs. Colby. He's going to take my little boy." A single tear slipped down her colorless cheek before she could swipe it away with the back of her hand. "I can't let him do that."

Sympathy tugged at Victoria's softer side—the side that hadn't hardened over the years in this cutthroat business. If Clarence Taylor had sent Miss Larson to her, Victoria would certainly do all she could to help her. "All right," she offered. "I will consider your case, but you have to tell me *everything,* Miss Larson."

"Thank you." Rachel's voice cracked with emotion.

Victoria opened her notepad and removed her gold pen from its holder. "I'll need to know as many details as possible about the stalker." She glanced up from her pad. "First, do you know his name?"

Rachel licked her lips, then swallowed visibly. "I believe your agency has worked on a case involving him before. His name is Gabriel DiCassi. They call him—"

"Angel," Victoria finished for her, the name barely more than a whisper. She shuddered with remembered dread. Several years, but not nearly enough, had passed since she heard that name. Not since…Sloan had left.

"Detective Taylor thought that one of your investigators might have experience dealing with…him," she said uncertainly.

Taking her time, Victoria placed her pen on the blank

notepad, then leveled her gaze on Rachel's. "Unfortunately, I do know him."

Despair reigned supreme in the young woman's features. "Then you know that this is no ordinary situation."

"Yes," Victoria agreed gravely. "Angel is a highly paid assassin whose reputation boasts a perfect record of kills. He's ruthless. If you're his target, he won't stop until you're dead."

"Please tell me you'll help me." Desperation weighed Rachel's weary tone. "I have to find a way to protect my son."

A frown tugged at Victoria. Somehow the part about the child didn't quite gel. "Why would Angel want to take your son?" Victoria thought briefly of the small dark-haired boy sitting in her outer office under her secretary Mildred's watchful eye.

Rachel looked away for a moment. "Because he's Josh's father." Her lips trembled with the effort it took to force her next words. "Five years ago, we were… involved."

"Involved?" Victoria heard the contempt in her own voice, and immediately regretted it. Humiliation clouded Rachel's expression.

"I was very young. It was a mistake." She squeezed her eyes shut and shook her head slowly from side to side. A soul-deep pain clouded her gaze when she opened her eyes once more. "He used me to get to my father."

"Yet you're still alive." Victoria arched a speculative brow. "That's not Angel's style. He never leaves loose ends."

"He would have killed me…" Rachel blinked furiously at the tears glittering, then shrugged. "I was lucky to escape. I've been running ever since. Later, he found out about Josh, and now Angel wants him."

If her story were true, Rachel Larson was as good as dead. Angel allowed nothing to stand between him and what he wanted. Anyone who tried to stop him was accepting a death sentence. Though Victoria employed the very finest in their fields, tracking down a man like Angel would take resources she simply could not risk. She had learned that lesson too well seven years ago.

Victoria braced herself for what she knew had to be said. "Regrettably, Miss Larson, the Colby Agency cannot provide the services you have requested."

Rachel stiffened. "You won't help me?"

"I don't mean that at all." Victoria pulled open her right desk drawer and flipped through her files. She removed a manila folder and scanned its contents. Satisfied with what she found, Victoria turned her attention back to Rachel. "There is only one man, to my knowledge, who knows Angel well enough to be of any assistance to you, and he doesn't work for me anymore." Victoria copied the name and address from the folder onto the back of her business card. "I can't guarantee that he'll be willing to take your case, but he's your only possible hope at succeeding. Tell him I sent you."

Rachel accepted the offered card. "Who is he?"

"Someone who used to work for this agency." Victoria leveled her gaze on Rachel's. "Someone I would trust with my own life. His name is Sloan."

"He must be the investigator Detective Taylor mentioned."

Victoria dipped her head in acknowledgement. "Sloan was the best investigator the Colby Agency has ever had the privilege of employing." Regret trickled through her. "As I said, he doesn't work for me anymore. Although this agency has utilized his services from time to time over the past couple of years, Sloan is very selective in the offers he takes these days." Victoria paused before continuing. "Considering the circumstances, he might not want to take your case at all."

Rachel searched Victoria's gaze. "If he's willing, how can he help me?"

Memories Victoria would rather not have recalled played in the private theater of her mind. "He knows Angel. He knows how the man operates and what motivates him."

Frowning, Rachel hesitated at first, but then asked, "How is it that Sloan knows Angel so well?"

Victoria sighed her own hesitation. What would it hurt to tell her? If Sloan could help the woman, Victoria rationalized, understanding would make dealing with him somewhat easier. "Seven years ago Angel assassinated two very prominent businessmen here in Chicago," she began. "The Colby Agency was called in to consult on the case." Victoria tamped down the guilt that quickly surfaced. "I assigned Sloan to support them. He possesses an uncanny ability to read people. He studied Angel's case, tracked him for months." Victoria met Rachel's unsuspecting gaze knowing that what she would say next would only add to her growing fear. "When Sloan got too close, Angel retaliated in a particularly ruthless manner. Recognizing the kind of man Sloan was and what would hurt him most, Angel murdered Sloan's wife and took his three-year-old son."

Rachel gasped and her eyes widened in horror. "Oh God."

"The child's body wasn't discovered for a while, and during that time Angel taunted Sloan with telephone calls of his son's recorded cries for daddy...." Her voice drifted off as the painful memories of that seemingly endless year of tracking Angel sifted through Victoria's thoughts. Sloan had pushed himself beyond any man's physical and mental limitations, and found nothing. Then, finally, they'd discovered the small body burned beyond recognition. Something had snapped inside Sloan then and he'd simply disappeared. Months later, Victoria learned that he'd resurfaced as a private contractor in Mexico. He hadn't allowed her close since. But he was still the best in the business of tracking and protection.

Rachel's complexion turned a whiter shade of pale. "How will I ever stop him?"

Victoria studied her a long moment before answering. Perhaps Angel had had some sort of twisted reasoning for allowing Rachel to live just as he had when he spared Sloan's life. Living with the loss was much more difficult than dying. Gabriel DiCassi was evil incarnate.

Victoria pointed to the card in Rachel's hand. "Talk to Sloan." If even a small part of the man she once knew lived behind that hardened, go-to-hell armor he wore, Sloan would never be able to turn this woman and her child away. And maybe the opportunity would allow him to lay his own demons to rest. "And don't let his attitude scare you off," Victoria added. "If there is anyone who can help you, Sloan can."

RACHEL STOOD on the street corner in downtown Chicago and stared at the card in her hand. Los Laureles Cantina in Florescitaf, Mexico. That's where she would find this man named Sloan. What sort of man used a cantina for his business office? Maybe she didn't want to know. Rachel shivered despite the August sun beating down from the clear blue sky. No amount of heat would ever make her feel warm inside knowing what lay ahead of her.

But she had no choice…she had to do something.

No matter how far and fast she ran, Angel always found

her. He wanted her son. Angel only allowed her to take care of Josh for the time being because he felt the boy needed his mother. He had said those very words to her on more than one occasion. One day though, he intended to take Josh. Rachel shuddered at the thought. She had to do something before that day came.

"I'm hungry, Mommy."

Rachel's attention jerked back to the here and now. She smiled at the little boy whose hand she held tightly in her own. "I'm sorry, honey. We'll have lunch soon." Satisfied, Josh smiled back at her. Somehow she had to find Sloan and convince him to help her.

No matter what it took.

Where the bond of family, tradition and honor run as deep and are as vast as the great Lone Star state, that's...

TRUEBLOOD, TEXAS

Texas families are at the heart of the next Harlequin 12-book continuity series.

HARLEQUIN®
INTRIGUE

is proud to launch this brand-new series of books by some of your very favorite authors.

Look for

SOMEONE S BABY
by Dani Sinclair
On sale May 2001

SECRET BODYGUARD
by B.J. Daniels
On sale June 2001

UNCONDITIONAL SURRENDER
by Joanna Wayne
On sale July 2001

Available at your favorite retail outlet.

HARLEQUIN®
Makes any time special ®

Visit us at www.eHarlequin.com

HITT

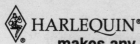

HARLEQUIN®

INTRIGUE

opens the case files on:

TOP SECRET
BABIES

Unwrap the mystery!

January 2001
#597 THE BODYGUARD'S BABY
Debra Webb

February 2001
#601 SAVING HIS SON
Rita Herron

March 2001
#605 THE HUNT FOR HAWKE'S DAUGHTER
Jean Barrett

April 2001
#609 UNDERCOVER BABY
Adrianne Lee

May 2001
#613 CONCEPTION COVER-UP
Karen Lawton Barrett

Follow the clues to your favorite retail outlet.

HARLEQUIN®
Makes any time special ™

INDULGE IN A QUIET MOMENT
WITH HARLEQUIN

Get a FREE
Quiet Moments Bath Spa

with just two proofs of purchase from
any of our four special collector's editions in May

Harlequin® is sure to make your time special this Mother's Day
with four special collector's editions featuring a short story
PLUS a complete novel packaged together in one volume!

Collection #1 Intrigue abounds in a collection featuring *New York Times* bestselling author Barbara Delinsky and Kelsey Roberts.

Collection #2 Relationships? Weddings? Children? = *New York Times* bestselling author Debbie Macomber and Tara Taylor Quinn at their best!

Collection #3 Escape to the past with *New York Times* bestselling author Heather Graham and Gayle Wilson.

Collection #4 Go West! With *New York Times* bestselling author Joan Johnston and Vicki Lewis Thompson!

Plus Special Consumer Campaign!
Each of these four collector's editions will feature a
"FREE QUIET MOMENTS BATH SPA" offer.
See inside book in May for details.

Only from

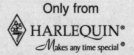

HARLEQUIN®
Makes any time special ®

Don't miss out! Look for this exciting promotion on sale in May 2001,
at your favorite retail outlet.

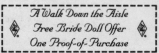